what he
always
knew

BOOK TWO

D1738686

Copyright © 2018 Kandi Steiner
All rights reserved.

No part of this book may be used or reproduced in any
form or by any means, electronic or mechanical, including
photocopying, recording, or by any information storage and
retrieval system without prior written consent of the author
except where permitted by law.

The characters and events depicted in this book are fictitious.
Any similarity to real persons, living or dead, is coincidental
and not intended by the author.

Published by Kandi Steiner

Edited by Elaine York/Allusion Publishing,
www.allusiongraphics.com

Cover Design by Staci Hart

Formatting by Elaine York/Allusion Publishing,
www.allusiongraphics.com

what he

always

knew

BOOK TWO

KANDI STEINER

This is book two in the *Best Kept Secrets Series*,
and it picks up right where the first book left off.

"IN THE END,
WE WERE LIKE GHOSTS

HANGING ON
TO THE ROOF OF THE EARTH.

HALFWAY BETWEEN WORLDS,
TOO AFRAID TO LET GO."

BEAU TAPLIN

prologue

CHARLIE

L eft or right.

It was as simple as that, except it wasn't simple at all.

If I went left, the road would eventually lead me to the house on the east side of Mount Lebanon — to the man I promised my life to, the one I'd imagined building a family with, the one who'd done everything in his power to try to keep me.

If I went right, the road would take me to a house not so familiar — to the man I used to only know as a boy, the man who came back unannounced, the man I loved first, before I even knew what love was.

I didn't have any more tears to shed. They were all dried on my face, inky lines of mascara marring each cheek like scars. I was at the fork I knew I'd eventually get to all along, the decision I never wanted to make between two choices I never knew I had before two months ago.

The truth was simple.

I loved them both.

My heart was forever severed, destined to exist in two equal halves — one with each man. But one half beat stronger, one half had the vein that ran deepest, and one half held my choice in silence well before I ever admitted it out loud.

The other half would always be a part of me, but in a softer way — a more subdued beating, a quieter presence, a different kind of life support.

A different kind of love.

My chest ached with the realization of what I had to do, of the words I had to say, the heart I had to break. Though the snow had cleared and spring was beginning to paint the earth green all around me, I still felt the harsh bite of winter nipping at my heels as I fled from it — from the cold, from the hurt, to a new beginning, to a new me.

Left or right.

It may not have been a simple choice, but I knew with every beat of my severed heart it was the right one.

So, I took a deep breath, let it out slowly, and turned the wheel.

chapter one

CHARLIE

Two months earlier

The first thing I noticed when I came to the morning after the spring concert was the splitting headache.

My ears rang, loud and shrill, and I creaked one eye open first before the other. When I tried to sit up, a sledgehammer smacked me back down. I groaned, massaging my temples as I laid back into the pillow.

The reality of what had happened the night before filtered in slowly through the waves of my headache, seeping in like frigid ice to my veins. I pressed into my temples, and then I saw a flash of Reese in the closet at school. I pinched the bridge of my nose, and then I saw Cameron's glossed eyes as he begged me to stay.

It was a nightmare, one I'd agreed to subject myself to for two more months.

I was giving Cameron the chance to keep me, but it was Reese who held my heart now.

"Hey."

I opened my eyes again, finding Cameron standing in the doorway of our bedroom. He was already fully dressed for work, his jaw clean shaven, tie fastened at his neck and dark hair styled neat. He balanced a steaming cup of tea on a tiny saucer plate, and when he crossed to sit on the edge of the bed next to me, I saw two small pills next to the mug.

"Ibuprofen," he said, handing me those first. "Figured you might need these."

My eyes were heavy from crying, heart heavy from fighting, and I pushed to sit up as slowly as I could before tossing the coated pills in my mouth. I swallowed, shaking my head when Cameron offered me the tea to help wash them down. He set the mug on our nightstand, exactly where the cup he'd brought me the night before had gone cold.

"How are you feeling?"

Cameron's hand reached forward for mine, cupping over my fingers, and I stared at that point of contact as another sharp pain ripped through my head.

"Tired," I answered. It was the best word I had to wrap up everything I felt. I was exhausted — from the night, from the past couple of months, from the last five years. I wanted to sleep until my nightmare was over. I wanted to cry at just the thought of what I had yet to endure, at the fact that I couldn't just wake up to a new, brighter day where life was simple again.

Cameron squeezed my hand.

"Maybe you should stay home today."

I shook my head before he'd even finished his sentence, throwing the covers back. "No. I want to go."

"I think everyone would understand after last night if you—"

"I want to go, Cameron."

I said the words with finality, and his brows bent together. He knew why I wanted to go, or rather, *whom* I wanted to go to. But he didn't let me see his heart break as that truth settled in.

"Okay," he said with a slight nod.

He stood first, holding out his hand to help me up. I wobbled a little, my head swimming, but Cameron held onto me and kept me steady. When the dizziness passed, I opened my eyes and took him in. My husband. The man I'd promised forever to.

The promise I wasn't sure I could keep anymore.

Cameron pulled his phone from his pocket, tapping a few buttons on the screen before setting it gently beside my tea on the nightstand. A soft, slow melody filled the room, a song I wasn't familiar with, and Cameron pulled me into his arms just as the first verse began.

He swayed me gently, but I was stiff in his arms, my eyes catching on the clock. I needed to get ready.

"I should get dressed," I said, but Cameron still swayed, his hand on the small of my back rubbing gently.

"Just one dance."

"You're going to be late for work."

"They'll live."

I looked at him then, just as the chorus swept over us, and I tried to remember the last time he put me before work. When was the last time he said work could wait, and I was priority number one?

I couldn't remember.

And now, it only felt like he was doing so because he knew he'd lost me.

It was too late, and only now was he waking up.

"Cameron, about last night..."

He shook his head firmly, pulling me closer until my head rested on his chest. He wrapped me up tighter, like that embrace would make me stay, like he could be the anchor that would keep me home.

"We don't need to talk about that right now," he whispered. "I know it was a lot of me to ask, and a lot for you to give. And I know it doesn't mean anything will change." Cameron swallowed then, stopping our dance long enough to pull back and look me in the eyes. "But I won't waste this chance, Charlie. I won't let you go without doing everything in my power to make you want to stay."

He looked younger then, in that morning light. Like the man I fell in love with.

"All I'm asking is that you try, that you let me in again. Just... give me this time with your heart before you decide to give it all to him."

The pain that had reverberated in my head all morning zipped down through my chest, and my next breath was haggard and harsh. I didn't know what to say, didn't know how to feel about the fact that he wanted me.

It wasn't long ago that I would have fallen into his arms overwhelmed with joy at his proclamation. I would have sobbed, would have sighed with relief at him finally coming back to me.

But now, I only felt pain — and anger.

Because it wasn't until he'd lost me, until I'd found comfort in Reese's arms that Cameron had noticed me again.

Cameron pulled me back into him, resting his chin on my head as we swayed, my left hand in his right, my ear to his chest. I closed my eyes, listening to his heart beat, and the longer the song played, the more I felt him. My breaths came a little lighter, the pain in my chest receding, and I sighed.

I still loved him.

I knew that last night. I knew it all weekend, even when I was with Reese, even when I knew I would leave Cameron I also knew I still loved him. I wasn't sure that would ever change, no matter what happened next.

He was the father of my children, the stealer of my heart, the comforter of my soul. He was my family. He was my home.

I just didn't know if that was enough.

As the song ended, Cameron hugged me tight to him, and I blinked away the tears threatening to fall.

"I need to get ready," I said after a moment, my voice low.

It must have killed him, to hear those words when I was in his arms, to know I would get dressed and go to another man. But Cameron just nodded, kissing my forehead before letting me go.

"Okay. Can I make you something for breakfast?"

I shook my head. "The tea is fine."

Cameron's gaze swept over our nightstand.

"I promise I'll drink it," I added, hoping to ease at least that part of his worry. "And I'll eat at lunch. I just need to let my stomach stabilize a little."

He forced a smile, but it fell quickly, and he straightened his tie with a look of resignation. "Okay. I'll see you tonight?"

I forced a smile back. "Mm-hmm."

"Okay." He nodded, hands sliding in the pockets of his slacks. He looked around like he didn't know what to do next before leaning in for a kiss.

My lips met his briefly, just a peck, and then I skirted behind him to our closet.

A few minutes later, I heard the front door close.

I ripped the first blouse I saw from the hanger, throwing it on haphazardly before pairing it with a simple navy skirt.

My hair was back in a bun in the next breath, and I didn't even check the mirror to assess my tired eyes. I knew they were puffy and underlined with deep purple skin, but it didn't matter.

I needed to get to Reese.

As tough as the night had been for me, I knew it must have been torturous for him. He had no idea what happened when I got home, no idea what I was thinking, or feeling, or what would happen next.

He would be angry when he found out, that much I knew. He'd be hurt. I'd promised Cameron a chance. I'd given him my word that, at least for the next two months, I'd stay.

And where did that leave Reese?

That was the question he'd have for me, and I only had the ten-minute drive to school to figure out the answer.

REESE

Blake sat at my kitchen bar, one foot propped under her on the stool while the other hung below her. Her bright blonde hair was piled in a messy bun on top of her head, a few strands hanging down to frame her face. That same hair had been sprawled over my chest when we woke that morning, and all I could think when my eyes opened and I saw it there was that it was the wrong color.

She shoved another bite of cereal in her mouth, her eyes on the fort in the living room.

"Do you mind if I clean that up today?" she asked, nodding to where the sheets hung from the fort Charlie and I had built. "I'll wash all those sheets and get this place looking somewhat decent. I figured you hadn't hung a single thing on the wall," she added with a chuckle. "I'll spend the day making a plan and I can start shopping tomorrow, start making this place feel more like a home."

"That's fine," I answered, though my fists curled at the thought of her touching the fort. Still, I knew she needed something to do, something to fix. That was who she was. And I was one of her favorite projects.

"Great. I was thinking plum, white, and gray for the bedroom. Just a dash of plum, though. Nothing too dark. And for the living room, I'll get some throw pillows to brighten up that dark couch. What do you think of mint?"

She kept talking, but I couldn't register a single word. I just nodded along, giving her permission she wasn't really even asking for. I needed a cigarette like I needed blood in my veins, but I'd promised Charlie I'd try to quit. That was when she was still in my home, in our fort, in my arms.

Now, she was gone, and Blake was in her place.

I still couldn't believe she was here, in Pennsylvania, in the house I'd had Charlie in just hours before Blake had shown up on my front porch.

She was New York. She was bright city lights and lonely broken nights. She was a chapter I'd already read, one I'd turned the page on when I left the city. It didn't feel right that she was here, in a place she never existed to me.

But I couldn't be mad she'd shown up. Not really.

Because we'd never technically ended our relationship when I left.

I met Blake a couple of years before my family died. I was piss ass drunk at a dive bar on the lower east side, causing trouble with one of my buddies from Juilliard.

It was a normal night for me — play piano at the restaurant all night for rich people who didn't hear me anyway, meet up with Ben at his place, hammer down some whiskey and stumble into the first bar we found. Crashing karaoke bars was our favorite, because we could make fun of other drunk assholes and feel a little better about the fact that we were thirty years old and still partying like we were twenty-one.

Neither of us were in a relationship, neither of us had kids, and neither of us had plans. We were the perfect pair.

But on that particular Friday night, Blake had stumbled into the same bar with a group of her girlfriends. She'd gone on stage solo and sang the most beautiful version of Fleetwood Mac's *Dreams* I'd ever heard in my life, and I'd declared on a stomach full of whiskey that I'd marry her one day.

We went on our first date a week later.

Blake had never really been my girlfriend. She was more of a friend who liked to get naked as much as I did. We'd meet up every now and then, sometimes going months between seeing each other, and every time we got together, we lost ourselves in each other. There were long nights spent in my apartment, smoking cigarettes and making out between stories. She'd always be gone the next morning before I woke up, and I never really knew when I'd see her again. I just knew that I would.

But when my family died, everything changed.

Blake had been there for me. She was the only one. She'd helped me with everything — the funeral, the will, the reporters, my bills, my job. There was so much to do, to handle, and I could barely get out of bed in the morning. In fact, on most days, I didn't. But Blake was there, handling all of it. She'd even tried to save me from myself when I was blowing through my inheritance, begging me for a small portion of it to invest.

That was all that was left of it now.

She hadn't just been there to handle the paperwork, either. She'd been there on the long, torturous nights where I'd break down into tears and drink myself stupid trying to mourn my loss. It was in that time that I realized those nights we'd slept together, the nights she'd shared my bed, we'd also shared a deeper part of ourselves.

She loved me. She loved me enough to be there for me in one of the darkest times of my life. And in that time, I realized I loved her, too.

Blake moved in with me a few weeks after my family passed just to make sure I wouldn't hurt myself. She took care of me like a mother, like a sister, like a friend, and like a wife.

So, I made her my girlfriend.

But when it came to moving, I hadn't thought twice about her. It was shitty, and I hated to admit it out loud. But that was just the way we were. She had never told me she loved me, and I never told her. She was there when I needed her, and I was there when she needed me. But she was busy with her own life just as I was with mine, and though we lived together, it was almost more as roommates than anything.

Sure, we had the title, but it didn't feel like anything had changed between us. We were still the same boy and girl who slept together and didn't talk for months at a time, except now we still shared a bed.

So, when I left, I didn't even consider the fact that she might want more.

I just thought that was where it ended. We had a few conversations about keeping in touch, about seeing each other when I came back into town, but we never said we would stay together. We never said we would do the long-distance thing, or that she would move, or I would come back.

Then again, we never said we were done, either.

And so, I couldn't really be mad that she's surprised me, probably thinking it'd make me happy to see her. And in a way, I was. Blake was perhaps my only *true* friend I had anymore.

But I had no idea how to explain her to Charlie, or vice versa.

And I had no idea what her being here meant.

"I need to get going," I said after she'd run off a list of all the things she wanted to accomplish that day. I dumped what was left of my coffee in the sink and swiped my coat off the counter. "I'll leave the spare house keys hanging on the hook by the door, and just text me if you need anything."

"Okay," she said with a bright smile. "I'll make dinner tonight, too. What time do you think you'll be home?"

"Not sure." My mind shot to Charlie. "But I'll let you know."

Blake smiled, hopping off the barstool and skipping around the kitchen island until she was in my arms. I had no choice but to catch her, to pull her into me, and when she leaned up to press a kiss to my lips, I kissed her back.

And I felt like absolute scum.

By the time I made it to school, it was only ten minutes before the first bell. It was the latest I'd been since I started, and I knew without a second guess that it was too late to talk to Charlie before the day began.

Still, I bolted to her classroom, and when I saw her standing at her whiteboard with her teacher's aide, I didn't know whether to sigh with relief or crumble from the pain. Her eyes flicked to mine as she ran over the day's plan with Robin, and they didn't give anything away before they were gone again. I watched her intently, waiting, watching the clock behind her, knowing there wasn't time to hear all I hoped to.

When Robin nodded and began distributing workbooks to each table, Charlie walked slowly and calmly over to where I stood in her doorway.

"Mr. Walker," she said, loud enough for Robin to hear. "Good morning. How are you?"

"Very well," I answered automatically. "Wanted to come check on you after last night. Feeling okay?"

"Yes, I'm okay. Thank you for asking. It was a wonderful spring concert, by the way. I'm sure Mr. Henderson is very proud of all your hard work."

I forced a smile, but my stomach turned as I searched her face for a sign of something — *anything* — to let me know how she was truly feeling.

I found nothing.

"I was wondering if you have plans for lunch. I wanted to go over the concert with you, talk about ways to improve for next semester."

"Oh," Charlie said, and she glanced briefly over her shoulder at Robin, who seemed oblivious to our conversation, anyway. "Sure. I'll see you in the café then?"

"Perfect."

I stood rooted to that spot, my hands in my pockets wrapped into tight fists to keep from reaching for her. I wanted to kiss her so badly I felt the pain of it like a thorn in my heart. Her hair was in a bun at the nape of her neck, her eyes tired and dark, her expression weary. I wanted to pull her into me, to play her any song she wanted to hear and then make love to her in our fort.

In our fort that Blake was currently taking down.

My stomach rolled again. I knew I had to tell Charlie about Blake, and I felt that Charlie had something to tell me, too. I had no idea what happened after she fainted at the concert last night. Did they fight? Did she tell him she was leaving? Did he make her cry?

I searched her eyes with my own, begging her to give me some kind of sign.

And then, slowly, purposefully — she smiled.

It was just a small smile, but it was a real one, one that told me we would talk later. I didn't know what that conversation would hold, but that smile gave me hope — it gave me something to hold onto.

I sighed with the relief it brought, offering her a smile of my own.

She was still mine. She was still with me. There was hope.

"Have a good morning, Mr. Walker," she said, and her eyes softened, her own hand twitching forward for me before she clasped it over her opposite wrist, instead.

"You too, Mrs.... Pierce." I swallowed, lips flattening. "See you at lunch."

When I was clear of her, I took a full breath, letting it out like a frustrated bull.

Four hours. I had to wait four hours to talk to her.

I watched the clock all morning.

Charlie was late to lunch.

I'd already piled up a plate with a hot sandwich that was rapidly turning cold as I sat at the table in the far back corner of the teachers' café, waiting for Charlie to show. I checked my phone for a text from her, but there was nothing.

There *were* several texts from Blake about the house, and dinner, and movie options for after dinner. But I couldn't think about her — not yet, not before I talked to Charlie.

She finally rushed in twenty minutes after I'd already been there, and I threw my hand up to wave her back. She blew out a sigh, shoving her phone into her pocket like she'd just ended a call.

"Sorry," she said on a breath as she slid her bag into one of the empty chairs at the table I'd claimed.

I waited for her to tell me who was on the phone, but she didn't offer anything past the apology.

"It's okay," I said, but my eyes drifted to her pocket, wondering if it was Cameron who had called. "Grab a plate and we can talk?" I suggested.

She looked at the bar of food like eating was the last thing she wanted to do, but she nodded. "Yeah, I should probably try to eat. Let me just grab a bowl of soup."

I couldn't take my eyes off her as she moved through the line of teachers, and I kept them there as she took the seat across from me, the steam from her soup drifting up to her nose.

"Hi," she said once she seated.

"Hi."

She smiled.

I smiled.

Then, her brows bent together, her hand sliding up to rest flat on the table.

"I missed you last night," she whispered.

I laughed, blowing out a breath. "To say I missed you, too, would be the understatement of the century." I shifted. "What happened, Charlie?"

Her face broke a little more, and she glanced around us. There were only a few other teachers still in the café, most had already eaten and made their way back to their classrooms.

"I don't know," she said with a sigh, running a hand up to smooth over her hair. "We talked. He took care of me after I fainted."

"I would have, too."

"I know," she said. "That's not what I meant. I just mean he took me home, made me some tea. And we talked." She swallowed. "I told him I wanted a divorce."

My heart stopped, kicking to life again with a newfound hope. It was unbelievable, that she'd told him about us, that she'd told him she was done. So much so that I questioned if I'd imagined hearing her say it, at all.

But there she was, sitting across from me, telling me she would leave her husband and be with me.

It was real. She wanted me.

Charlie Reid was finally mine.

My hand slid up onto the table to mirror hers, and I pushed it forward. There were still at least twelve inches between our fingertips, but I felt the charge between them like we were holding hands. I wished so desperately to pull her into me, to kiss her, to tell her she was making the right decision.

That I would love her better.

"What did he say?" I asked once my heart had settled.

Charlie looked down at her soup.

"He asked me for two months."

And just like that, all the hope drained.

Those words hung between us like smoke, and my gaze dropped to Charlie's soup, too. I couldn't look at her when I asked the next question.

"What does that mean?"

Where does that leave me?

Charlie's eyes stayed on the soup.

"He said you'd been back in my life for two months," she said. "He said he wanted the same amount of time to show me I should stay."

"Bullshit."

Charlie reddened. "Reese..."

"No, it's bullshit. He's had years, Charlie. *Years.*" I shook my head.

The logical side of me echoed my thoughts with *of course he asked for more time, he loves her and doesn't want to lose her, dumb ass*. But the side of me that had tasted Charlie, the side that had felt what it was like to own her — *that* side said bullshit.

He didn't deserve her. He'd naïvely believed he could treat her the way he had for five years and she'd just stay. He thought she'd never leave. And then when she finally told him she was going, he begged for more time.

Bullshit.

"Why should he get another two months?" I asked.

I was fuming, nostrils flaring as Charlie slipped her hand back from where it rested in front of mine and picked up her soup spoon, instead. I felt the loss of that energy between

17

us, and I reached my hand forward, begging her to keep the connection.

"I don't know, because he wants a chance, I guess," she said with a shrug. "He wants more time."

"And what do you want?"

She closed her eyes on a breath.

"I don't know, Reese. I'm just... I'm confused. I love him, too." Her eyes opened again, the pain in them mirroring mine. "I'm sorry, but I do. This is all... it's so much."

She dropped her soup spoon before even attempting to take a bite, sitting back in her chair.

My hand inched forward again, and she watched the movement, her eyes stuck on my fingertips before they found me again. I needed to touch her. I needed to hold her, to remind her what it felt like when she was in my arms this weekend.

Watching her sitting there so close to me, yet so far away, it was almost as torturous as the night she left me in the fort we'd built. And with the next words she spoke, the same longing ache I'd felt that night ripped through me like a knife.

"I told him yes."

Her voice was just a whisper, but it might as well have been a train.

"I gave him two months."

I closed my eyes, pushing a breath through my nose as I tried to hold onto what hope was still left.

I wanted to scream, to flip tables and demand for her to leave him tonight. The rational side of me didn't exist when it came to Charlie. There was only the mad man inside me, the one who had wanted her for so long — *too* long — and now that he'd had her, there was no satiating him.

She had to be mine. That was the only answer.

But I knew I couldn't have her if I didn't give her the time she needed, the space to make the decision on her own.

She had to choose me, too.

After a moment, I leaned back in my own chair, my hand still flat on the table, though there was too much distance between us now. "I understand," I finally said.

"You do?"

"I do."

Charlie sighed, leaning forward, her hand on the table again. She spread her fingers over the cool surface, her eyes on mine.

"Thank you," she said, fingers inching forward.

We watched each other, and I asked her without words what this meant for me — for us. When her hand reached just far enough for her middle finger to touch the tip of mine, my heart squeezed.

It didn't change anything for us. That small touch told me so.

Hope trickled back in.

"There's something I need to tell you, too," I said, and I swept my hand over hers.

But before I could say another word, Mr. Henderson swung into the café, his eyes lighting up when he spotted us in the corner.

I pulled my hand from Charlie quickly, running it back through my hair and forcing a smile as he approached. Charlie arched a questioning brow, but when Mr. Henderson came into her view, she sat up straighter, finally taking the first bite of her soup.

"Afternoon, Mr. Walker," he said, greeting me first before

nodding at Charlie. "Mrs. Pierce. I'm so glad I found you two together. I have great news."

Charie's cheeks were tinged a deep pink, and she only smiled up at Mr. Henderson briefly before taking another bite of her soup.

"What news is that?" I asked.

He clapped his hands together excitedly, his eyes doubling in size. "Well, I just received confirmation that we have two seats at the Star Schools Conference again this year. Are you familiar?"

He didn't wait for me to answer before he continued.

"It's a high-end conference for teachers at model schools, mostly private, some public. Incredible speakers and break-out sessions, one of the best conferences in the nation. This year they're in Miami, and, well..." Mr. Henderson gave us both a toothy smile. "I hope you two like the beach!"

Charlie and I exchanged a look.

"Are you saying that you're sending *us*?" Charlie asked.

"I am! How could I not send two of my award-nominated teachers?" he said.

That earned him more blank looks from us.

"I'm so happy to be the one to tell you that you have *both* been nominated for awards at our annual Westchester Year End Gala. Reese, you have been nominated for our Bright Beginning award, which is reserved for teachers who have joined us in the last eighteen months. And Charlie," he said, turning to her with the most prideful smile I'd ever seen him wear. "You, my dear, have been nominated for Teacher of the Year." He chuckled. "And if it counts for anything at all, you've already got my vote."

Charlie covered her mouth with the fingertips I'd just

touched, her eyes finding mine before they drifted back up to Mr. Henderson. "*Me?*"

"Yes, you." Mr. Henderson extended his hand for hers. "Congratulations."

She shook his hand deftly, shock still painting her face. "I'm... honored. Thank you."

"You're quite welcome, I'm so happy I had the pleasure of telling you. Now," he said once he had finished shaking Charlie's hand. "The conference is in less than three weeks. I'll work on finding substitutes for your classrooms, as it takes place on a Thursday, Friday, Saturday. You'll fly back Sunday. Mrs. Trumane at the front office will email you all the details, as well as your travel information."

Charlie still couldn't speak, so I thanked Mr. Henderson for us, and after swiping a cupcake from the bar, he was gone.

"Congratulations, Charlie," I said, reaching forward for her hand. This time I took it greedily, squeezing it in my own, wishing I could do so much more. "I'm so happy for you."

"Thank you," she whispered, shaking her head. "I just... I can't believe it." Then, her eyes caught mine. "And we're going to a conference."

"We are."

"Just the two of us."

I smirked. "Indeed."

The first bell rang, signaling the end of the lunch hour, and Charlie's attention snapped to the clock on the wall before she jumped up.

"I didn't realize how late it was. I have to get back."

"Wait," I said, standing with her. I stepped a little closer, lowering my voice.

"I have to run. We can talk more at dinner tomorrow night?"

"Dinner?"

She smiled. "I figured they hadn't told you. Pretend to be surprised, please? My parents invited Cameron and I to come watch you play at the restaurant."

A flurry of thoughts and feelings assaulted me at her surprise — happiness that her parents wanted to see me play, relief that I'd get to see Charlie outside of school, anger that Cameron would be there with her, and complete dread at the fact that I likely wouldn't be able to keep Blake away.

"Can we have lunch again tomorrow?"

Charlie was already rushing toward the door, her bag slung over her shoulder. "I can't, meeting with Robin to discuss a few lesson plans. I'll need to make a plan for when we're out for the conference now, too."

Something had shifted in Charlie since the beginning of lunch, likely due to her award nomination. She smiled so brightly, her cheeks rosy pink, hazelnut eyes wide and light.

I hated that I had to share her.

She seemed to read that emotion on my face, because she checked over her shoulder that we were alone, then she stepped into me, lifting up onto her toes to press a kiss to my lips.

I stiffened, eyes still open and searching behind her, but the other teachers had gone already. So, I melted into her, pulling her flush against me and sucking her bottom lip between my teeth. She grinned against my lips, sealing the kiss with one last peck, and then she pulled back, flushed.

"For the record," I said, sweeping a fallen strand of her hair behind her ear. "I hate that you're going home to him tonight."

Her face crumpled. "Please... I need you to understand."

"I do," I assured her. "But it doesn't make me hate it any less."

She squeezed my hand in understanding, and I held that hand as she walked away, only letting it drop once she'd reached the doorway of the café. I watched her go, leaning against the doorframe until she disappeared around the corner of the hallway, and then I finally made my way back to my classroom.

Two months.

I shook my head, disappointed in myself that I'd thought Cameron would let her go so easily. I hated him for asking her for anything, most of all more time, but I couldn't blame him. He was playing his last cards, whatever ones he had left.

I would have done the same.

I would have done anything to keep her.

Still, I didn't know how I would get her alone now, how I would remind her of the way it felt to be together this weekend. Something happened in my house, in that fort, at that piano — it was like traveling back in time, but as the people we are now. I wanted to share all of my scars with her, and I wanted to heal all of hers in return.

That would be harder to do with Cameron holding on so tight.

The realization that Blake was in the picture now, too, made me curl my fists in the pockets of my slacks. I didn't know where to start with explaining her to Charlie, and I didn't know how to cut Blake *out* of the picture, either.

The truth was, I loved her, too. I didn't want to hurt her.

But I didn't want to *be* with her, either.

I sighed, running a frustrated hand through my hair. The truth would have to come out — to Charlie first, and eventually, to Blake. Would Charlie hate me? Would she understand?

Would this work in Cameron's favor?

I didn't have any of the answers, but I knew one thing for sure.

I had to get Charlie alone before tomorrow night.

chapter Two

CAMERON

When I was eight years old, I watched my father beat my mother to a bloody pulp — and then he went to jail for the rest of his life, and I went to live with my grandparents.

That was the sob story everyone wanted from me. Everyone. The girls who slept with me, the sports psychiatrist for the hockey team at Garrick, the coach who didn't understand why I didn't try to go pro — they all wanted the story. They wanted to solve the mystery, to know more about the man behind the mask.

Charlie was the only one who ever got it.

She was the only one who ever got the story, who ever got *all* of me.

I couldn't be sure why those memories were resurfacing as I sat on the edge of our bed Wednesday evening, watching Charlie put on her makeup in her vanity mirror. I used to follow her around when she was getting ready, back when we were younger. It'd take me all of ten minutes to be dressed and ready to go for a night out, but it always took her at least an hour.

So, I followed her around, playing music for us and talking about anything and everything.

I'd make her laugh, refill her wine, tell her she didn't even need any of the makeup she was so carefully applying. She'd tell me about her dreams and I'd listen. I always loved to listen to her, even when I didn't have much to say.

Somewhere along the way, I stopped doing that.

I started watching TV downstairs instead, or I'd sit in my office and work until the very minute she was ready to walk out the door. I couldn't name the year when I'd decided I didn't want to spend time with her while she got ready anymore. I couldn't remember what changed.

But tonight, I took my old seat on the edge of the bed, right behind her, and I watched with adoration as she carefully swiped her dark eyeliner over her lids, bringing it to a gentle point at the crease of her eyes.

And I also thought of my father.

Maybe it was because right now, staring at my beautiful wife, I couldn't imagine the kind of man who could beat someone he made vows to. I couldn't imagine hurting Charlie, couldn't bear the thought of seeing her cringe as my hand connected with her cheek, or hearing her scream as my hands wrapped around her tiny arms.

I couldn't fathom hurting her, and yet I had.

That simple fact might as well have been my father's fist, for how hard it sucker punched me in the gut, for the sting it left in its wake — a constant reminder, a chronic pain.

I may not have struck her to the ground, or raised my voice, or done anything to purposefully make her feel like she was anything but my entire world. But I had let her grieve the loss our sons alone. I had let her think I'd abandoned her, I'd failed to use my words to comfort her when she needed me most, and I'd let another man come between us and sweep her off her feet right in front of me.

If she wouldn't have agreed to give me two months to change her mind, I wouldn't have been able to live with myself.

Two months.

Those words circled my every thought as Charlie tucked her eyeliner away, pulling out my favorite red lipstick, next. Her eyes caught mine in the mirror as she rolled the bottom of the tube, the red stick emerging, and I smirked.

"My favorite."

Charlie blushed, leaning forward a little to smooth the stick over her top lip.

"I remember."

I couldn't help but watch her as she applied the last of it, rolling her lips together once both of them were coated. Then, I stood, towering behind her before I bent to whisper into the hollow point of her ear.

"Can't wait to help you take that off later."

Goose bumps sparked from where my lips touched her skin and spread like wildfire down her bare neck. I smiled, finding some sort of hope in the fact that I still knew that spot was one of her weak points, that it was where I'd whisper my darkest desires to her before I made them all come true later in our bed.

Charlie's eyes found mine in the mirror again, heated at first, but then slowly subdued, slowly saddened.

I realized then that I wasn't the only one she was putting the lipstick on for.

Maybe I wasn't even on her mind at all, anymore.

But I didn't question her, didn't let it show. I just kissed her neck, holding her gaze in the mirror as long as I could.

"I'll go get the car warmed up," I told her. "Meet you in the foyer?"

She nodded, her smile soft and meek. It was a mix of love and pity. I wasn't sure which one weighed more.

As I descended our stairs, I checked the time on my watch, and the irony wasn't lost on me.

Time.

It was something I'd never paid attention to before. It felt like an unlimited resource, something I had plenty of. I had time to work through our sons' death on my own, time to give Charlie her space, time to bring her back to me when she was ready, time to build a life with her — and to try to build a family again, too.

I thought I had forever.

Now, I only had weeks.

Once the car was started, I waited in the foyer, and Charlie came down the stairs in only the way she could — like an angel. She floated from step to step, her long black dress trailing the wood, her neck decorated with a simple strand of pearls that I'd bought her for Mother's Day when she was pregnant. I waited until she stood in front of me at the bottom step, then I took her hand in mine.

"You're beautiful," I told her.

"Thank you, Cam."

She smiled, squeezing my hand, and I wrapped her coat around her before walking her to the car.

On the drive to the restaurant where we would watch Reese play piano, I squeezed her thigh and told her I loved her.

She told me she loved me, too.

I believed her, and I knew that was what I needed to hold onto — that love. I had to bring it back to life from where it hung on with futile breaths now. Time was working against me, and I had years to make up for, with just days to do it. Days and weeks and two insufficient months. It wasn't enough time, but it had to be.

The only thing I could know to be true was that she still loved me.

I hoped that love was enough to bring her back to me, too.

CHARLIE

I thought about Jane again on the drive to dinner Wednesday evening.

It hadn't yet been a week since I'd let her loose, since I'd opened our bedroom window and told her to fly free. The more time passed, the more I missed her.

As I stared out the window on our drive to dinner, I wondered if she was out there, staring right back at me from a distance.

Cameron's hand rested easily on my leg, just above my knee, his fingers keeping the inside of my thigh warm as we drove. He'd watched me get ready that evening, from the time I started doing my hair until I applied the very last of my lipstick. It was something he used to do — *before*.

Every time I looked in the mirror and found his gaze staring back at me, my stomach warmed.

It had always been so special to me, that he would just follow me around while I got ready. It never took him long, and he could have easily done a number of other things. But he always stayed, watching, talking, laughing.

It was like every minute he got to spend with me was a precious one.

Just like on our way to dinner two months before when I couldn't remember when his hand had stopped finding my knee in the car, I couldn't remember when he'd stopped watching me get ready. But tonight, he'd done both again.

It should have made me swoon. It *would* have, just weeks before. I stared at his hand and willed myself to feel that same fluttery joy I'd felt the night after my parents' house, the night I thought we'd have sex again. I tried to remember what it felt like the night he claimed me after I'd been at Happy Hour with Reese. I searched for the love and adoration I'd felt when I walked in on him redoing my library to surprise me.

But I came up empty.

And if those feelings were the needles, the excitement I felt over seeing Reese was the hay that made the stack. *Those* feelings were bountiful. The very knee that Cameron held onto bounced with anticipation of seeing another man — one I couldn't stop thinking about.

We hadn't had the chance to be alone since Monday night, since before Cameron surprised us both on stage at the spring concert. Thankfully, I'd been able to talk to him during school yesterday, but we hadn't had a single moment in passing today. There were several times he'd tried to catch me, to talk to me, but we'd been interrupted every time. I couldn't wait to see him, to finally be able to have more than a crossing of paths.

I wondered how he'd look tonight, what tuxedo he would wear, how he'd style his hair. I wondered if he'd look at me while he played. I wondered if he'd find a way to steal a moment from me.

I wondered if hell was nice, since all signs pointed to me going there now.

My husband was in the car with me, begging me for my attention, and I couldn't stop fantasizing about Reese. I'd waited so long to have this want from Cameron, to have him look at me the way he used to, to hear the words he'd always held silently in his heart.

And when my mind wandered like that, I thought about Jane, my beloved Budgie that I'd set loose.

I wondered if she still loved me and thought of me, too. I wondered if she was thankful I'd set her free, or if she was devastated that I had let her go. In two months, I'd be in her place, only I'd have the choice — fly out the window to a new life, or stay inside with the one I've known for years.

I was only two days into the two months I'd promised Cameron, and I already felt the truth of it all like it was a necklace I never took off — one I didn't have to examine to know what it looked like, to know it was there.

Two months wouldn't be enough.

Still, when we arrived at the restaurant and Cameron circled the car to my side at valet, opening my door for me and helping me out with his hand in mine, I made a promise to myself that I would at least try. I would at least hear him out. I would at least give him the chance I promised him.

At least then, at the end of it all, I could say I'd made the right decision.

I looped my arm in Cameron's as we made our way inside The Kinky Starfish, a swanky dinner and cocktail spot in the heart of downtown Pittsburgh. I'd never been before, though Mom and Dad had spent a couple of anniversaries there. All I knew was that one dinner there cost about as much as our entire electric bill, and the dinner was served slowly and purposefully over the course of four hours.

It wasn't just food. It was an experience.

With Reese playing the piano that evening, I had no doubt it would be one I'd never forget.

I could feel how tense Cameron was as he opened the door for me, ushering me inside and out of the cold. We checked our coats, and when I threaded my arm through his again, I squeezed his forearm. No matter what was going on in my head right now, I knew it was a huge sacrifice for him to be here. He knew we were coming to watch Reese play, the man whom I'd spent the entire weekend with.

I knew without a doubt that I couldn't do the same if our roles were reversed.

It felt a little like masochism to me, that Cameron not only agreed to let me go tonight, but that he came with me. I wondered if it was just so he could keep an eye on me, so he could keep Reese and me away from each other, or if he was just trying to show me that he wasn't going anywhere.

It suddenly occurred to me that I hadn't even asked how he was feeling.

Tugging on his arm, I pulled him to the side of the hostess stand before he could tell her the name of our reservation.

"Are you okay?"

Cameron's brows knitted together. "I'm fine. Are you okay?"

"No, I mean... are you *okay*? With being here."

Cameron swallowed, his eyes catching somewhere behind me before they found mine again. "I'll survive."

"We can go," I offered, but my stomach sank at the thought. "If you don't want to be here. I understand."

His jaw flexed, and he grabbed my hands in his, pulling me closer.

"You want me to be honest right now?"

I nodded, smoothing my thumb over his.

Cameron looked at me for a long moment, his eyes searching mine like he was the one who'd asked a question and I had the answer inside them. It seemed almost like he was debating whether he could tell me the truth or not — whether it would matter. Or maybe he didn't even know what the truth was, himself.

Finally, he let out a long breath, shaking his head. "The truth is nothing matters more to me than your happiness," he said, voice just above a whisper. "And I can see as clearly as that lipstick on your lips that being here makes you happy. So yes, I'm okay." He squeezed my hands. "I'm more than okay."

His admission made my heart ache, and I squeezed his hands in return, because I knew while that may have been a truth, it wasn't the *entire* truth.

He was hurting. Being here hurt him.

And he was taking the pain for me.

I couldn't wrap my mind around that kind of selfless love, not when I was in the middle of what was possibly the most selfish time in my entire life. But I didn't have time to overthink it before Cameron leaned forward to softly kiss my lips, and then he led us to the hostess, who took us immediately to the table.

Mom and Dad were already there, and they jumped up as soon as they saw us, Dad rushing to shake Cameron's hand as Mom wrapped me in a hug. They were going on and on about how excited they were for all of us to be there, but I was too busy staring at the stranger at our table to hear anything they were saying.

It was a woman.

A woman who, if I had to guess, was not much older than me. She had platinum blonde hair, straight as a pin and hanging down to the middle of her back. She pulled it over one shoulder as she smiled, waiting patiently behind my parents as they greeted us. Her bright blue eyes were heavily lined, her lips the same red shade as mine, and she wore a tight, beige dress that hugged all of her curves and showed off her beautiful tan skin.

My first thought was that she was someone new to the country club, a new trophy wife Mom was trying to make feel welcome. Then I thought maybe she was a new employee at Reid Energy Solutions, or perhaps a client Dad was trying to schmooze.

But something inside me, something low in my gut, told me the reason she was there wasn't for my parents.

"Oh!" Mom said when our greetings were done and she noticed the woman standing behind them. "Where are my manners? Charlie, Cameron, I'm so excited to introduce you to Blake Springthorpe. She's joining us all the way from New York City."

"So nice to meet you both," she said, her smile taking over her entire face as she leaned forward to shake my hand first, and then Cameron's. "It's nice to know Reese still has such amazing childhood friends that would come see him play on his first night."

I lifted one brow, the sinking in my stomach growing more as we finished shaking hands. "Oh, you know Reese?"

Blake laughed a little, the sound light and angelic as she shared a knowing look with my mother. Behind her, I noticed Reese crossing the room toward us from back where the bathrooms were, and his eyes doubled in size when he saw me.

Just before he joined us, Mom confirmed that feeling in my gut was there for a reason.

"Of course she knows him, sweetie." Mom chuckled. "This is Reese's girlfriend."

chapter three

REESE

I f hell was a place on Earth, I was literally walking into it in a tuxedo.

I'd told myself to wait, to not go to the bathroom until after Charlie and Cameron had arrived. I was going to try to pull her aside before she got to the table, though I hadn't exactly figured out how I would do that yet. But it didn't matter now — she was standing right next to Blake.

And judging by the steam coming from her ears, I wasn't going to have the chance to explain a damn thing.

"Ah, there's the man of the night!" Maxwell said as I approached the group. He clapped me hard on the back, squeezing my shoulder with a proud grin. "Are you open for requests yet, son? You must play *The Way You Look Tonight.*"

Gloria beamed. "That's our wedding song."

"Exactly, dear. That's why he must play it."

He leaned in to kiss her blushing cheek, and I swear Blake melted into a puddle on the floor watching them.

Charlie, however, was shooting lasers at me with her beautiful brown eyes.

"Anything for you, Mr. Reid," I said, clearing my throat. "Nice to see you, Charlie." I clenched my jaw, trying to keep my smile in place. "Cameron."

"Oh, we wouldn't miss it," Cameron said, his grin wide and confident. Clearly he'd caught on to the fact that Charlie didn't know about Blake, and he didn't have to say anything for me to already know what he was thinking.

This would work against me, and play right into his plan to convince Charlie to stay.

"Mom was just introducing us to your *girlfriend*," Charlie said next, and the woman didn't show a single card as the words left her lips. They were light and airy, riding on a beautiful smile — one that I knew hid all the questions she had for me.

And likely a few curse words, too.

"Why am I not surprised you haven't told them about me yet?" Blake teased, threading her arm in mine and leaning up on her toes to kiss my cheek.

Charlie watched that kiss with murder in her eyes.

"Reese always was the perpetual bachelor," she explained to the group, a charming smile firmly in place. "I don't think the word *girlfriend* left his lips in at least ten years before he made it official with me."

Maxwell and Gloria laughed at that, and it was a perfect segue for Gloria to tell the story of how she and Maxwell had met and started dating. I smiled and nodded as she did, but my eyes kept finding Charlie's, and hers never left mine.

I wasn't sure if she wanted to cry or kill me.

It felt a little like both.

I cursed the time on my watch that told me I had to make my way to my piano. I wouldn't get my first fifteen-minute break for at least an hour, and that meant an hour of playing and not talking to Charlie. It meant an hour of her not knowing why I kept Blake from her, and how I felt about her.

It also meant an hour with Cameron.

And an hour for Blake to make things even worse.

I gritted my teeth, knowing I had no choice but to wait for that break. I had to figure out a way to get her away from the table when that time came.

"Well, it's time for me to start," I said. "I'll join you for a drink after this first set."

"Oh, good luck, babe!" Blake said excitedly, kissing my cheek again before taking her seat next to Gloria.

"Break a leg, son," Maxwell chimed.

And with one last, longing look at Charlie, I made my way to the piano.

———

It was the longest, most torturous hour of my life.

While playing the piano for someone other than a student again should have brought me nothing but joy, all I could do was force a smile as I played through my set list, all the while checking the time on my watch for an acceptable amount of time to pass for me to take a break.

When I wasn't charming the crowd with the occasional wink and smile, I was staring at Charlie.

Blake seemed to be the one filling all the conversation at the table, and the more she made everyone else laugh, the more I watched Charlie drink. The more she drank, the more her brows lowered as she glared at me.

It was literally the worst-case scenario, and I cursed myself more and more each passing minute for not making time to explain to her before the night had arrived. Trying to catch her at school earlier today had been impossible, but I should have somehow found a way to make it work. I should have waited to use the damn bathroom until she was here.

Rookie mistakes, ones that would cost me.

Still, I wasn't out of cards, and I played one I hoped would salvage the night as I rounded out my set list.

"Ladies and gentlemen," I said, fingers softly grazing the keys as I addressed the crowd. "It's time for me to take a short break. But don't worry, I'll be back soon to continue playing your requests. Before I go, here's one last song. This one is an original, one I wrote for a very special girl." I smiled then. "I think that's how all the great love songs start, isn't it?"

The crowd chuckled a bit at that, and I found Charlie's eyes once more, wondering if she was starting to recognize the tune as my fingers moved. Blake pressed a hand to her chest where she sat beside Gloria. She thought the song was for her.

But I didn't have to say for Charlie to know.

It was the same tune she'd woken up to, the one I'd written after I'd had her for the first time, after I'd touched her, kissed her, existed inside her. And when the first crescendo played, I saw recognition hit.

Charlie's frown faded for the first time that night, and I begged her with my eyes across that crowded room to listen. I tried with the only tool I had to bring her back to that night, to the weekend, to the night not so long ago before everything got even more complicated between us.

That night seemed so far away now.

Had it really just been days before? Was it really only Wednesday now? For some reason, that first night we shared seemed like years ago, and my chest ached with the need to bring it back to Charlie. I wanted to take her home. I wanted to hold her. I wanted to remind her how she could be loved, if she chose me.

Cameron had forgotten their anniversary. He had forgotten to be a husband to Charlie when she needed him most. Now, he begged her for more time, but he didn't deserve it.

He didn't deserve her.

Then again, I was the one with a "girlfriend" sitting at the table with her right now. As much as Cameron had hurt her, now I had, too.

I just hoped the song would reach her.

Charlie watched me as I played, her face stoic, hand reaching for her wine every now and then. I still cast my gaze over the entire crowd, but I found her more than usual that song, trying to read her, trying to hold her with the song since I couldn't hold her in my arms.

Near the end, I watched the candlelight catch in her eyes as they glossed over, and she shook her head before standing abruptly, whispering something to Cameron before dashing back toward the bathrooms.

There was another full minute in the song, but I ended it early, thanking the restaurant for their applause all the while making sure I didn't lose Charlie in the crowd. Once I'd taken my bows, I stopped by the table long enough to ask Blake to order me a drink and thank the Reids for their kind compliments.

Then, I excused myself for the bathroom, chasing after the only girl who mattered.

CHARLIE

I flew into the women's bathroom with steam rolling off my skin in waves.

Stomping into the first open stall, I slammed the door closed behind me and fisted my hands at my sides. If it wasn't such a nice restaurant, I would have screamed. I would have cursed. I would have probably cried.

Because I'd been duped.

Reese had done nothing but look at me like I was the only woman who mattered in the world for the last two months. He'd taken his time, slowly making his way inside my heart, and once he'd had it, he'd dug his claws in deep. I believed every word he said — how could I not with the sincerity I found in his emerald eyes?

But Blake Springthorpe was living proof that all of it was a lie.

Reese had a girlfriend, and suddenly everything that had existed between us felt like the reflection of a fun house mirror. It was warped — a fat, distorted version of the truth.

He'd lied to me, he'd kept any mention of Blake out of every single conversation we'd had, and even worse — he'd cheated on her.

With me.

A married woman.

A new rush of anger flooded me at the realization, at how stupid I had been, how careless, how completely naïve. I let it take me over, my body bending with that rage, until it faded and left behind the real cause of my grief.

Hurt.

I was hurt.

I was jealous and scared, angry and sad, and more than anything, I was confused. Why would he say the things he did, and do the things he'd done, if he was in a relationship? Was he ever going to tell me about her? Was he ever going to end it with her?

Or was I just a conquest?

My fingers ran up through my hair, twisting and gripping until the pain I felt in my chest transitioned to my scalp.

It occurred to me then that while I knew the Reese Walker who existed fourteen years ago, the one I'd stayed up late with talking and listening to him play piano, I hadn't a clue who he had become over the years — or who he really was now.

How could I believe him as the boy I used to know, when that boy no longer existed?

I forced several breaths in the bathroom stall before slowly moving to the sink. I washed my hands calmly, reapplying my lipstick and fixing my hair. For a moment, I just stared at the woman gazing back at me, the woman I didn't recognize. I saw so many things in that reflection: a wife, a daughter, a cheater, a liar, a lost little girl, a selfish woman.

I wondered what other people saw.

When my heart was as calm as it could be, given the circumstances, I opened the door that led back into the restaurant. But before I could take two steps, a hand wrapped around my wrist, and I was yanked into the mens' bathroom.

Panic surged through me as Reese tugged me inside, pressing my back into the door and covering my mouth with his hand as he locked it behind us. When I realized it was him, I narrowed my eyes, biting his middle finger until he yanked his hand back.

"Ouch!" He shook his hand out. "What the hell, Charlie?"

"You were messing up my lipstick," I said flatly, pressing my hands into his chest. I shoved him off me, crossing the empty bathroom to the mirror to fix the mess he'd made.

Reese just watched me, and I knew what he wanted — he wanted me to make a scene. He wanted me to cry, to beg him to tell me who Blake was and what she meant to him, but I refused to give him the satisfaction.

Instead, I acted completely unfazed, wetting the corner of a paper towel before wiping away the small smudges around my lips.

"Charlie," he started, moving into the space behind me. "I'm so sorry about Blake. I can explain."

"Oh, don't worry," I said calmly. "She's told us plenty of stories over the last hour. I think I know all I need to know."

"It's complicated."

I scoffed. "I'm sure it is."

Reese blew out a frustrated sigh, stepping a little closer until my eyes found his in the mirror.

"When I left New York, yes — she was technically still my girlfriend. But only because we never talked about what we were. Ever. She was more a roommate than anything. We never agreed to be long distance, and we never agreed to keep seeing each other."

"But you never called it off either, did you?"

He swallowed. "No, but—"

I just laughed, shaking my head. "That's rich. I suppose you were never going to tell me about her then?"

"I didn't think I needed to."

I spun then, stepping into his space until there were just centimeters between us. He stared down his nose at me, and our chests brushed, sparking a heat low in my stomach that made me even angrier.

I hated that he affected me that way.

"You didn't think you needed to mention you had a *girlfriend*?"

Reese clenched his jaw. "Like I said, it's complicated. And I'm going to address this with her."

"Oh, are you?" I laughed again, crossing my arms over my chest. "Well, that's just great. Let me know how that goes."

"Damn it, Charlie," Reese snapped. "Stop acting like that and listen to me."

"Acting like *what*?"

"Like you don't care. Like you're not upset right now," he said, stepping into my space again. He lowered his voice. "Like you don't want me to kiss you."

A chill swept over me, electricity sparking low and hot between my thighs. My eyelids fluttered, and then anger surged in like a riptide, masking the desire.

"You are unbelievable." I scoffed, throwing my hands up as I crossed the bathroom. "I'm going back to the table."

"Did you forget that you're the one who's *married*? That you just asked me — *yesterday* — to be okay with the fact that you're staying with him for at least two more months?"

"EXACTLY!" I spun on him again, unwelcome tears flooding my eyes. They only made me angrier. "I'm married. And you have a girlfriend. So why didn't you just leave me alone?"

"Because I love you."

My heart sank, falling into a sad heap on the floor below us as my face twisted with the agony his words brought.

"Don't say that to me," I whispered, the tears spilling over now. I wiped them away quickly, furious that I'd let them fall at all. "Don't lie to me anymore."

"It's not a lie, and you know it." Reese stepped into me, his thumb replacing my own as he dried my tears. Then, he lifted my chin until my eyes met his. "I'm sorry I didn't tell you about her, Charlie. I am. I don't have any valid excuse as to why I didn't. And I know I have to handle things with her, but just like you, I need a little bit of time, okay?"

His eyes pleaded with mine, but my heart was already bruised by his hands, and now it cowered away from where it once ran to him for comfort.

"What are we doing?" I whispered, shaking my head. "We're hurting them, we're hurting *each other*. Why?"

"Because we know what we feel is real," he answered simply. "Because you're my home. Because I'm your happiness. Because I love you, Charlie. And you love me. And if there's anything in this world worth making a mess over, worth fighting for, it's that."

My stomach twisted with pain again, but my heart responded to his words with a hard, steady beat. I didn't know if what he said made any of this right, but I knew it was true.

Where did that leave us?

"I don't know what to believe anymore," I confessed. "I feel like I'm in a dream. A nightmare."

"Trust what you felt with me this weekend," he said. "What I know you *still* feel."

"*How*?" I shook my head. "How do I know what's real anymore?"

Reese's knuckle lifted my chin, his lips lowering for mine, and I held my breath wishing for that kiss. I just needed something — anything — to bring me back to him, to the way it had felt over the weekend, to the relief and love I'd found in his arms.

But before his lips met mine, a hard, loud knock sounded at the door.

"Charlie? Are you in there?"

I pushed Reese away, wiping away what was left of the tears on my face before quickly crossing the bathroom to unlock the door.

Cameron stood on the other side of it once I swung it open, and I watched his face twist as confusion and concern for me morphed into a solid, unrelenting rage once he saw Reese standing behind me.

"Your parents were worried," he said flatly, not taking his eyes off Reese. "As was I."

"I'm fine," I said with a croaky voice. I cleared my throat, sliding my hand into his. "I was just coming back."

Cameron nodded. "Did he hurt you?"

"Are you fucking kidding me, man?" Reese said incredulously.

"No, of course not," I added quickly. "Come on, let's go back to the table."

"I think we should go." Cameron's grip on my hand was strong, his eyes still narrowed at Reese.

Reese started toward us, but I turned to warn him with my eyes not to press.

"I still have another set," he said.

"I think we've heard enough." Cameron's words were final, and he tucked me under one arm with the punctuation of them, guiding me out of the bathroom.

I didn't look back.

"Are you okay?" Cameron asked once we were moving through the crowd.

"I'm fine."

"You sure?"

I nodded, crossing my arms over my middle. "I just want to go home."

Cameron walked me to the front first, giving the valet our ticket and wrapping me in my coat before excusing himself to go back to our table. I watched him from across the restaurant as he let everyone know we were leaving, that I wasn't feeling well. He made his way back to me quickly, just as Reese took the piano again, and my eyes flicked between the two of them.

I hated them both.

But I loved them both, too.

And for that, I hated myself.

chapter four

CAMERON

Nothing killed me quite as much as the sight of Charlie crying.

Maybe that was why I'd had to use every ounce of willpower in me not to smash Reese's face into the bathroom sink at The Kinky Starfish. That's what I told myself, although I knew the bigger part of that was the fact that he had my wife locked in a bathroom with him.

Alone.

And she was crying.

My fists tightened around the steering wheel at the memory of it, and I cracked my neck, reciting every calming word I had to keep my cool. Every cell in my body wanted to combust with the rage I felt toward that man, toward what he'd done to my wife — to my marriage.

I wanted to forbid her from ever seeing him again, to move us across the country and away from him, but that wouldn't fix anything.

The truth was I couldn't tell Charlie what to do, or what *not* to do. She didn't belong to me.

I'd lost that privilege, and even when I'd had it, I never would have used it.

I respected her too much.

I didn't want her to do something because she felt obligated to, least of all stay with me, or stay away from him. All I truly wanted was her happiness. Did I yearn to be the one she found it with? More than anything. But if she didn't, if her happiness was with him at the end of it all, I would bow out as gracefully as I could and wish them well.

But tonight, he hadn't made her happy. He'd made her cry.

And I wanted to murder him.

Charlie was still sniffling as we drove into our housing development. My hand had found her knee when we rounded the last corner before our driveway, and I squeezed gently, letting her know I was there.

"Want me to run you a hot bath?" I asked when we were parked.

She shook her head softly, eyes on her hands as she sniffed again. "I'd just like to go to bed."

My stomach knotted, but I squeezed her knee again in understanding before pushing my door open. I circled the car quickly to grab hers next, helping her up and out, and she held onto me as we walked inside.

I had to reach her.

That's all I could think as I watched her kick out of her heels, abandoning them on the hardwood behind her as she made her way upstairs. I followed, my eyes stuck on her delicate spine she'd revealed as she swept her long hair over her shoulder, and blood pumped through me harder at the thought of touching her.

It was the only way I could get to her tonight.

I didn't have words — I never did. Tonight was no different. What could I say to possibly comfort her from the pain *another* man had caused? And there wasn't a single thing I could think to give her in that moment that would make her feel any better — nothing I could build, nothing I could cook, nothing I could buy.

The only way I knew to make her feel my love was to use my hands, my lips, my body to show her I was there. I was always going to be there.

A small sigh left Charlie's lips when we made it to our bedroom, and she pulled all the rings from her fingers, save for the one I'd given her the night I proposed at her parents' house. She unclasped her pearls next, and as she set them on her vanity and made to move for her zipper, I slid up behind her.

"Let me," I breathed, and my fingers covered hers momentarily before she conceded, letting me undress her.

I took my time, sweeping her hair away from where it had fallen back and pulling the zipper down slowly. Charlie stiffened when my fingers grazed her lower back under the fabric, and I swallowed, just the sight of her skin eliciting that same carnal reaction in me that it always had.

Chills raced down her back next as my hands moved up and over her shoulders, sliding the straps of her dress down, and when she let her arms rest at her side, the entire dress fell into a puddle of silk on the floor.

She hadn't worn a bra, and I let my fingertips trail leisurely over her shoulders and across her thin collarbone before they dipped just a little lower, grazing the small swell of her breasts. We were standing in front of the same vanity mirror I'd watched her get ready in before dinner, and my eyes found her in the reflection just as she closed hers.

She was still stiff under my touch, but I took my time warming her up, stepping closer as my lips found the back of her neck. I kissed her gently at first, my lips tender and feather-light against her skin, but when her lips parted, a sigh leaving the space they left, I palmed her breasts in my hands and softly bit her neck.

Charlie arched her back, leaning into my touch, and the reaction I had to that movement, to that sigh, was automatic. I hardened instantly, pressing that arousal into her backside to let her feel me. She gasped again, but then she leaned away.

"Cam..."

I spun her, hand finding the back of her neck and pulling her mouth to mine before she could say another word. My lips devoured hers greedily, tongue sweeping in to claim her as my hands tightened around her waist. The way she fit there in my arms, the way her mouth moved with mine, it was like the sweetest, most familiar dance. We both knew the music well, and it sang straight to our hearts, bringing us back together, if for only that small moment.

My hands swept up into her hair, tugging gently, just enough to make her head drop back and allow me better access to her mouth. I kissed down her jaw, up to the lobe of her ear, across her neck, her collarbone, before crawling my way back up to her lips once more.

She was fighting it, fighting me, but the more I kissed her, the more she melted.

Yes, I thought, *come back to me.*

I pleaded with her to do just that with every touch, every kiss, every moan. Steadily, carefully, I wrapped my arms around her until I could lift her, carrying her to our bed. She hit the comforter with a soft *whoosh*, her legs spread for me, and I slid between them with my lips still fused to hers.

When my left hand slipped between us, trailing down until I felt the wetness of her core on my fingers, she sighed.

I plunged one finger inside her, soft but deep, and her hand shot out to wrap around my wrist.

"Please..."

Her request fueled my fire, and I slid another finger inside her, growling against her neck.

But she shook her head, gripping my wrist harder.

"Please, Cameron," she said again, this time waiting until my eyes met hers. "I'm tired."

And with those two words, my blood ran cold, draining the heat from me in a slow, torturous current.

I still held her there, my fingers inside her, my eyes searching hers for what those words truly meant. It was the first time Charlie had ever rejected me, the first time I'd ever known the feeling, and I realized then how badly I must have hurt her all those nights I'd pushed her away.

But it was only because I didn't know how to touch her, anymore. Not after what happened.

Not after I filled her with love, love that became our babies, babies that were never born.

Slowly, carefully, I withdrew my fingers, wrapping her in my arms as I watched her.

"Okay," I said after a moment.

"I'm sorry."

Her cheeks tinged pink, her eyes falling to my chest, but I just shook my head.

"It's okay, sweetheart."

Say something, I urged myself. *Tell her you love her. Tell her why you love her. Tell her everything she means to you. Tell her you've been hurting, too. Tell her the truth about what she thinks she knows. Tell her it's killing you that she's in your arms thinking about him.*

But the words wouldn't come.

Charlie forced a small smile, one that fell quickly as she lifted to plant a quick kiss on my lips. Then, she rolled out from under me, grabbing a nightgown from her top dresser drawer and disappearing into the bathroom.

I wasn't sure how long I laid there, but it was long after Charlie had come back from the bathroom, long after she'd turned down the lights, and long after her breaths had steadied out as she fell asleep. I was still there in that same spot, fully dressed, and it felt like the first time I'd blinked in hours when I finally came to around midnight.

The thoughts that swirled in my head during that time were like the nastiest tornado, sweeping me up at the granular level before funneling me up into the catastrophic tunnel above. I thought of the time I had left, the time I'd wasted, the woman I loved, the woman who didn't just love me anymore. Up and up I went, further into the storm, each thought worse than the one before it as I let the worst-case scenarios play out in front of me.

I could try as hard as I could, and still lose her.

I could lose her to him.

And the worst part was that I felt helpless, like even though I'd asked for time to bring her back to me, there was no possible way to do it. How could I make her stay when I couldn't open my mouth and give her the reasons, when I couldn't tell her all the things she needed to hear?

I climbed out of bed quietly, careful not to wake Charlie as I changed into sweatpants and a t-shirt and made my way downstairs. I slipped into my office after making a cup of tea, and the steam was the only thing that warmed me as I pulled up the search engine window on my computer.

If I was to lose Charlie, I'd be damned if I'd do it still holding onto words I needed to say, to truths that could possibly make her stay.

So, for the first time in my life, I buried my pride and faced my fear.

I booked an appointment with a therapist.

chapter five

REESE

A week and a half after the disastrous night at The Kinky Starfish, I drank coffee at my kitchen island while Blake packed up her things for the weekend.

"I'll be back Sunday afternoon," she assured me again, stuffing her tablet into her backpack. "Call me if you need me to get anything on my way home."

Home. I hated that she called my house that.

"I will."

"Are you sure you can't come with me?" she asked again, pulling her long blonde hair over her shoulder as she assessed her bags.

"Sorry, I've got a couple of tutoring sessions tomorrow afternoon," I lied.

The truth was, I'd cleared my schedule for the weekend in hopes I could steal Charlie away. It had been nine long days and nights since we'd fought, since she'd found out about Blake, and I was so desperate to get her alone I was ready to lock her in the janitor's closet at school.

She'd barely said two words to me since that night, and it was slowly killing me from the inside out. I had no idea what Cameron was doing when he had her alone, but I knew it wasn't anything working in my favor.

Charlie and I had had the most perfect weekend together. We'd figured everything out. She'd finally admitted that she loved me, and we were going to be together. We just were. It didn't even scare me that Cameron wanted two months — not really — because I knew there was nothing he could say or do that could erase how Charlie felt for me.

At least, I hoped.

But then, everything went up in flames the night of the dinner. Blake had thrown the biggest, ugliest wrench in our plan to be together, and now everything I'd built was in danger of crashing to the cold, hard ground below.

Charlie was right — why should she believe me when I'd kept the biggest secret of all from her? Why should she trust me with her heart any more than she trusted Cameron?

The more the days dragged on without her feeling that connection from me, the more time Charlie spent with Cameron and away from me, the more worried I became. And I realized that it wasn't just two months for Cameron, it was two months for *me*, too — to make that rocky foundation we'd started on a more sound and solid one, one she could depend on.

I loved Charlie, I *needed* her, and I missed her.

I wondered if she missed me, too.

With Blake going out of town for the weekend, I finally had a chance to see Charlie — to have a night with just her and me. I didn't plan to waste that opportunity.

"Okay," Blake said, and with a sigh, she rounded the kitchen island until she was standing in front of my barstool.

She wrapped her arms around my neck, finding my eyes with hers.

"I guess I'm all ready to go then..." She swallowed, her voice lowering to a whisper as vulnerability slipped over her. "I'm scared."

At that, my heart cracked.

I pulled Blake into me, smoothing her hair with one hand as I hugged her close with the other.

The night after the Reids came to watch me play at the restaurant, Blake had finally told me the reason she'd come into town — the *real* reason.

Her father had fainted at work, and when he'd been admitted to the hospital, they'd found a tumor on his brain.

Blake didn't seem to know much about what was going on, other than there was a hospital in Pittsburgh that specialized in the specific kind of issues her father was facing.

So, when he'd flown out to check into that hospital, she'd flown out to stay with me.

She'd told me that the very same night I'd planned to tell her to leave.

It'd been impossible then.

She'd broken down in my arms, so scared to lose her father, and here I was the same man she'd helped survive the loss of *his* father — and entire family — just three years ago. There were too many nights where Blake had peeled me off my bathroom floor and out of my whiskey-stained clothes, putting me to bed and holding me while I cried. She'd seen more of me in those few months of grieving than most people had in my entire life.

I remembered one night waking up, not remembering how I got home, how I got to bed, and there she was. She was sleeping right next to me, still completely dressed, and she was holding me. Her legs wrapped around mine, her hand on my chest, her hair sweeping up and over my own pillow.

And in that moment, I remember being overwhelmed with gratitude that she hadn't left me alone. Everyone else had. Everyone else had moved on with their lives after they sent me flowers or brought me casseroles. But not Blake. She stayed.

And the simple truth was that Blake needed *me* now, and I would be there for her.

I knew, eventually, I'd have to tell her about Charlie. I'd have to clear up what Blake and I were — and what we weren't. But with Charlie giving Cameron his two-month time-frame, I didn't feel the need to rush that. For now, I could be Blake's friend.

I owed her that.

"It's going to be okay," I told her, holding her a little tighter. "They've been running tests and I bet you'll all get good news tomorrow. There's a reason they moved him here, right? To these specialists?"

Blake just shrugged in my arms.

"It's because they know what they're doing. He's in good hands, just trust that."

She pulled back, sniffling a little as she nodded. "You're right. I just don't know what I'll do if... if..."

"Don't think like that," I said, cutting her sentence short. "Positive vibes, okay?"

"Okay."

Blake smiled at me, her blue eyes still glossed with unshed tears.

"Thank you for being here for me," she said. "I don't know how I would do this without you."

I swallowed, guilt simmering low in my gut as I squeezed her hand in mine. "You could, but I wouldn't let you."

Her smile grew at that, and she leaned in, pressing her lips to mine before I had the chance to stop her.

I'd been careful with my actions around her, steering clear of any kind of affection that went past friendship. Every now and then she'd steal a kiss, but I'd always end it early, and I did the same on that Friday morning.

"I better get going," I said, pulling back with my hands on her arms, but Blake pressed into my space more.

Her lips latched onto mine, her tongue sweeping inside my mouth as she gripped me hard over my dress slacks. And it didn't matter that all I could think about was Charlie, or that it was *her* I wanted to rush to that morning — when Blake touched me like that, my body responded.

"Blake," I warned, grabbing her arms a bit harder to push her back. "I really need to go."

"Please, Reese," she begged when her eyes found mine again. They were still shiny and wet, her face twisting with the pain from the trip she had to make into the city. "I need this. I need you. Please."

I closed my eyes tight as her hand ran the length of my hard-on again, her little body rolling into mine as she kissed my neck.

"Not right now," I tried, my hand stopping hers from where it was undoing my zipper.

"Why not?" Blake searched my eyes. "You haven't touched me since I've been here. Do you not want me, anymore?"

"It's not that," I breathed. "It's just..."

"What?" she probed, and her hand was already working under mine again. "Please, just let me make you feel good. *I* need to feel good, too. Just for a little bit. Please, Reese. *Please.*"

"Jesus Christ," I cursed as she wiggled her hand under my pants and over my briefs below. I gritted my teeth, trying to find a way to get her to stop, but unless I told her the truth, I had nothing.

And I couldn't break her heart. Not yet. Not today.

So, I relented, dropping my grip on her wrist and letting her take what she wanted.

I let Blake fuck me as I sat on that barstool, working herself to a release in my lap that would take away whatever pain she was feeling. I hated myself so much as I drove myself to school afterward that I considered taking my car right off the bridge.

Because I'd taken Blake's pain, but I'd also given more to Charlie, in return.

She would hate me when she found out, and she *would* find out — I'd tell her that day. I had to. I owed her that honesty, and that respect.

Once I explained, she'd understand. Once I got her alone, she'd feel me again. Once I had her again, I'd never let her go.

I just needed one night.

———

I couldn't get Charlie alone until after the last bell rang that Friday.

I tried before school, but I'd been too late, and she was nowhere to be found at lunch, either. I wasn't surprised, not after a week and a half of her avoiding me. She was pissed, and she had the right to be.

But I would change that this weekend.

I rapped on the doorframe of her classroom once the car pool was clear, watching as she tidied up the tables.

"Need some help?"

She stiffened at the sound of my voice, one hand sweeping up to tuck a fallen strand of hair behind her ear, but she continued working without so much as a glance in my direction.

"Nope."

The word left her lips with a pop, and I grimaced, sliding into the room like the snake I was.

"Okay, how about some company, then?"

"I prefer to work alone, actually."

I chuckled, taking a seat at one of the tables, my knees riding up comically high as I tried to fit into the tiny chair.

"How long are you going to stay mad at me?"

"Forever."

"Charlie..."

She huffed, finally looking at me as she stood straight with the new pile of workbooks tucked under one arm. "What do you want, Reese?"

"I want to explain."

"Explain what? Your girlfriend? Like I said, I think I've got the picture."

"I don't think you do."

"Blonde hair, big boobs, legs for days. You guys met at a bar on karaoke night, you've been dating for *years*. I think that's plenty of knowledge."

"She was there for me," I said loudly, cutting Charlie's rampage off. I paused, watching her eyes with my own, begging them to hear me. "When... after my family died, she was there. She saw me at my worst, Charlie, and yes, I loved her. I still do. I always will. But not like that." I swallowed. "Not like you."

"And how do you love me?"

"With every beat of my stupid, fucked-up, irresponsible heart."

I held her gaze, but no sign of warmth passed her features. She simply watched me until I patted the tiny chair next to me, signaling her to join me.

She blew out a sigh, shaking her head as she let the workbooks hit the table with a slap. Then, she sat next to me, though she looked like she actually fit in the chair that made me look like an overgrown clown.

"What were you going to do?" she asked. "Did you just... *leave* her in New York City? Did you just assume she'd know it was over?"

"Honestly?" I asked. "In a way, yes."

Charlie grimaced, but I reached for her hand, and when our skin finally connected after so long of being apart, I know she felt the spark, too. She calmed, waiting for me to continue as my thumb rubbed the palm of her hand.

"Look, Blake and I... we were always complicated. For years, it was so casual I honestly just thought we'd always be friends. We hooked up sometimes, but even then, it was primitive. It was just... I don't know, there were no feelings attached. We took what we needed from each other, and then we'd go *months* without even so much as a text message."

Charlie was so stiff under my touch, like she didn't trust it anymore. I hoped my words would thaw that ice around her heart once more.

"But when my family died, Blake was there. She was the *only* one there. She helped me handle everything, Charlie — the funeral, their will, my inheritance, my apartment, all my bills. She even called my bosses for me, both at the restaurants I worked at and at Juilliard. And she made sure I ate, made sure I didn't just exist on cigarettes and whiskey." I paused. "She loved me. And she was the first one to ever tell me that, not just with her words, but with her actions, too."

I shrugged, memories of Blake holding me in the dark resurfacing. I could still smell the shampoo she used then, could feel her small hands on my shoulders and back, her lips on my forehead.

"And yes, I loved her. I still do. But when I left New York, neither one of us knew what we wanted. She works for one of the fitness magazines based in the city, in social media, and she loves it. Even though she can do her job remotely the way she is while she's here right now, she didn't want to *permanently* leave New York City, and I never would have asked her to. I was looking for a new start, anyway."

Charlie lifted one brow. "So, you moved away, and she stayed, and no one asked the question, 'What happens now?'"

"I know it sounds crazy," I admitted. "But that's just how we are. We don't ask questions like that. We don't talk about feelings or future plans. We just figure it out as we go. So, when I left, I think we both had this sort of mutual understanding. We'd keep in touch, but past that?" I shrugged. "There was nothing really to say."

"Except that there was," Charlie argued. "Because she showed up on your doorstep two months after you moved thinking she was still your girlfriend."

I ran a hand through my hair. "Yeah, well, she's going through something. Her dad is in the hospital here in Pittsburgh, something about a brain tumor they found. They're not sure how serious anything is yet but... I guess she needed me."

Charlie's eyes finally softened at that, and I squeezed her hand, praying to any god that would listen for her to believe the next words out of my mouth.

"I care about her, Charlie. And I want to be there for her the way she was for me. But, she's not my girlfriend — not the way she thinks. And I promise I will clear that up and I will tell her about you, when the time is right."

"When the time is right," she deadpanned.

"Yes. And I don't see any sense in rushing that, seeing as how you've given Cameron his time. Am I right?"

Charlie narrowed her eyes then, pulling her hand from mine. "Don't turn this on me. I was honest with you when I agreed to give Cameron time, and it shouldn't have mattered, not if what we'd felt was so solid. But you lied to me, Reese. How could I ever trust you now?"

"Has Cameron never lied to you?" I deflected. "You gave him your trust when he didn't deserve it. At least give me the chance to earn it back, too."

Charlie's shoulders rounded, her little eyes sad under bent brows. "That's low, Reese."

"I'm sorry," I said quickly, pulling her hands into mine again. "Just... please. Give me another chance. I'm still the same guy you've been with since January. I'm still the same boy you used to have a crush on."

She smirked. "So cocky. How do you know I had a crush on you?"

It was me who cocked a brow this time. "You're kidding, right? Miss Red Cheeks."

On cue, she blushed, rolling her eyes before she let them settle on mine again. They were wide then, searching for something. "I wish I could have been there for you, when everything..." She swallowed. "I didn't even call."

"We've been through that," I told her, squeezing her hands. "You had your own life here, Charlie. It's okay." I shrugged. "Now, I just need you to understand that I had my own life before you, too. Or rather, *after* you — and before we found each other again. The in-between. But it doesn't change anything about how I feel for you now. It doesn't change the fact that this," I said, gesturing between us. "*We* are real."

Charlie pulled her little mouth to the side, considering me.

"Let me back in," I begged her. "Please."

She sighed, her brows pinching together like she was still a little unsure. But she smiled, and that smile let me take my next breath.

"Fine," she said. "But, no more lies, okay? I mean it. I'll be honest with you, and I expect the same."

"I promise."

A pang of warning zipped through me as I gave my word to her, knowing what I needed to say next would likely ruffle any feathers I'd managed to smooth in the last ten minutes.

"With that in mind, I need to tell you something."

Charlie's smile slipped. "Okay..."

"This morning, Blake was really upset..." I scratched my neck, praying the words would come out right. "She's going into the city to see her dad, and she's scared. And well... the way she used to help me, sometimes, it would get... physical. It was just the way we sort of made the pain go away. On both ends. And..."

Charlie's lips were flat now, her hands turning cold in mine.

"God, Charlie, please don't make me say it."

"You slept with her."

I cringed, trying to hold her hands tighter but she ripped them away, swiping the workbooks off the table as she stormed across the classroom.

"*God,* Reese. What the hell is wrong with you?" She slapped the workbooks on her desk, hastily shoving her personal items in her messenger bag before throwing it over her shoulder. "You just fed me that... that load of complete *garbage* not even a full twenty-four hours after you slept with her?" She shook her head. "You're unbelievable."

"It didn't mean anything," I said, stumbling a bit as I stood from the awkward position I'd been in at the kids' table. I caught the crook of her elbow just before she reached the door.

"Let me go."

"No."

"Let me *go,* Reese."

"I can't!" I yelled, eyes glancing in the hall behind her before I pulled her more into the classroom, more into me. "I can't let you go, Tadpole. Not after I've known what it's like to hold you."

Her eyes glossed then, and her gaze dropped to the floor between us. "I can't believe you slept with her."

"You haven't with Cameron?"

"Not since you." Her eyes met mine immediately, unwaveringly, the truth one she was proud to state. "How could I, after what we shared?"

My heart broke and beamed all at once. She'd refused her husband for me. Even though she'd promised him more time, she hadn't slept with him, at least not yet.

I hoped she never would again.

I wanted to be the only hands that got to touch her, and that's when I realized that it didn't matter if my morning with Blake was meaningless. It still hurt.

It was still wrong.

"I'm sorry," I whispered, brushing Charlie's cheek with my knuckle. "I won't let it happen again. I promise. I give you my word. Just... stay with me this weekend. Blake is gone. Tell Cameron you're going somewhere, or hell, tell him the truth, I don't care. Just..." I lifted her chin, our lips just centimeters apart as I whispered my plea into her skin. "Be with me."

She considered me, her eyes searching mine before they flicked to my lips and back again. But then she sighed, pulling away until we no longer touched, until there were feet between us instead of inches.

"I'm sorry, I just don't know how I feel right now," she said with a sniff. "I need some time to think. To process. Besides," she added. "Cameron is taking me somewhere this weekend."

Dread seeped through me slow and mercilessly, followed quickly by a hot, jealous anger. I clenched my jaw, testing my next words carefully in my mind before letting them out.

"Where is he taking you?"

"I don't know."

"Tell him no," I said without hesitation, as if it was the only solution. "Say you don't want to go. Say you want to be with me, instead."

"I can't," she said on a sigh. "I told him I would go already. I promised him I'd give him this chance."

Her eyes met mine then, and they were hard again, like the eyes I'd seen the first day I'd been in town, only this time they weren't empty. They weren't dead.

They were alive with a fire I knew I'd lit.

"And, honestly?" she said. "I don't want to be with you right now."

"Don't sleep with him."

Charlie's mouth popped open, and she blinked several times, as if she'd imagined what I'd said. "You're joking."

"I'm as serious as an obituary. Don't sleep with him."

"Wow." Charlie adjusted her bag on her shoulder, shaking her head. "Fuck you, Reese."

With that, she was out the door, on her way home, on her way to him.

And there was nothing more I could do.

chapter six

CHARLIE

How was it that I'd managed to wake up in someone else's life?

I flipped open the top of my old suitcase with that thought on repeat, my fingers running the intricate stitching on the sides. I hadn't touched the suitcase in years, since before I'd been pregnant. There were no vacations happening once we'd found out, and definitely none that were even *considered* after we'd lost the boys.

That suitcase had been a wedding gift from my parents, one I'd opened with an unmatched joy as I thought of all the places it would see. I imagined it stuffed under a plane on its way to Paris, loaded in the back of our car for a weekend getaway, packed to the brim with souvenirs from a new city we'd see each year.

And that suitcase *had* seen a lot, at least, in those first few years of our marriage.

It'd touched down in Las Vegas the night Cameron and I flew there on a whim, and it had seen the beach when Cameron and I spent our honeymoon in Hawaii. It had even lost a zipper at the old cabin we booked with Graham,

Christina, and my parents for Christmas three years after we'd married.

It had seen nothing but the inside of our closet since that trip.

But, here I was, cracking it open after years of it collecting dust, my clothes and shoes piled on the bed around it as I tried to figure out how to make it all fit. And all I could think as I packed was that I must have somehow slipped into someone else's life, because I knew it couldn't possibly be mine I was living.

It couldn't possibly be me, Charlie Pierce, caught in a confusing web of lies and truths, trying to decipher it all and make what seemed like an impossible decision.

It couldn't be me in love with two men. It couldn't be me with two men doing all they could to have me.

But it was, and I wished I could break down the facets of that reality as easily as I'd chosen what to pack for the weekend, but it was useless. So, I focused on that packing, on that easy task, on something that felt like it could be tackled, since my thoughts couldn't be.

Cameron was taking me on a trip.

I didn't have any other details outside of that. He gave me a small packing list of things I would need, and told me we would leave tonight after he got off work. He also said we wouldn't return until Sunday evening.

I had no idea where we were going, but it didn't really matter.

All I knew was that I didn't want to go.

I sighed as I tucked my shoes in first, following Cameron's guidelines to pack casual, comfortable, and warm clothes. And as the methodical task of playing Tetris in that suitcase took over my hands, my mind slipped away, taking me to the one place I dreaded more than wherever it was Cameron was taking me.

To thoughts of Reese.

Just a simple whisper of his name in my subconscious made me shove my clothes in harder, wedging them into the spaces with a curl in my lip. It had been just hours since he'd told me about what he'd done, and those hours weren't enough for me to cool down from the boiling temperature he'd set my blood at.

He'd slept with her.

Not only had he slept with her, but he'd fed me another baking sheet full of bullshit cookies *before* telling me that he'd slept with her. He'd actually had me, too. He'd had me in the palm of his hand, eating up every lie he told, believing that he didn't love Blake like he loved me, that she didn't mean anything.

Stupid.

He begged me to believe him when he said it was meaningless, the morning they had shared, but how could I? Everything he'd said to me felt hollow and fake now, especially without his hands and lips to seal the promises he whispered against my skin.

Reese Walker had betrayed my trust, just like my husband.

And yet I loved him still.

That was the most frustrating part, I realized, as I shoved another pair of boots into my suitcase with a grunt. He wanted me to believe him, and as much as I didn't, I wanted to. It was there, that yearning to trust him, to let him take me in his arms and erase all the pain like he had just a few weeks before.

Had anything changed since then?

It felt like everything had. Between Cameron asking me for more time and Blake showing up as the unforeseen plot twist in my nightmare, I didn't know which way was up anymore. Nothing made sense.

Except that when Reese touched me, when he took my hand in his, I felt it.

I remembered.

That small touch alone took me back to that night, to that fort, to that weekend. It took me back to the Incline, to the fundraiser, to every moment since he'd shown back up in my life and reminded me what it was like to be loved.

To be wanted.

He confused me more than quantum physics. I didn't understand how I could hate him and yet still want him with every breath I took.

And then, there was Cameron.

My hands slowed at the thought of him, and I paused completely for a moment before I continued packing, tucking my panties into the side pockets of my suitcase with care.

He had been so patient with me since the night I'd agreed to give him time, and even more so since the night I'd rejected him.

I knew how badly that hurt.

It was the first time he'd been on the receiving end of that hurt, and now that he knew what it felt like, I wondered if he understood the pain I'd endured over the last five years. It wasn't that we'd never had sex, but he had rejected me more times than I could recall.

Each one left a deeper cut, and none of those had formed scabs yet. They were all still fresh and raw, their pain just as present as it was the first night it existed.

For the past week and a half, Cameron had been more quiet than usual. He was staying later at work again, but as soon as he would get home, he would sit with me at our dinner table and talk for hours. He would tell me about his day, ask me about mine, and fill the silence between us with conversation that seemed so meaningless, yet made me feel at home again.

I thought what I really wanted was to be alone, but when Cameron talked to me, I realized it wasn't true. I actually looked forward to dinner with him — as much as I could, anyway.

And the truth was, I couldn't remember the last time we'd talked like that.

Even if it wasn't anything substantial, just hearing his voice again, seeing his laugh — it had brought a warmth to my heart that had been absent for far too long.

And then, last night, he'd asked me to take this trip with him. And I'd agreed.

"How's it going in here?"

His voice startled my thoughts, and they scattered away like birds, flying back to the little cages of my mind reserved for each of them as I zipped up my suitcase.

"All packed up," I said, heaving my suitcase off the bed as I turned to Cameron.

He was already rushing to my side, taking the suitcase from my hand with a smile so big it made a new ache split my heart.

He was so excited, and I only wanted to crawl into bed and not see him for the rest of the night. Hell, the rest of the weekend.

"I'll get this in the car, then. Do you need anything else?"

I shook my head. "I'll just freshen up and meet you downstairs."

"Okay," he said, bouncing a little as he leaned in to kiss my cheek. "You look beautiful, by the way."

"I don't have any makeup on," I pointed out. "And my hair is a mess from school. And I'm exhausted."

Cameron's eyes circled my features as I pointed them out, but he just smiled wider.

"Exactly. And you're still beautiful."

I flushed, a long breath leaving my chest as Cameron took my bag and headed for the stairs.

After I'd used the restroom, I checked our bathroom mirror, staring at the reflection Cameron had called beautiful. My eyes were heavy, the skin puffy underneath them, and my hair was piled into a messier bun than usual on top of my head. I wore just a casual, mint green, long-sleeve shirt and jeans with my favorite pair of brown boots. There was nothing particularly special about how I looked or what I wore, yet he had called me beautiful.

He'd said that the day I gave birth to our sons, too.

A flash of his smile on that day hit me out of nowhere, like a lightning bolt set to kill, but I shook it off, packing that memory away along with the clothes in my suitcase. I'd take it with me this weekend, and, as I'd promised Cameron, I'd try.

I'd try to give him the chance he'd asked for.

But as I turned out the lights in our room, fingers trailing the wood of our staircase as I made my way down, I couldn't hide the hurt that underlined my intention. Because what played in my mind on repeat each time I was with him was that he hadn't wanted a chance to keep me — at least, not until he'd lost me in the first place.

And that was one truth I couldn't pack away.

chapter seven

CAMERON

I had less than two hours in the car to breathe some life into Charlie.

Ever since the evening of our dinner at The Kinky Starfish, she'd been like a turtle that had retreated into her shell, refusing to poke so much as a toe out, let alone her head. She woke up, went to work, came home, ate dinner, gave me what little energy she could in our conversations, and then she was right back to bed.

And I was running out of time.

Two months wasn't long, and here I'd already lost almost two weeks. I needed to get her away from the house, away from the every day... away from him.

My heart had done a little jump for joy when she agreed to let me take her out of town this weekend, but it would be a pointless trip if I couldn't reach inside the shell she was hiding under and coax her out.

"We've got a couple hours in the car," I told her once we were outside the Mount Lebanon city limits. "Feel free to kick off your shoes and get comfortable."

"Okay," she said softly, but her tired eyes stayed glued on the trees we passed outside her window. She was leaning so close to her door that I couldn't reach over and rest my right hand on her knee, but I left it open on the center console — just in case.

Ideas for how to get her to laugh popped through my mind like lottery balls as I drove, and I waited for one to jump out and stick. I should have asked Patrick if *he* had any ideas before I left, since it had been his suggestion to take the trip. Then again, my time with Patrick was already packed, and I needed every minute he had to filter through my own shit.

I met with Patrick for the first time the very next evening after Charlie rejected me in our bed, and I'd been with him every day since — save for Saturday and Sunday. Charlie thought I was working late again, and as much as I hated it, I let her believe that was the truth. I didn't want to tell her I was talking to a therapist until I had something more substantial than that to say.

Like that it was helping.

The first session had been the most difficult, my head hung between my shoulders as I wrung my hands together and confessed what a horrid husband I'd been to my wife since we lost our children.

It felt a little like the one and only time my father had dragged me to church with him, when I'd sat outside the confessional as he told the man inside it all of his transgressions. He'd been tasked with a handful of Hail Mary's to absolve his sins, but I knew there was nothing I could do to ever make peace with mine. I only wanted to try — not for me, but for Charlie.

I wanted to be the man she deserved, though I'd never be the one who deserved her, in return.

Patrick had sent me away with homework after every session. Sometimes it was to write about a memory, something from my childhood, and other times it was answering a list of questions I'd never even thought to ask myself. One of them that stuck with me long after I'd let the pen drop on the page I wrote on was, "What do you love about your wife, and what do you think she loves about you?"

Answering the first half of that question was like adding one plus one together. Loving Charlie was effortless — it always had been.

Since the moment I met her, I knew she was unlike any other girl I'd known before her. The way her cheeks tinged when I held her hand, the way she smiled fully only to bite her lower lip like she wished she could take part of that smile back, like she was showing all her cards at once, the way her soft eyes searched mine every time she asked me a question, like she was hearing the answer I gave and also the one I didn't at the same time — it was all part of what made Charlie the one and only girl I ever let inside my head.

Because I trusted her to see me, the real me, and not run away.

Those small truths were what had drawn me into Charlie, what had made me want her, but it was what I found after months of spending time with her that made me love her.

It was how intelligent she was, how she was always reading and learning, talking to others like they were more of a lesson than anything she could find in a classroom. It was how she cried for stray dogs and cheered for couples getting engaged at the park we used to walk in together, even when she had no idea who they were. It was how she held me the night I told her what happened with my father, and instead of saying she was sorry, she told me she was thankful to him.

Because everything that had happened in my life, whether good or bad, had somehow led me to her.

Then, she told me she loved me, and I knew my life would never be the same again.

My reasons for loving Charlie were endless, and each sentence I wrote about her brought me back to the fact that I could *not* lose her. But in order to keep her, I knew I had to dig deep, into a part of myself I never wanted to touch, or see, or let *be* seen. That's what I was doing with Patrick — even when it hurt.

The second part of that night's homework had been impossible to answer.

I knew Charlie loved me. That was perhaps what I loved most about her, the *way* she loved me. The way she saw me, cared for me, understood me. But to answer the question of *why* she loved me, of what she loved about me — it was impossible.

Because I didn't understand it. I never had.

I didn't see anything inside me worth loving. I was an unwanted child, both by my mother who was killed and my father who killed her — even by my grandparents who were stuck with me after the murder. They cared for me, they loved me enough to put me in hockey and get me thinking about college, but even still, I knew I was something they never asked for. I was a burden.

I'd tried to love Charlie right.

Since the moment I realized I loved her and she loved me in return, I vowed to be everything she needed in life — and that was well before our wedding day. But I'd failed her, and for that reason, I couldn't think of a single reason why she should love me.

But maybe, just maybe, I could change that.

"Are you hungry?" I asked when we were a little over an hour into our drive.

Charlie shook her head, gaze still fixed out the window. I wondered what she was thinking.

"I'm okay."

I frowned. "Are you sure? We haven't eaten dinner yet, and there's a stop coming up that STRIPES!"

The word flew out of my mouth before I could stop it, and Charlie jumped a little before looking over at me with wide eyes.

"What?"

It had been habit, calling out the object marker sign as we passed by it. The yellow and black stripes slanted at an angle toward the road, indicating an obstruction, and I drove slightly to the left to avoid a small breakage in the road just before a bridge. Charlie still stared at me, and even *I* was surprised I'd called it, but I realized it may be the perfect opportunity to break through to her.

"You heard me," I said, feigning confidence. I adjusted my hold on the wheel and turned to her with a wry smile. "Stripes. Whatcha taking off, first?"

Charlie's mouth popped open, a mixture of emotions crossing over her features as she processed. She went from shocked, to confused, to marginally amused, and back to disbelief again.

"You're kidding, right?" she said, leaning up in her seat.

But she was smiling. That was a win.

"Stripes," she deadpanned. "As in, the car game we used to play when we were in college."

"The one and only."

It was a road trip game we played, mostly when traveling to parties off campus or making our way across country for spring breaks. Any time you saw that stripes sign, you called out *STRIPES*, and everyone who *didn't* call it first had to take off an article of clothing. First person to call stripes three times won, and everyone else had to strip completely at that point.

Charlie laughed, crossing her arms as her eyes found the road in front of us. "That's ridiculous. I'm not playing that. I'm thirty years old," she pointed out. "And you're thirty-one. We're adults."

"So? You still have great tits, and I want to see them. Strip."

Charlie's jaw dropped again and I belly laughed, tossing my head back before meeting her eyes with a challenging gaze.

"Did you just say I have nice *tits*," she said, but already she was laughing, too. "I don't think I've ever heard you say that. Ever."

"Well, it's true," I confessed. "Now, are you going to strip, or is my girl backing out of a challenge because she's *too old*?"

Charlie laughed incredulously, her arms still crossed as she shook her head at me. She opened her mouth to argue again, but then simply closed it before she leaned up and stripped off her socks from her feet. She'd already taken her boots off earlier, and she sat back with one eyebrow cocked, popping her feet up on the dash.

"There," she said. "Happy?"

"I mean, I would have much preferred the shirt, but I'll take what I can get," I teased.

Charlie chuckled, looking out the window again as her now-bare feet bopped along to the song on the radio.

She was peeking out of her shell, and I knew I had to make another move while I had the chance.

I slipped my phone from the center console, thumbing through it until I found the song. Once *Ain't No Mountain High Enough* started playing, I tapped the plus volume button on my steering wheel, watching Charlie as I did.

At first, she didn't respond, other than to cast me a confused glance as to why the music was suddenly so loud. But as the melody floated in and she recognized the familiar intro, she smiled.

"This always makes me think of the summer before our senior year," she said. "Remember? When we all drove up to Erie?"

"I do," I said. "Ready for the duet?"

She scoffed. "Oh, *please.* Like you'll sing. I tried to get you to for years and—"

But before she could finish the sentence, I was already belting out Marvin Gaye's first verse, and for the third time, Charlie's mouth hung open.

I finished the first verse, using my right hand to grip an imaginary microphone as I tilted it toward her.

But she didn't sing. She just gaped.

"Come on, don't leave me hanging," I said as Tammi Terrell's part faded out. I sang Marvin's next little part, still holding the microphone for her to jump in, and then, just before the chorus hit, I saw another sign.

"STRIPES!" I called out, and then I pulled the microphone back, belting out the first part of the chorus as Charlie whipped around just in time to see the sign pass by.

She turned on me, mouth open in a surprised smile, but she only paused a moment more before she ripped her shirt over her head and spun it around like a rodeo rope as she joined in on the chorus. We both laughed our way through the words, though I was more than a little distracted now that her simple, nude bra was exposed. My hand drifted over with the microphone, but as she leaned to sing into it, I dropped down lower and cupped her breast with a squeeze.

Charlie swatted my hand away, still laughing as the second verse kicked in, and then she threw her hand up and pointed out the window.

"STRIPES!"

I'd seen the sign, too, but not before her. So, I held the wheel steady with one hand, stripping out of my sweater before peeling it off that arm and tossing it toward Charlie. She caught it on a laugh, and then the second chorus started.

We sang loud and entirely off key, but neither of us cared. And when I looked over in the passenger seat, I saw Charlie — all of her.

I saw her when she was nineteen and nervous, her hands tucked between her thighs in my old Pontiac.

I saw her eyes wide and lips parted as I slid inside her for the first time.

I saw her under a white veil as she promised to love me for the rest of her life.

And the way she looked at me, the way she tilted her head to the side just an inch, I couldn't be sure what she was thinking, but I did know one thing.

She still loved me.

Even if I didn't know *why*, I knew she did.

The song faded out, both of us still bopping along, and she leaned one elbow on the console with her hand propped on her chin.

"Kiss me," she whispered.

I slowed, glancing at the road once more before my eyes found hers. She watched me with brows bent together, like being near me hurt her as much as it healed her. I framed her chin with my pointer finger and thumb, lowering my lips to hers slowly and purposefully, as if that kiss was my only chance to keep her outside of her shell. I'd finally coaxed her out, and now I needed her to stay.

My eyes found the road again, ensuring I was driving safe before I glanced back at her. She was still watching me, a small smile on her lips now.

"I love you."

I rubbed her lower lip with my thumb, tracing where I'd just kissed her. "I love you, too."

When my eyes glanced back to the road, I smirked, leaning in to press my lips to hers once more.

"And Charlie?"

"Yes?" she breathed.

I smiled wider, kissing her nose.

"Stripes."

Charlie tilted her head again, then she whipped around just in time to see the sign fly by.

"Damn it!" she yelled on a laugh, then she poked my ribs over and over as I laughed, too, trying to dodge her jabs. I memorized her laugh in that moment, the way it left her lips at different decibels, the tone of it sweet and song-like.

I wanted to bottle it up and keep it forever, just in case I ever wanted to take a sip of this night again. Later. In another time.

In a time when maybe she wouldn't be mine anymore.

"So, I have to strip now?" she asked.

I just lifted a brow, because she already knew the answer.

Besides, I was too busy tracing the lines of her face, tacking them to the foam board of my memory, hoping to keep her there forever.

But when she reached behind her, eyes on me as she unclasped her bra, everything else faded away.

And I prayed to God for more time.

———

CHARLIE

"That was so fun," I said as Cameron unloaded our bags from the trunk.

He threw them over his shoulders, closing the trunk and reaching for my hand as my mind ran over the memories that resurfaced from the evening.

"I can't believe how much the campus has changed," I added, offering to take my bag from him. He just shook his head, tightening his grip on my hand. "The old bonfire pit is gone. I mean... *gone*."

"Guess they needed a Science Center more than drunken bonfires."

"They've got their priorities wrong."

He chuckled at that, opening the door that led into the hotel lobby. When I stepped inside, a wave of familiarity washed over me, and I frowned.

"I've been here before."

Cameron smirked, dropping our bags by my feet as he dug out his wallet.

"I'll go check us in. Be right back."

He made his way to the desk as I looked around the run-down lobby, wondering why it felt so familiar. I also couldn't help but question why it had been the place Cameron chose for us to sleep that night. To say it was a little shabby for his usual taste would be an understatement. The carpeted floors were stained, the lighting low and dingy, with various bulbs burnt out and not replaced. We were one of very few cars outside, which didn't surprise me being that our university was pretty much in the middle of nowhere. Still, I was surprised we hadn't driven back into the city for the night, to a more grand hotel.

Then again, I'd given up on trying to figure out any of Cameron's moves that night.

From planning a spontaneous weekend trip to singing in the car on the ride out to Garrick, he'd surprised me. What had surprised me *most* was how he'd managed to turn my entire night around — maybe even my entire week.

It had been surreal, driving around campus, seeing all that had changed since we were students there. He'd wanted to take me to the old bonfire pit at the end of the night, after dinner at the small diner on campus, of course, but the pit had been demolished and replaced by a modern, all-glass and steel building.

So instead, we'd sat at the edge of the dock on the campus lake and recounted all the nights we'd spent around that fire pit, from the night he'd nearly punched one of his fraternity brothers for ogling me to the night he'd told me about his parents.

That was the night I told him I loved him.

He'd taken almost three months to say it in return.

I didn't mind waiting for him, though — not back then. With Cameron, his word meant something to him. There was so much thought and intention behind every sentence that left his mouth, and I knew that if and when he did tell me he loved me, he would mean it.

Maybe more than anyone had ever meant it before.

And when he did tell me, I'd felt every part of my heart squeeze at his words. We were napping between classes one lazy, rainy afternoon, and he woke up before me. I opened my eyes to find his there staring back at me, and he swept my hair out of my face, told me he loved me, and leaned in to seal that confession with the sweetest kiss of my life.

I was smiling at that memory when Cameron returned from the front desk, holding up a key card between his thumb and index finger.

"Come on," he said, picking up the bags again. "Let's get you to this room."

"Anxious to get me alone there, Mr. Pierce?"

Cameron eyed me. "You were stark ass naked in the seat next to me for the last half hour of our drive into campus, and I couldn't touch you. Does that answer your question?"

I flushed, biting my lower lip as he reached for my hand and dragged me down the hall to the elevators. "It was your idea to play Stripes," I countered. "To be fair."

"There's nothing fair about you being naked when I can't touch you."

I laughed, but inside my stomach flipped inside out. The last time he'd tried to touch me, I'd rejected him — the same way he'd rejected me so many nights in the last five years. It wasn't that his touch didn't still elicit a need within me, but that night, Reese had been the main man on my mind.

I didn't want to touch Cameron when I was thinking of Reese.

We shot up to the top floor of the hotel, and I stared at the buttons in the elevator, something about them triggering a memory, too. But it wasn't until Cameron opened our door and ushered me inside our room for the night that it hit me.

"Oh my God…"

I balked at the horrid floral wallpaper lining the room, a wallpaper I couldn't forget even if I tried. My eyes trailed the large bed next, the white comforter lined with a red bed liner at the bottom, rose petals spread across both. I found the wide balcony next, but just barely glanced at it before my eyes stuck on the large jacuzzi tub in the corner.

"Cameron, is this…?"

"The room we stayed in after our first bonfire at Garrick together?" he finished for me.

"It is, isn't it?!" I laughed, running my fingers over the wallpaper as I looked around. "God, it hasn't changed a bit."

"It might be the only thing," Cameron said.

"I hated this wallpaper then. It's even worse now."

"So bad," Cameron agreed, but he dropped our bags on the bed and crossed to where I stood, pressing me against the papered wall. "But it was the last thing on my mind that night."

"And tonight?" I breathed, eyes falling to his lips.

"I hadn't even noticed it until you said something."

Cameron looked at me in that moment as if he'd walked through the desert and I was an untouched, natural spring. I flushed, and he leaned in slowly to press his lips to mine, that kiss sending a jolt of electricity to my core. I arched into his touch, his hands pinning my hips to the wall as he kissed me harder, but he broke the kiss before the flame could catch.

"I thought we could take a bath," he said. "Like that night."

I smiled. "That sounds nice."

"I'll get the water running. Why don't you pop that champagne over there?" He nodded to a bottle cooling in an ice bucket.

But when he moved away from the wall and I pushed forward, half of the wallpaper came with me.

It stuck to my sweater, the ripping sound the only thing I heard before my eyes were wide and staring at Cameron, who was trying his best not to laugh. I turned, feeling where the paper was stuck to the back of my shirt, little strips of it connecting me to the wall behind me.

"Not exactly the magical place it used to be, is it?" I asked, laughing with Cameron.

He helped me unstick the paper before I peeled off my sweater, still wearing my blouse beneath it. Cameron's eyes caught on my chest before he ripped them away and made his way over to the tub.

For a moment, the only sound was the water running as I untwisted the metal top on the champagne and prepared to pop the cork. I felt Cameron's eyes on me, like they had been all night, but the anxiety they brought when we first left our house was gone, replaced by an easy comfort.

I was having fun.

The trip I'd been dreading with the man I didn't want to spend time with was turning out to be exactly what I needed. I was out of the house, out of the town I hadn't left for a while, and back in a place where I felt connected to Cameron.

But as much as I loved it, it also hurt.

Because now that I was alone with my husband, I couldn't remember why I ever let Reese in my heart in the first place.

I thought back to when he first came to town, to how I was feeling then. I remembered still wanting Cameron, even on the night Reese opened up to me about his family at my parents' house. But somewhere along the way, Reese showed me how unhappy I was. It wasn't that I hadn't felt that way before Reese came back, but he just put a magnifying glass to it.

And he asked me to do something about it.

He asked me to not settle, to not be okay with being unhappy. And so, I'd found happiness in him.

And I loved him, too.

That was the truth. I had wanted him when I was younger and those feelings were only multiplied now.

But he had Blake, and he didn't tell me about her. *That* was what weighed most on my mind now when I thought of him. I could no longer see him dropping to his knees to touch my scars at the Incline, or feel his hands on me under the sheets of our fort, or hear his voice whispering my name the first time he had me.

They were all muted by the woman he kept a secret.

My eyes met Cameron's from across the room where he filled the tub. He offered me a small smile, and I knew without a doubt that he would have told me about Blake, had he been Reese. But he wasn't Reese. He was Cameron — my husband, my family.

Then again, he'd kept secrets from me, too.

I poured the champagne into two flutes, dropping a couple of strawberries from the bowl next to the bottle inside each one before crossing to Cameron. He was frowning, his focus on the water when I handed him his glass.

"It's not as hot as I remember," he said, one hand feeling the water still as he took the glass in his other.

"I'm sure it's fine."

He lifted a brow. "Feel for yourself."

When I did, I laughed. "Oh, my God. It's lukewarm."

"At best."

I chuckled, but I saw the frustration shading Cameron's face. He was trying so hard to make the night magical, to relive an evening that had meant so much to us years ago.

Carefully, I sat my glass on the edge of the tub, stripping out of my blouse and letting it fall to the floor before my fingers began working the buttons on my jeans. Cameron's face smoothed when he saw me undressing, and he swallowed, eyes catching on my lace panties as I dropped my jeans to the floor next.

"We'll make it work," I said, unhooking my bra with an arched brow. "You going to let me get naked all alone?"

Cameron smirked, shaking his head as he watched me a moment longer. Once my bra was unclasped and dangling from one finger, he stood, stripping with me. We watched each other with only the sound of the water running, and once we were both bare, Cameron cut the water off and thumbed through his phone until a soft melody started playing through it.

He grabbed his glass first, settling back into the water with his legs wide enough for me to sit between them. I crawled in carefully, but it was useless, the water sloshed over the sides as I sank down, taking my seat in front of him.

"It's almost cold," I said on a laugh, and Cameron blew out a frustrated breath from behind me. "But I still remember what it felt like that night," I added. "How hot it was, and the bubbles — remember?"

"I do," he said in my ear, one hand holding his glass while the other trailed circles on my knee. I leaned back more into him, letting his body envelop mine.

For a while we just sat there, silently sipping on our champagne and touching each other gently. I would reach back for Cameron's hair, running my fingers through it, and he would trail the skin of my collarbone, making me shiver under the touch. Eventually, our hands met in the middle, and our fingers folded together as I leaned my head back on a sigh.

My eyes caught on the old chandelier in the middle of the room, its bronze paint chipping, only half of the bulbs lit. I chuckled again, lightly enough that I don't even think Cameron noticed.

"Why did you bring me here tonight?" I asked after a while. "Back to Garrick? To this hotel?"

Cameron pressed his palm flat to mine, his fingertips slipping between mine slowly until we were holding hands again.

"Honestly?"

I nodded.

"I wanted to bring you back to a simpler time, I guess," he said on a breath. "And maybe I wanted to come back to this time, too. So much has changed since we fell in love here — good and bad. I thought maybe if we could come back here, to the beginning, we could remember what that felt like. What it was like just falling into each other and not having to think about anything else." Cameron chuckled. "A time before bills and houses and steady, nine-to-five jobs."

I smiled, leaning my head back on his chest.

"I think you've said more on this trip than you have in the past five years."

He paused.

"Well, I should have been talking to you more. I should have let you in more."

Cameron squeezed my hand, and I squeezed his in return, my eyes closing at the truth behind his words. "I know it's hard."

"It is," he agreed quickly. "But I'm your husband, and I should have been there for you. When everything..."

Cameron's voice broke, and he cleared his throat, adjusting his position behind me.

"I've been seeing someone," he said, and instantly, my heart froze, the beat stuck under my rib cage. But before I could draw any conclusions of my own, he clarified with, "A therapist. His name is Patrick."

I sat up, twisting a little until I could see Cameron's face. "How long?"

"A little over a week," he said, and I felt the tremble in his hand still intertwined with mine.

Cameron hated talking, hated opening up and feeling vulnerable, and here he'd been doing so with a stranger — and now, with me. I leaned against him again, this time curling into him, my cheek against his chest as I wrapped my arms around his middle.

"There's so much I want to tell you, Charlie," Cameron said, his hand running over my damp hair before he pressed a kiss to it. "So much I *need* to tell you, things you need to hear, but I may not be able to say it all at once. I may not get it all out tonight, but I promise you, I'm trying. And I will tell you everything. I will."

"It's okay," I tried, but he shook his head.

"It's not. And I could start in a lot of different places, but the first thing I want to say to you is that I'm sorry. I'm so fucking sorry I left you to battle the grief over losing Derrick and Jeremiah on your own. I was stupid to think you needed space and time. You're right — you needed me, and I wasn't there."

Emotion strangled me like a noose, its hands wrapping tight around my throat as I wrapped my arms around Cameron tighter. He was so warm, yet he was shaking, and I tried as much as I could to make him feel comfortable.

The words he was giving me, they were more than he'd given me in years — and I knew how much they hurt for him to say.

"I was devastated," he said, his voice just above a whisper. "When we lost them, I felt like somehow it was *my* fault — like I had failed you and them in some way I couldn't even be sure of. And I wanted to help you, to make you feel better, but I didn't know how. I was useless. I tried rebuilding your library and packing away any memory of our boys..." He swallowed, voice thick with emotion. "Like I could make them disappear. Like I could fix your pain by removing any reminders of the reason it existed, instead of facing it head on with you."

My heart broke with his admission. Here I'd felt like it was my fault, like I was the one who'd failed by not carrying our boys into a healthy birth, and Cameron felt that same pressure.

It was all too much for us. For *both* of us. Why hadn't I ever thought to ask him if *he* was okay?

"When I told Patrick about what happened, he asked me how I felt about losing them," Cameron said. "The boys. And at first, the answer was easy. I was sad, I was angry, I was devastated and heartbroken. I blamed God, blamed myself, blamed my shit father even though I haven't seen him since I was eight. Somehow it was his fault, too, and that's when Patrick helped me realize something I hadn't before."

My breath caught, and I held it in my lungs as I waited for Cameron to continue.

"The truth is, I was more angry than anything when we lost the boys, Charlie. I couldn't handle the pain, or the thought of not having them in our lives, but I could spend hours and hours every night being angry. And what Patrick helped me see was that I wasn't mad at you, or at me, or at the doctors or the stupid grieving books your parents gave us," he said, shaking his head. "I was angry because it wasn't fair. I was angry because of the injustice of my life, of being an unwanted child who, in turn, couldn't have the children he wanted more than anything."

I closed my eyes, tears I hadn't even realized were building rolling down my cheeks in two symmetrical lines.

"Oh, Cameron," I whispered, holding him tight. "You weren't unwanted."

"Yes, I was," he said louder, his voice strong and sure. "And it's so, *so* fucked up that they could have me when they didn't even want me. A druggie mother, an abusive, asshole dad. They didn't want a kid, and yet they got me."

He was shaking, and I smoothed my hands down his lower back where I held him, lips pressed against his chest.

"And here we are, two people who love each other more than anything in the world, and we couldn't have our boys." He swallowed. "*That's* what I played on repeat, over and over, until my thoughts were scrambled and knotted. All I could think was how we wanted those boys and we couldn't have them. But we deserved them, Charlie. Damn it, *you* deserved them."

Cameron grabbed my arms, pulling me up until my eyes met his. He ran his hands up and over my shoulders, my neck, until they framed my face as his eyes searched mine, begging me to hear him.

"You will be the most amazing mother one day," he said, his voice breaking. "Whether with me or..."

But he couldn't finish the sentence, and I hated myself for ever making it a sentence he thought in the first place.

"You will be the best mom in the world. I know it. And I'm just so sorry those boys didn't get to live long enough to have you as their mother because they would have been the luckiest boys in the world." He sniffed. "And I would have been the luckiest man." At that, he choked on a laugh. "I still am, at least for now."

"Shhh," I said quickly, leaning in to kiss him, and we both exhaled together once our lips met.

I wrapped my arms around his neck and pulled him into me, twisting in the bath as the water sloshed over the sides again. I straddled him the best I could in the space we had, our chests fused together as he kissed my lips hard enough to bruise them.

"I'm so sorry, Charlie," he said between kisses. "I just wanted you to know that. I was hurting, too. I lost them, too. But I'm sorry I wasn't there for you the way I should have been. I'm sorry I haven't been here, not really, since the day they left."

"It's okay, Cameron. It's okay. I understand." I kissed him again, softer this time — longer. "There's no right way to handle what we went through, okay? We were both just doing what we could. That's all we had to give, and it's okay."

"I'll never forgive myself," he whispered. "But I had to tell you. I wanted you to understand. And more than anything, I need you to know that I have always loved you, Charlie. Always. That never wavered — not ever."

"I know," I said quickly, but in my heart, a familiar pain stung me like a wasp. Because though I knew he'd always loved me, he had wavered — he had strayed from my love and into the arms of another woman.

And I still didn't know why.

But I pushed those thoughts from my mind, choosing to focus on the little ray of light Cameron had chosen to shine on his darkest thoughts that night. He'd let me in, he'd let me see, and I wanted to live in that light as long as I could.

"Cameron," I said, running my hands back through his hair until his chocolate eyes connected with mine.

"Yes?"

"Do you want me?"

He blew out a long breath, shaking his head as his forehead leaned in to mine. "More than anything."

"Make love to me," I whispered.

Cameron's hands gripped me tighter, his lips finding mine with a sigh of relief and passion. I rolled my hips against him, making waves in the water around us, and I felt those waves washing away any and everything that wasn't us in that moment. For now, for tonight, we were only man and woman, husband and wife — and he was all I wanted.

"I've been aching to touch you all night," Cameron confessed, his hand snaking under the water to cup my ass. "But I'm not doing it in a lukewarm bathtub."

I laughed, head falling back before he pulled my lips to his again. He helped me turn carefully, until we were both facing the faucet again, and then he stood as I leaned forward in the tub. He stepped out first, grabbing a towel off the rack, but when he turned to where I still lay in the tub, he paused, shaking his head.

"*God,* Charlie," he groaned, eyes devouring every inch of my skin. "You are so... beautiful. Crushingly so."

I blushed, following his gaze to where my nipples peeked out of the water, to where my thighs were visible, too. With my eyes snapping back to his, I rolled, giving him a view of my backside as I bit my lower lip.

He groaned again, holding the towel in one hand and offering his free one to me. "Come here."

There was something about having my husband look at me that way again — like it was that first night he'd taken me to that hotel room, like he wanted me more than oxygen in his lungs — and it gave me a confidence I hadn't had in years. Maybe ever.

So, instead of reaching up for his hand, I rolled to my back again, letting my knees fall open as one hand slid between my thighs. I kept my eyes on him, watching as he grew harder for me at the sight of me touching myself, and when his eyes found mine, I gasped, letting out a long moan as I slipped one finger inside me.

Cameron inhaled a stiff breath, and I creaked one eye open to see him watching me. His lower lip was pinned between his teeth, his cock rock hard now, and the hand that had been offered to help me out of the tub was now wrapped around his shaft. He pumped once, flexing his hips into his touch, and the sight of him touching himself sent a jolt through me.

I'd never seen Cameron stroke himself, never walked in on him watching porn or relieving himself before bed. There was something about the way his eyes almost closed, the heat that lay within them as he watched me, the pressure of his hand as it slid over his wet crown and down his shaft to the very base of him. I knew every inch of him, every curve, every vein, and every sensitive spot.

That man was mine. He always had been.

When my fingers moved up to circle my clit, Cameron growled, dropping the towel altogether and reaching into the tub until I was cradled in his arms. I giggled as he lifted me, but his lips suppressed that laugh quickly, and he carried me blindly to the bed, dropping me into the comforter with every inch of me still dripping wet.

"Open," he commanded, tapping the inside of each of my knees. He was still standing at the edge of the bed, stroking himself as I did as he said, and once I was spread open for him, he dropped to his knees.

His hands wrapped around my hips, tugging me toward him until my thighs hit his shoulders, and his tongue licked the water from the inside of my thigh first before his mouth fused with my core. I fisted my hands in the sheets at the feel of his hot mouth on my clit, his tongue circling, teeth nibbling with just the slightest pressure as he sucked and kissed.

Just as I knew him, Cameron knew me — he knew all the right places to touch, the right ways to tease, the right spots to hit. After all these years, he still remembered, and I knew he always would.

And just when I wanted it most, he carefully slipped his middle finger inside me, turning his wrist toward the ceiling and curling that finger until I arched off the bed with an insatiable moan.

That moan fueled his passion, his tongue swirling faster as his finger worked me closer to a release. It never took long for Cameron to get me there, not when he knew exactly what I needed — exactly what I craved. But before I could catch the fire I chased, he slowed, withdrawing his finger with a soft kiss to my clit before he stood again.

Seeing him standing there at the edge of the bed, the floral wallpaper and half-full bath tub visible behind him, it was almost like traveling back in time. I blinked and saw him at just twenty years old, his hair a little longer then, face a little rounder and more baby-like. Then I blinked again, seeing how age had changed him, how the stubble grew on his chin now, how his eyes were a little more worn.

I thought I loved the boy I had in this room more than ten years ago, but it was nothing compared to how I felt for the man who stood before me now. He was my protector, my lover, my best friend.

And maybe I'd lost him for a while, maybe we'd drifted apart, but tonight, we were coming back together. Tonight, we would try again.

Tonight, I was his. And he was mine.

Cameron stroked himself once before he crawled onto the bed with me, helping me maneuver back into the pillows. When he settled between my legs, we both moaned at the feel of his hardness sliding between my wet lips. But he backed off a bit, kissing me softly until he balanced on his hands above me.

"Roll over."

Again, I did as he said, heart racing with anticipation of him being inside me. When my stomach was on the bed, he pulled my hips up just a bit, lifting me with a low arch in my back and his crown at my center. His hands massaged my cheeks, spreading them wide so he could see all of me before he positioned himself at my entrance, and with careful, slow measure, he flexed forward, and my husband filled me.

For a brief, fleeting moment, I thought of Reese.

Not because I wanted him in that moment, but because I couldn't help but compare how different it felt when Cameron slipped inside me. I knew the feel of him, I knew the way he curved inside me, and yet it was like a new man touching me that night. It was the man he'd revealed to me, the man I'd been trying to reach since our sons died, and now he was here — he was present — and he let me see all of him, *feel* all of him, like never before.

Cameron withdrew his hips with a low groan, sliding back inside me again a little slower, hitting a new depth as I tossed my head back. One hand came up to fist my hair then, and he held that fistful tight as his lips lowered to my neck. He kissed and bit his way down to my shoulder, his hips working a little faster, every nerve in my body awakening to his touch.

"Yes," I moaned when he slid in at a slight angle, hitting the spot within me that drove me closer to release. "Right there. Yes, Cameron. *Yes.*"

His breath was hot in my ear as he moved, and I felt each flex, each centimeter inside me, each hand of his — the one in my hair, the one bruising my hip. He shifted me a little more to the left, a trick he'd learned years ago, one that let him reach that perfect spot inside me. And when he did, my moans grew louder, more erratic, my hands fisting in the sheets as I lost control.

There were no words as my orgasm built fiery and fast, three pumps of his hips getting me to the top before I soared over the edge. He stayed deep when he felt me shaking around him, flexing his hips in smaller pumps that hit that spot over and over as I came. And I couldn't breathe, couldn't think, couldn't do anything other than feel him in that moment.

It was the sweetest release, and at the end of it, I collapsed to the bed, hips dropping into the comforter as my back ached in the best possible way.

Cameron slowed, releasing my hair from his grip as he kissed gently down my back. I shivered under his feather-light kisses, shaking more when he withdrew, and he kissed my lower back softly before helping me roll to my back.

He took his time climbing back up my body, his lips and tongue savoring each stop along the way — my thighs, my stomach, my ribs, my breasts, my collarbone, my neck, before he finally settled between my legs and tasted my mouth with his own. I moaned into that kiss, arching up toward him, aching for him to fill me again until he found his own ecstasy.

He pulled back from our kiss, hand sweeping my hair away as his eyes searched mine, and in that moment, I saw it — the pain. It pained him to touch me, to have me, when he felt like he didn't deserve to. He swallowed, brows bending together, and as he lowered another kiss to my lips, I replied to what he couldn't say out loud.

"I love you, too, Cameron," I whispered. "I love you, too."

He sighed, shaking his head just once before his lips found mine again, hot and needy, and his thighs spread my own so he could slide inside me once more.

I was tighter now, my climax making me swell with want, and we both groaned at the way it felt when he stretched me open for him again. I ran my hands through his hair, tightening my grip and holding on as he flexed into me, over and over, slow at first before picking up a steady rhythm.

And he didn't watch my modest breasts as they bounced when he came, nor did he curse or groan. He just watched me, his eyes fixed on my own, his mouth falling open as a longing sigh left his lips and landed on mine. He pulsed out his release inside me, his hands gripping me tight, as if I'd float away once the moment was over. And when it was, my name was all he whispered before he kissed me.

He rolled to his side, taking me with him, his lips still soft on mine as he stroked my hair back away from my face. His eyes were closed now, and when he pressed his forehead to mine, our breaths slowing, I let my eyes fall shut, too.

And though he was all I wanted that night, and though I was sated and satisfied, I couldn't ignore the familiar, lonely ache that crept its way up through my chest. Because Cameron had opened up to me that night, he'd let me in, and so I felt closer to him, yet still so far away — like we had both crossed our ends of the bridge, but were still separated by a five-foot jump between the two.

He had given me so much that evening, but there was still so much he held.

Could I find comfort in what he'd offered? Could I hold onto that small bit of light, hoping it would eventually grow tenfold and show me everything he'd hidden away over the years? And even if he could, I wasn't naïve enough to believe that one happy night with Cameron was enough to erase what I'd felt with Reese.

Even now, laying in Cameron's arms, I wondered if Reese was thinking of me. I wondered when I would see him next, and what I would feel when I did. It didn't matter that I was angry with him, or that he'd kept Blake from me — I still wanted him.

Because though Cameron had made me happy tonight, Reese had made me happy first — after years of being dead inside, and well before Cameron had even woken up to see he was losing me.

And was that the only reason he was trying? Was he only doing what he thought he had to do to keep me, or was it what he wanted, too? Would it all stop if I stayed, if I came home to him? Would we slip back into that numb existence Reese had found me in just over two months ago?

I couldn't be sure, but I tried with everything I had to let what he'd given me be enough. And for the first time in years, as I fell asleep in my husband's arms that night, I tucked my thoughts away, and I felt at peace.

For the first time in years, he felt like home.

chapter eight

CAMERON

There were two things I was constantly aware of when it came to time.

One was that I didn't have much of it. That one had been something I'd recognized early and easily. Two months wasn't long — no one would dispute that. But the second reality that I had learned later was that time was also fragile.

My weekend with Charlie had been everything I'd wanted it to be — maybe even more. She'd come back to me, opened up, let me in, and I'd crawled into her like a shelter from the darkest storm. Bringing her back to Garrick had the exact effect I wanted. It reminded her of a time when it was just us, when we fell in love, and I knew that — at least for the weekend — she was mine. All mine. Only mine.

But time had passed.

Now, it was Wednesday. We unpacked our bags late Sunday night, crawled into bed together, and fell asleep with content smiles on our faces. But on Monday morning, she came back here — to Westchester.

To him.

And ever since then, I'd felt her pulling away again.

The heels of my dress shoes clicked through the vacant halls as I made my way to Charlie's classroom. It had been so long since I'd been there, but I still knew the way. I used to surprise her all the time — for lunch, for holidays, for no reason at all, flowers in hand.

But just like with watching her get ready, I'd stopped coming to Westchester somewhere along the way.

And now, it was *his* territory, and I felt like the first soldier crossing over enemy lines.

Tomorrow, she would get on a plane and fly down to Florida to spend an entire weekend with Reese. It killed me, *literally* I felt my heart threaten to stop beating any time I let myself really think about it. But it was happening, and I couldn't control that.

I needed to find something I *could* control.

My anxiety had festered like an infected wound since Monday, my hands itching for something to do to make her stay with me. I knew she had to go to the conference tomorrow, but how could I stay in her mind, in her heart, when she was away with him?

In a strange way, the universe had given me something last night. When I got home from work, Charlie told me her check engine light had come on. So, I let her take my car to school and I took hers into the shop. It was so small, so easy, but it was something I could do for Charlie. It was something I could take off her plate and put on mine. It was a way to show her my love.

And there was another way I'd show her, too — a plan I was putting into action for while she was away. When she came back to me Sunday night, it wouldn't be just me she would come home to.

But that plan had to be shelved until she left.

For now, I used the energy from the weekend to keep her with me for as long as I could.

The halls filled with kids on their way to the lunchroom as I walked through the school. They filtered out slowly at first, a few classrooms dismissing early, and then the halls were crawling with little eyes and voices. I watched them all pass with a smile on my face, and when I recognized one of them, that smile split my face in half.

"Mr. Pierce!"

Jeremiah flung himself out of line and into my arms, which earned him a stern reprimanding from Robin, Charlie's aide. When she saw it was me, she paused, holding the line in place for just a moment as a small smile found her lips, too.

"Hey buddy," I said, bending to my knee to catch him. I managed to move the flowers I'd brought Charlie out of the way before he could crush them, and I squeezed him in a hug before he pulled away again. "How have you been?"

"Good," he said quickly, his eyes still bright and round. "Mom said you guys are starting on our house soon!"

"We are. Are you going to come and help us start building on groundbreaking day?"

Jeremiah nodded. "Uh-huh. Mom said she's gonna get me my own shovel!"

I chuckled, ruffling the hair on his head.

And for just a flash, I felt my unborn son like it was him staring back at me through Jeremiah's eyes.

"Well alright," I said. "Can't wait to see it. I bet you're going to be a big help to us."

"I will be! You can count on me, Mr. Pierce!"

He was still bouncing a little when Robin coaxed him back in line, and I waved her a thank you as the line began to file away again.

The halls grew quieter as I closed in on Charlie's classroom, and when I rounded the corner and saw her through the open doorway, I couldn't help but stop and smile.

This was Charlie in her element.

I wished I could have caught her in time to watch her with the kids, the same way I had the first time I'd surprised her at work. But even now, watching her tidy up the classroom while she hummed softly to herself, I could feel the joy radiating off her.

Her smile was genuine as she swept through the classroom, and I watched greedily, soaking up what that smile did to me, in turn. To some, they'd look at her and say she was "just a Kindergarten teacher." But for Charlie, there was no better job in the world. There was no better time to teach children, to help them form habits, to comfort them as they transitioned from home life to school life. This was her calling, it was what she was *made* to do.

School made her happy. Teaching made her happy. And, more than anything, those *kids* made her happy.

I was reminded again that one day, she would be the best mother the world had ever seen.

I hoped I'd be there to witness it first-hand.

Charlie caught a glimpse of me when she was stacking up workbooks, and at first, her mouth seemed to flatten at having a visitor. But when she did a double-take, she paused, her brows pinching together.

And then her smile lit up the room.

"Cam?" She shook her head, abandoning the workbooks she'd stacked up on her desk. "What are you doing here?"

"Surprising you. Did it work?"

I handed her the flowers, and she laughed, inhaling their scent with eyes closed before they fluttered open and found mine again.

"I'm very surprised," she said, placing the vase of flowers on her desk. She fiddled with a few of the stems before turning to me again, slowly trailing her hands up my arms to hook behind my neck. "Thank you."

I kissed her. Because there was nothing else to do in that moment. When she looked at me like that, when her eyes lit up for me and not for him, I had to find a way to seal that snapshot of time in her mind.

"I can't remember the last time you came to Westchester," she said, her big eyes searching mine. "I mean, other than the concert. I guess what I mean is I can't remember the last time you came here, to this wing."

"To your room," I finished for her.

She smiled, nodding. "Yeah."

"Well, I took your car into the shop. They're going to take a look and get back to me. But they gave me a rental until then, and I already took off work, so I figured I'd surprise you for lunch. Can you sneak away to go off campus? If not, we can just go to the café."

Charlie shifted.

"Um, maybe I could run down and grab something for us, and then we could eat here."

"In your classroom?"

She nodded, her eyes skirting to the open door behind me.

And that's when I realized.

She was supposed to have lunch with *him*.

I swallowed, heat creeping up my neck. "Okay. Should I wait here?"

But before she could answer, there was a knock on the frame of her door, and I turned to find Reese gaping at us just as Charlie pulled back.

She cleared her throat. "Hey, Reese. Cam surprised me for lunch," she said quickly. "I know we were supposed to go over plans for the conference, but I figured we could talk more on that in the morning?"

Reese was still staring at me, like he couldn't believe I was in my own wife's classroom. It was like I didn't belong, and I guessed that, in a way, for him, I didn't. This was where he'd had Charlie alone. It was where he'd gotten her to open up to him.

In his eyes, I wasn't supposed to be here.

I smirked.

Reese narrowed his eyes at that, stepping into the classroom with his hands slipping easily inside the pockets of his slacks. "Hey, Cameron, nice to see you," he said, a fake smile finding his lips.

"Likewise," I managed.

Reese evaluated me, his jaw tense. "Those flowers from you?"

I didn't answer. We both knew they were, and I wasn't dealing into whatever game he was trying to play.

He sniffed. "They're nice. I didn't realize you liked lilies, Charlie."

At that, I glanced at the flowers, and then at Charlie.

She didn't like lilies. She liked daisies.

How could I forget that?

Charlie ignored the dig, her arms folding over her chest. "We're going to go off campus to eat. Can you let Robin know I'll be a little late getting back? She knows the rest of the plans for the day."

Reese swallowed at that. "Sure. Is seven still okay for me to pick you up tomorrow, then?"

I frowned, finding Charlie. "I was going to take you to the airport on my way to work."

She cringed. "Well, I just knew that would make you late for work. Reese offered to pick me up, since it's on his way, and we're both going to the same place."

"Oh," I said, as calmly as I could manage. "I guess that makes sense. I don't mind being late for work, though. If you want me to take you."

"It's really no problem," Reese said, and my fists clenched at my sides.

"I wasn't talking to you. I was talking to my *wife*."

"Oh, sorry. I guess I just didn't realize what that looked like, since it's such a rare occurrence."

I blew out a breath through my nose, taking a large step toward him, but he only laughed as Charlie pressed her hands into my chest.

"Come on. Let's go get lunch." She turned to Reese then, and she looked even more pissed than I was. "Maybe you should use this time to call *Blake*. I'm sure she'd love to hear from you."

Reese's smile fell at that, and I saw the look in his eyes, one I knew all too well. He pleaded with Charlie for something in that moment — but for what, I wasn't sure. Forgiveness? Understanding? Either way, Charlie didn't seem keen to give it to him. She grabbed her purse from the hook behind her desk chair, leading the way out of her classroom.

"See you tomorrow," she called behind us, but she didn't turn, didn't so much as glance at Reese again before we were out of her room and down the hall.

We were both silent as we walked to the rental car, and once we were inside it, Charlie buckled up and let out a long breath.

I followed her lead, strapping on my seatbelt, but then I paused with my hands on the wheel.

"Are you sure you don't want me to take you tomorrow?"

"It's on his way, Cam," she said. "And we're both going there. No sense in going out of your way."

"I don't mind."

"I know. But it's fine, I can just ride with him."

My stomach turned. I knew they'd be together all weekend, so in the grand scheme of things, a car ride didn't make much of a difference. Still, I hated it.

I started the car, but still didn't put it in reverse.

"I'm sorry," I said softly. "About the lilies. I know you like daisies, I don't know why I didn't—"

"Cam," Charlie said quickly, leaning over in her seat until her hand could reach my leg. She squeezed, making me look at her. "Don't. I love them. Truly. They were such a wonderful surprise." She smiled. "And you delivering them in person was icing on the cake."

I let out a sigh, nodding, though I was still upset with myself.

"Thank you," she said, leaning over and pressing a kiss to my lips.

My left hand wandered from the steering wheel then, framing her face and holding her mouth to mine. I kissed her as long as she let me, and when she finally pulled back, she clicked on the seat warmers and stared out the front windshield.

"We need to hurry back, okay? I sprung this on Robin, and I don't want to leave her alone for too long."

And once again, I was reminded that time was my biggest enemy of all.

chapter nine

REESE

I hadn't slept in days.

It was the day of the conference, and I was supposed to be a representative of our school. I was supposed to be on my A game, the best of the best, and I looked like I got jumped in an alley last night. My eyes were heavy and lined in purple, my hair a mess no matter how I tried to style it.

I should have gotten rest. I should have been more prepared for today.

But how could I sleep knowing I had to wait to get Charlie alone, knowing she was going home to Cameron every night...

Knowing something had changed.

As if the weekend hadn't been bad enough with Charlie being on some sort of trip with Cameron, it had been even worse once she'd returned. Because she was different that Friday afternoon she left school than she was Monday morning when she returned.

Before she left, it had been like she was dreading the trip. I knew she would stay with me, if she could, if she hadn't promised him she would go with him wherever it was he asked her to go. But when she came back, I knew it was as a different woman. Her eyes were lighter, her smile wide, her laugh spritely and easy.

Something had happened. Cameron had made a move. And I knew I wouldn't have a chance to make mine until the conference.

So, I'd waited, three long days, just trying to bide my time until today. I'd somehow managed to talk her into having lunch with me yesterday, to go over the conference, and that little nibble of cheese was all I had.

And he stole it away.

Seeing him at Westchester, in a place that belonged to me and Charlie, it was like watching a concert where the lead band had stolen all my songs and claimed them as their own.

That was *our* place. Cameron already got to have Charlie every night at home, and now he had crossed over into my territory, into the one place where I had her without him. But as much as it ticked me off, it also reassured me that though he was trying, he still didn't know Charlie like I did.

She'd only told me once what her favorite flower was — sixteen years ago, on her fourteenth birthday, when I'd given her a notebook with daisies on it.

I'd never forgotten, and he had.

It didn't seem like a big deal at first glance. It was just flowers, just one small detail. But that's the way I loved Charlie — completely, with every fiber of my being. I loved her with every memory in my heart, with every song in my soul, and maybe Cameron had loved her that same way once before.

But where his love had faded, mine hadn't — not even when I'd never really had her as my own.

That was what I held onto as I tried and failed to sleep, knowing I would see her today, knowing I would finally get her alone.

Blake handed me my bag after I shrugged on a light coat, and she sighed when I opened the front door.

"I wish you didn't have to go," she said, running a hand through her long, messy hair before tucking her arms around her middle. "Not that I'm not ecstatic they chose you to attend in your first semester, but selfishly, I'll miss you."

My throat thickened. "I'll miss you, too. But I'll be back Sunday."

"Seems so far away."

"You'll blink and I'll be here again," I assured her, leaning in for a hug. She snuck up on her toes and pressed a kiss to my lips before I could stop her, but I broke it quickly.

"I should get going."

"Hey," she said, pulling my arm to stop me before I could make it through the door. "Are you sure you're okay? You've seemed so... distant, lately."

I swallowed. "I'm good. Just have a lot on my mind with the conference and all."

She nodded. "Yeah, I get that. It's a lot of pressure as a new teacher, I'm sure." Then, her lips curved into a seductive smile, and she trailed her fingertips over my bicep. "Are you sure you don't want me to help relieve a little of that pressure?"

My stomach rolled, Charlie's face when I told her about me and Blake sleeping together just once flashing in front of my eyes. That pain she'd worn would haunt me forever, and I vowed to never be the one to put it there, again.

"I really have to get going, Blake."

"It won't take long. You know how quick we can be when we want to be."

She licked her lips, and I peeled her off me, clearing my throat.

"Save that energy for when I get back, okay?" I said, praying I could just buy some time. I'd fake sick when I got back if I had to, but I knew one thing was for sure — I wouldn't touch Blake again.

I wouldn't betray Charlie.

"Have a good weekend," I offered as I wiggled past her, jogging down the porch steps.

"You, too," she said on a sigh.

I felt her eyes on me the entire walk to my car.

Once I was out of our neighborhood, I turned the radio off and ran through the words I would say to Charlie.

The last time I'd seen her, we'd fought. She wasn't happy with me, and I couldn't blame her. But the whole thing was just so... messy. It was complicated. Charlie of all people should understand that. I just needed to get her alone, talk to her without all the chaos surrounding us.

A beach in Miami seemed like the perfect place to do it.

I couldn't help but feel like I was losing her, and that feeling was strengthened when I pulled into her driveway and she made her way to my car. She didn't look excited to be going to the conference, and she definitely didn't seem happy at the sight of me.

Her long hair was pulled into a high bun, her eyes level, plump lips in a flat line as she dragged her suitcase down the driveway. I jumped out to take it from her, but she stopped me short.

"Don't."

I paused in front of her, hands up, and she moved around me to lug her suitcase into my trunk before slamming it shut. I opened her car door for her and she slid inside the passenger side seat without so much as a glance in my direction.

But someone else was staring at me.

Cameron stood in the doorway, his arms crossed as he leaned against one side of it and watched me make my way to my side of the car. I stared back, gaze unwavering.

The way he wore a cocky smirk told me he thought he'd won. It was the same smile I'd worn when he'd been at school the day before, except mine had been more like defensive armor than anything I was actually sure of. The truth was, I'd been scared shitless when I saw him in her room.

Something had changed. Cameron had made a move. I didn't know what it was, but I knew I had my work cut out for me to bring Charlie back to me.

He thought I was out of the picture, my bridge burned, my chance shattered.

But he had years of mistakes to make up for, and I only had one.

He underestimated me, but I only smiled back, because the truth was it was better that way.

I wanted him to think I was easy competition, that I'd fade off without putting up any kind of fight. Because what he failed to see was this had nothing to do with him. I didn't give a shit about him. It was Charlie I cared for, and her happiness.

Only now, I *knew* I could make her happier than him, that I could treat her better, and I wouldn't stop until she was mine.

I cocked one brow in Cameron's direction before opening my door to slide inside. Charlie still didn't look at me, not after I shut the door and not after I put the car in drive. Her eyes were on her husband.

I had to make her see.

He was only fighting for her because he lost her in the first place, but he didn't love her like I did.

No one loved her like I did. No one ever would.

She watched him until he was out of her sight, then her eyes found the road, and a deafening silence fell over us.

"I don't know about you," I said once we were clear of her house. "But I am beyond ready for sunshine and drinks on the beach."

"We'll be inside the hotel almost the entire time," she said, her expression blank as she stared out the front window.

"Not the whole time. We have breaks. And Saturday, the conference ends at noon, and we have the whole rest of the day and that night before we leave Sunday."

"Yeah, well, the beach isn't really my thing."

I sighed, reaching a hand over for hers, but she leaned away from the touch.

"Come on, Charlie," I pleaded. "We have an entire weekend away together. Alone..." I glanced at the road before reaching over farther to place my hand on her knee. "Don't spend it being mad at me."

"How's Blake?"

She whipped around to face me with that question, her lips pursed, and I swallowed at the way her eyes bore holes into mine.

"Honestly?" I asked. "Not good. Her dad's tests came back this weekend. The tumor is cancerous, and it's terminal."

Charlie's eyes softened, just the tiniest bit, and she turned back to the window with her arms crossed tight over her chest.

Saying the words out loud hurt me more than when I'd heard Blake say them.

But I had to tell Charlie, I had to let her in on the full situation so she would understand. No, I hadn't been honest about Blake, and yes, I had fucked up by sleeping with her.

Just like Charlie was giving Cameron time, I needed her to do the same for me. Blake needed me, and I could be there for her as a friend without crossing any lines — but Charlie had to trust me.

And I knew I didn't deserve that trust from her, not when I'd already betrayed it.

"It's complicated, Charlie," I said after a moment. "I told you that. But I made good on my promise to you. I haven't touched her since that day, and I won't again. I'm just trying to help her through this time, okay? And I'm going to tell her about you. About us. Just let me decide when that time is right." I paused. "Give me the time that I'm giving you with Cameron."

She scoffed. "Whatever."

My fists tightened around the steering wheel. I ran through all the words I'd wanted to say to her, but none of them felt adequate. She hated me, and she wasn't going to let me in — not yet.

I had to figure out a way to break through.

But every rational thought was sucked out into the cool March air when she kicked open her door at the airport, not even looking at me as the last words I expected flew from her mouth.

"I slept with him."

Then, she slammed her door, yanked her bag from the trunk, and made her way into the airport without checking to see if I followed.

CHARLIE

My mom used to say to me, "Be careful what you wish for."

I never understood it, not until I wished for nothing but chocolate one year for Christmas. My parents delivered, as did "Santa" and my grandparents. I had more chocolate than I knew what to do with, and I ate as much of it as I could in one sitting.

Then, I got violently ill.

I still remember sleeping in the bathroom, hugging onto the toilet and telling my mom I never wanted to taste chocolate ever again. I begged her to take what I had left and give it away, and she'd just chuckled, reminding me of that warning she'd given.

"Be careful what you wish for."

That lesson came back into my mind as I glanced over to where Reese sat, across the room from me. I didn't understand how he could look so artistically beautiful, even under the horrid fluorescent lights of the conference ballroom. It was like resisting chocolate, trying not to stare at him, but it didn't really matter — because *his* eyes hadn't found mine since the car ride to the airport yesterday.

It didn't matter that our hotel rooms were right next to each other, or that we'd been in several of the same small group break-out sessions, or that we'd been at the same dinner and the same after-party. Reese had avoided me every minute of the conference so far, and from the outside, it looked like he was having the time of his life.

Everyone loved him after just day one, which was a half day, and I couldn't blame them. He was charming, lively, the life of the party even at a conference.

He made everyone laugh — except for me.

As if his thoughtful insight and perfect comical timing during the conference wasn't enough, he was the center of attention at the mixer last night, too. He even played the keyboard at the little beach bar we all ended up at, with everyone gathered around him and singing along.

It wasn't even nine before I skipped out of the event, no longer wanting to be in the same room with him — especially since it seemed like he'd completely forgotten I existed.

I'd told him about Cameron because I knew it'd piss him off, and I'd been right.

I'd wanted him to leave me alone, and he had.

But now, all I wanted was to get inside his head, to know what he was thinking.

It was immature and childish, pushing his buttons just to get a rise out of him. It was the same game I'd played with Cameron the night I'd gone out to happy hour and stayed out late. I'd wanted his attention, and it took drastic measures to get it.

But with Reese, he had *wanted* to give me his attention — and he'd wanted mine, in return. But I was still pissed over Blake, and betrayed, and hurt. He had apologized, offered to tell me more, begged me for understanding — and all I'd done was act like the eight year old I was when I first realized I had a crush on him.

I think in a way, I thought I really did want him to leave me alone. After my weekend with Cameron, I was on a high with him. I wanted to give him my full attention, and Reese would have blocked that. So, I'd tried to push him away, to make him angry.

And I'd succeeded.

Still, though I'd had an amazing weekend with Cameron, and I was happy he was seeing a therapist, I still felt like we were standing on a broken bridge. There were still scars we shared, ones that hadn't healed — ones we hadn't even talked about. He was trying, and so was I, but it didn't change the way I felt for Reese.

Reese drove me mad. He got under my skin the way only someone you love more than the oxygen you need to breathe can. He pushed me to limits I never knew existed, and he showed me a life I never imagined I could have — a love I never imagined I could feel.

He made me irrational, and yet, I wanted him.

But I'd pushed him away.

Was this it? Was it over?

Be careful what you wish for.

"Alright, everyone. That wraps us up for today," Cindy, our moderator, announced after the last keynote speaker. "We'll have a break for dinner on your own and then there is an optional mixer at Hulligan's, the same place as last night. Beach gear encouraged."

Everyone clapped before the room erupted into a mixture of conversation and laughter. I packed up my bag in silence, smiling at a few people I'd met that day before waving goodbye and excusing myself upstairs to my room.

My phone rang as I stepped off the elevator on our floor, and I swallowed at the sight of Cameron's face on the screen. It was a photo I'd snapped at the park downtown one afternoon years ago. His aviator sunglasses reflected the

Pittsburgh skyline, the sun bright behind it, and his laughing smile took up his entire face. He had just a hint of stubble, my favorite length, and I remembered that moment like it had just happened.

With a tap of my finger, the picture disappeared, the call ignored.

It wasn't that I didn't want to talk to Cameron, but more that I didn't want to talk to *anyone*.

After our weekend together, everything at home had been perfect. I felt Cameron again, the old Cameron, the one I fell in love with and married, the one I built that home with so long ago. We cooked together twice before I left for the conference, both nights filled with laughter and wine. He had surprised me at school, bringing me flowers and taking me out to lunch. And in Cameron fashion, he had taken care of my car when the check engine light came on — just so I wouldn't have to.

Even more than all that, he was talking to me — maybe more than he ever had.

By all counts, he was giving me what I'd always wanted.

But there was still one thing we hadn't discussed.

Her.

I shook off the thought as my phone buzzed in my hand, just as I slid my key card against the entry pad and slipped inside my room. I dropped my bag on the chair by the desk before sliding the message open.

- I know you're busy with the conference. Just wanted to check in on you. Hope you're having fun. -

I sighed, flopping down on the bed and kicking my heels off.

- It's very fun, but lots of people-ing. You know that's my favorite. -

- Oh boy. Forced conversation. Sounds like a blast. -

I smiled at his text, watching the little bubbles bounce beneath it as he typed out another.

- Well, I'll leave you to it. Was just thinking of you. I miss you. -

My heart twisted, one hand moving to press against that spot in my chest where the ache was most present. It seemed to be almost a permanent ache now, between Cameron and Reese.

- I miss you, too. Talk soon. -

My stomach growled as I tossed my phone face down on the comforter, and I frowned, debating my options for sustenance. Reese would be joining a big group for dinner, no doubt, networking the way I should have been. But now that I was in my room after a full day of talking and listening to presentations, the last thing I wanted to do was talk to anyone else.

So, I flopped on my stomach, reaching for the phone to dial room service. Once I'd ordered, I stripped out of my dress, ran the hottest shower I could manage, and pulled out my laptop to go through my notes from the day.

When I opened the first document, my computer warned me of low battery, so I hopped up to dig through my bag for my charger. It was at the very bottom, the head of it stuck under my books. I yanked, and when I pulled it free, I cringed at the sight of wires poking through the white protective tubing.

"Shit."

I plugged it in, anyway, finagling the wire after it was connected to my computer to see if I could get it in a spot to charge. I twisted the wires left and right, pinched them together at different areas, and even tried using a Band-Aid to fuse the tubing back together, but it was no use.

A frustrated huff left my lips as I debated my options.

Some would have taken it as a sign to go out after dinner, to be social, but even the thought of being around people made me want to shove my head in an oven.

I could run out to the store, I thought, but that would require putting on pants — and that sounded even worse than talking to people.

There was *one* easy way to get a charger, though "easy" was a relative term. I knew Reese had the same laptop, and his room was just next door. He'd definitely be out for the night, the charger of no use to him. All I had to do was ask.

And my pride hated that.

"Ugh," I groaned, but I rolled myself out of bed, anyway, not even bothering to put on shoes before I slung my door open. I propped it open with the lock at the top, blowing out a long breath as I knocked on Reese's door next.

It didn't occur to me that I maybe should have stopped to put on clothes — not until the exact moment Reese opened his door.

The cool air from inside his room rushed through my still-damp hair, and Reese just stood there, his eyes hard on mine before they slowly made their way down to my robe. He focused on the knot I'd tied at my waist, the one at the bottom of the V the robe left between my breasts, before his gaze drifted down again, to my bare legs. The ends of my robe didn't quite connect at the bottom, and that left him a view of my thigh, still glistening as it dried from my shower.

I pulled those ends together, clearing my throat as my cheeks heated. "Can I borrow your laptop charger?"

Reese's eyes were still stuck on the point where I held my robe together. His jaw clenched, and he tightened his hold on the door knob before finally finding my gaze.

"For tomorrow?"

"No, for tonight. I just wanted to go through my notes for the day, and my charger broke. Can I borrow yours?"

He didn't answer, his eyes taking in my wet hair now — hair that was down and hanging over my shoulders.

"I'll give it back," I added. "The charge should be enough to get me through the day tomorrow and I'll go to the store when we get home."

Reese still stared at me, a small smirk climbing on his face as he pushed the door open wider and stepped aside for me to come in.

I opened my mouth to argue, to say I could just wait there while he got the charger, but the way he lifted one brow told me that wasn't an option. So, I stepped inside, staying close to the door once it had closed behind us.

"You're not going out for dinner?" he asked, crossing the room to where his backpack rested on the desk. He was already changed for the night, sporting casual, baby blue shorts and a white dress shirt that had the top three buttons undone. The sleeves were rolled up to his elbows, and a beige blazer was thrown over the edge of his bed — an accessory I assumed would top off his look.

"I ordered room service."

Reese glanced at me, that same smirk on his stupid face as he shook his head and dug through his bag. "You should come out."

"I'm okay. Thanks."

The entire room smelled like him. He was freshly showered, his long hair a little damp at the ends, too, and he wore the same cologne I remembered him wearing the night we went up the Incline. I remembered that scent enveloping me as I broke in his arms, as I showed him my scars, and that same scent dusted the sheets of the fort we built in his home.

"What about after?" he asked, crossing the room to where I stood. He held the charger in his hand, but he made no attempt to give it to me. "You coming down to the beach?"

"I told you," I said, swallowing at his nearness. "The beach isn't really my thing."

Reese stepped into my space even more. "Okay."

He offered me the charger, his eyes watching me over the bridge of his nose. I swallowed, reaching for the white cord, but before I could pull away, his hand tightened over mine.

"So, is this it?"

My eyes flicked to where his hand gripped mine before I found his gaze again.

"This is the end? You're staying with Cameron, and I can just fuck off?"

"Reese..." I shook my head, eyes dropping to the floor between us.

"Just answer me."

"I don't *have* an answer," I said honestly, my voice squeaking at the top of the confession. "And I didn't say it was over. I just... I told you I slept with him. I wanted to be honest."

Reese's jaw flexed at the reminder of what I'd done, and he took another step, just centimeters between us now.

"You slept with him," he repeated. "Knowing that... hearing you say those words... it *kills* me, Charlie. It makes me want to murder him."

"That's not fair."

"I never said it was," he answered quickly. "But it's the truth."

Tears pricked the edges of my eyes, but I forced a breath, keeping them inside.

"I still love him," I whispered.

Reese swallowed. "So, does that mean you don't want me?"

My eyes traveled up until they met his chest, and I watched his breaths enter and leave, the speed of them matching that of my heart.

"You don't care about me?" he pushed further, his hand letting go of where it held the charger and mine. He moved it to frame my jaw instead, thumb tracing the skin there, his breath hot on my lips. "And everything we had, everything you felt with me..." he said. "You don't feel that anymore?"

"I..."

I couldn't answer, the words stuck like feathers in honey somewhere inside my throat. My head spun, the smell of him too much, the feel of his hand on me making me weak.

"And this..." he continued, his free hand trailing up the edges of my robe that lined the middle of my body. He pushed them aside gently, his finger just barely grazing the bottom of my breast as I inhaled a stiff breath. "This doesn't make you feel anything at all?"

"Reese..."

"Say my name one more time, and this robe will be on the floor."

I bit my lip, squeezing my eyes as my body screamed under his touch. He'd barely even brushed my skin and I was already on fire, writhing for oxygen.

"Yes."

"Yes, what?" he probed, and this time, his finger trailed up just enough to graze my pebbled nipple.

"Yes, I still want you," I panted. "But I'm just... I'm confused. I need some space, some time."

"I don't want space." He rolled the pad of his thumb over my nipple, his hand slipping all the way under my robe to grip my breast firmly. "And we don't have time."

"Reese..."

And just as he promised, my robe was on the floor in a snap.

He tugged one end of the loose knot I'd tied under my breasts, and the moment the robe wasn't between us any longer, he pulled me flush against him, his lips finding mine in a heated frenzy.

I gasped into his open mouth, but his tongue snuck inside in the next breath, and before I could register what had happened, my feet were off the ground. Reese pushed me against the wall, his hands pinning my hips against it as he kissed down my neck, sucking the skin between his teeth hard enough to leave marks.

Hissing, I arched off the wall and into his touch, the overwhelming feel of him taking me under like a tidal wave. I didn't gasp for air, didn't beg for oxygen — I simply let the wave take me down, down to hell, down to where my favorite sinner waited with open arms.

"You drive me absolutely *crazy*, you know that?" Reese growled, pressing the hard-on straining through his shorts against my naked core. The friction sparked a fire, and I whimpered, rolling my hips against him.

Reese hadn't touched me since the night of the spring concert, since he'd made me come for him in the costume closet. I'd had to be quiet then, but as Reese slipped a finger inside me, the loudest moan ripped from my throat. He groaned, withdrawing his finger before sliding it in again.

"So tight." He murmured against my lips, and he kissed me harder as he slid another finger in to join the first.

My hands pressed hard into the wall, trying to find something to grip as he pinned me there. Every sound was muted other than his breaths, his eyes all I could see, his hands all I could feel. Just like the first time he'd touched me, Reese overwhelmed every sense, demanding all of me.

Memories of the fort flashed behind my eyes, the feel of him touching me on his piano, the way he'd stretched me open more than once that night. And I wished it was only lust. I wished it was only his body that made me feel this way.

But it was him.

It was the lost boy I wanted to save when I was younger, the man I wanted to find home in now. It was the way he listened to me, the way he knew exactly what to say, the way he understood what I never had to explain.

Reese was my jagged little pill, one I wanted to swallow eagerly.

But unlike that first night Reese had touched me, Cameron still lived within my heart tonight, too. And it was the flash of his smile in the car on the way to Garrick that zapped me back to reality.

"Stop," I said, eyes popping open as I pressed my hands into Reese's chest.

He pulled back, smirking before his lips found mine again. He thought it was a game, a sexy round of cat and mouse. But I had to get out. I had to get air.

I had to get space.

"NO!"

This time, I pushed hard enough for his grip to weaken, and he dropped me gently to the floor with his face screwed up in confusion.

"Are you okay? I was just—"

"I have to go."

"Charlie."

I scrambled for my robe at his feet, tucking it haphazardly around me and fumbling with the door knob until I finally yanked it open.

"Charlie, wait!"

But I was already in the hall, and in the next instant, I pushed through my room door, slapping the lock stopper out of the way and shutting the door firmly behind me. I fell against it, my breaths erratic, and I jumped when Reese knocked.

"Come on, Charlie. Let me in," he begged, his voice muffled through the door. "Talk to me, for Christ's sake."

I backed away, still watching the door like he'd somehow find a way inside.

"He doesn't love you," he said after a moment. "Not the way I do. I know you know that. He's inside your head, your heart, but only because he lost you. It took that — losing you — for him to wake up and try to be what you deserve, Charlie."

He paused, and I stared at the peep hole on the door, wondering what he looked like in that moment.

"He's giving you everything right now, and I'm sure he's making you feel more than you have in years. But he's only making you feel that way because he wants you to stay. The question is, will he still make you feel this way, will he still treat you the same once he has you again?"

An ache surged through me, and I closed my eyes tight against the tears that threatened to fall.

I thought he was done, but Reese lowered his voice a little more before he asked just one final question.

"If you stay, and he goes back to the husband you've had for the past five years, will it be enough?"

My face warped, fighting against the emotion building in me. I felt Reese on the other end of the door, begging me to open it for him, but after a moment, I heard a sigh before his door opened and closed with a soft latch.

I cried, falling to the floor with my hands still clutching my robe as I tried to catch my breath. My heart thumped loudly in my ears where my head hung between my shoulders, each beat separating another thought as they ripped through me.

Thump.

What is wrong with me?

Thump.

Who have I become?

Thump.

What the hell do I do now?

And between those thoughts, I asked myself the same question as Reese.

"If you stay, and he goes back to the husband you've had for the past five years, will it be enough?"

It was the only question I knew the answer to.

chapter Ten

CHARLIE

The rest of the conference dragged by, each minute feeling like a day. By the time we ended the Saturday afternoon session, it was all I could do to haul myself upstairs, change, and make my way to the bar. I knew everyone would be at the final mixer being held in the ballroom next to where we'd had the conference, so I found my safe haven in the relatively empty beach bar out back.

I chose a seat at the bar, my sandy feet dangling off the tall stool as I ordered my first drink of the weekend. That drink quickly turned to two, and two to three, and before I knew it, the sun had set, the beach growing dark behind me as dusk settled in.

My fingers trailed the sugary rim of my fifth fruity margarita as a cool breeze swept into the bar. At least, I thought it was my fifth. I hadn't kept an accurate count, and I didn't really care as I lifted it to my lips, hoping the alcohol would burn away everything else that stung — like the fact that I was killing my husband, that I didn't know if I could stay with him, and that I still loved Reese, even when I wished I could stay away from him.

It'd been almost a month now since Cameron asked me to give him another chance, and the thought of enduring the pain I felt in my chest for another month made my stomach lurch. To make matters worse, I knew I wasn't the only one feeling that pain. Cameron had to be sick, knowing I was away with Reese, and Reese had agreed to wait for me — to respect the time I'd promised Cameron.

I didn't deserve either one of them.

Why did I think my happiness mattered anymore? The truth was they'd both be better off without me, and I should have to endure life alone. At least, that's what I wanted to believe.

But inside my heart, I didn't.

Under the bad decisions I'd made in the past few months, I knew my heart was pure and true. I had loved Cameron with every ounce of love and care I possessed. I had tried to wait for him, to let him come back to me on his own time. I had suffered through lonely nights, cold rejection, empty promises.

I may not have been perfect, but he'd hurt me, too.

And in the back of my mind, Reese's question played over and over. If I stayed and Cameron went back to the way he'd been the past five years, would it be enough?

No.

Not even close.

Thunder rolled quiet and low off in the distance, and I took another sip of my drink, head fuzzy as I tried to imagine my life. With Cameron, it was hard to picture anything other than what we'd lived since the boys died.

I could faintly remember a time before, when we were happy, when we were *blissfully* happy. He'd given me a glimpse of that the previous weekend, when he'd taken me back to Garrick, and back to a room we made memories in. And Cameron was opening up to me, he was letting me in, he was giving me a piece of himself he was never able to give before.

I loved him. I missed him. I didn't even want to leave for the conference because we were having so much fun at home. I wanted to stay in his arms, in that house where he was beginning to peel back his layers and let me inside.

Still, Reese had a point, and it stuck with me long after I left his room last night.

If I stayed, would Cameron be the old Cameron, the one I fell in love with, or would he go back to being the one who'd hurt me and let me feel like I didn't matter at all to him?

I blinked, imagining a different life, one where I was with Reese.

I saw us living in his quaint house, me sprucing up the front garden and choosing new linen colors in his bedroom. I pictured us as renowned teachers at Westchester, the couple everyone loved to talk to, the one everyone wanted to be. I saw late nights at his piano, heard our moans under his sheets, felt his arms wrapped around me.

But when I tried to see past that, to a family, to having children and joining my parents for Christmas, I couldn't. Because those memories had already been created by Cameron, and I didn't know how to erase him.

What if I never could?

I sighed, sucking a large gulp of margarita through my straw. I wondered if the answers lay at the bottom of this glass, since I hadn't found any in the last four.

I felt him take the seat next to me before he said a word. His presence was electrifying, one that buzzed with a mixture of invitation and warning. He tapped on the bar, and as soon as the bartender saw him, she smiled, whipping up some sort of drink without him saying a word.

Of course. Even the staff knew and loved him.

I stared at his forearm on the bar next to mine, tracing the lean muscles and dark hair.

"You've been in the sun," I noted, taking another sip through my straw. His skin was a golden tan, a beautiful bronze, the color of caramel.

"Spent the day on the beach after we were cut loose today," he answered.

His voice was thick and a bit raw, like he hadn't slept. I felt his eyes on me, but I kept mine on the bar — on his arm, my arm, how close they were, how much space they'd have to cross to touch.

"Speaking of which, I thought you hated the beach."

"I do," I confirmed. "But I love margaritas."

I took another large slurp, and Reese chuckled, his forearm leaving the bar next to mine for a second before returning. I imagined he ran his hand through his hair, or perhaps scratched an itch on his jaw. He'd let his beard grow in a bit over the weekend, just a little scruff. I wanted to touch it, too.

"It kills me, you know," Reese said after a moment, his voice low. "Watching you right now, knowing there's so much on your mind, so much that's hurting you."

I stopped drinking, but kept my lips on the straw, my feet still kicking under the chair.

"I wish I could crawl inside that mind of yours and face all your demons for you."

My heart squeezed, but I shook my head on a laugh.

"They're some mean motherfuckers."

"I believe that," he said quickly. "But, I'd fight them, anyway."

I propped one elbow up on the bar, leaning my cheek on my palm as I finally turned to face him. His face was just as tan as his arms, his nose a little red at the tip. I met his eyes, another roll of thunder sounding in the distance as I watched him.

"Why do you care?" I asked. "About me, I mean. I never talked to you after you left Mount Lebanon, not even when everything happened..." My stomach twisted. "Why do you still care about me?"

Reese smiled, his gaze falling to where his hands rested around his glass before it rose up to the thatch ceiling of the bar. "Why does rain fall in the desert? Why are diamonds made from dust?" He shrugged. "Some things just are, Tadpole — no matter how difficult or impossible the circumstances." His eyes found mine again. "I care about you because there is no other choice for me, and I love you the same."

Butterflies buzzed to life in my stomach at his words, and I smiled, nudging him with my knee under the bar.

"Such a poet."

"And I didn't even know it," he added with a grin, but it fell quickly, his eyes searching mine. "Talk to me."

I sighed, sucking down the last of my drink before signaling to the bartender that I'd like another. I knew the hangover in the morning would likely kill me, but it was worth it to numb the pain tonight.

"You might need a cigarette."

"I quit."

I frowned. "You did? When?"

"The day after you asked me to."

I thought back to the Sunday we'd spent mostly in his bed, the ending of our one and only weekend together. He'd lit a cigarette after we'd made love, and I joked about him needing to quit.

I couldn't believe he'd actually done it.

My eyes traveled back to where the bartender was mixing my drink.

"I'm sorry I locked you out last night," I said first, my voice as unsteady as the ice floating in my new margarita. "It's just... it's all so much for me right now. I can't think straight. Nothing makes sense. And the things you said, the truth of them, I couldn't handle it." I shook my head. "Cameron has been talking to me more."

Reese took a sip from his glass. "Yeah?"

I nodded. "Yeah. I know you don't want to hear this, but we had an amazing weekend together. He came back to me," I said, and then I shook my head. "No, it was more than that. He came back, but he also showed me layers of him I'd never seen before. We talked about how he felt after we lost our boys. He let me in on how it affected him. And we laughed, Reese."

"You deserve to laugh."

"It had been a while since I laughed with him," I confessed. "Truly laughed, anyway."

Reese spun his glass between his hands on the bar. He wouldn't meet my gaze.

Another rumble of thunder found us, this one stronger, the breeze picking up as the storm rolled in.

I sipped on the fresh drink the bartender delivered, cringing at the strength of it. But I sucked down more, anyway. I needed liquid courage for what I was about to say next.

"He cheated on me."

Reese stilled, his hands pausing on the glass, but he still didn't look at me.

"Cameron. It was about a year after we lost the boys. I... I walked in on him one evening at work, trying to surprise him. I wanted to take him out for dinner." I laughed, recalling the memory as if it were happening in that very moment. I could still see her navy pencil skirt gathered at her hips where she straddled him, could see her red manicured nails on his shoulders — the same color as her lips when she turned and smirked at me from where she sat.

"There's this girl he works with often," I said. "Natalia. She's from one of the sister companies my uncle founded in New York City. She comes here a lot, though, to the home office, and she and Cameron are always on the same projects together." I swallowed, stirring my drink with the straw. "She's gorgeous. Long, tan legs, bright blonde hair, and she has these... eyes," I said. "They're like a crystal green, almost like cat eyes. She's sexy." I laughed. "She's literally everything that I'm not."

Reese turned to me then, and he opened his mouth to argue, but I shook my head.

"No, seriously, Reese. It's a different level. And I don't know, maybe part of me expected it when I showed up that night. She was sitting on him in his chair, straddling him. I walked in, and when I saw them, I dropped my purse."

A flash of the sound of that, of my keys and purse hitting the floor, collided with the thunder at the beach bar.

I closed my eyes.

"Cameron threw her off of him, of course. Chased after me. He kept saying he was sorry, that he could explain, but when we got home that night, he had nothing to say for himself." I shrugged. "He just held me and begged me for forgiveness. He told me there was no excuse, and he would never forgive himself for hurting me."

"But *you* forgave him," Reese said. "Didn't you?"

"I did," I admitted, something between a laugh and a cry leaving my lips. "But I never forgot. And I think that's part of the problem, you know? This past weekend, I felt him — the old him. He made me laugh, he made me feel wanted, and I felt every beat of my heart still pounding with the love I've always had for him, for the love I always *will* have," I said. "But, I'll never forget what he did. And it's not even really the sex," I admitted. "That, I think I can forget. But I'll never forget that when I needed him most, he found comfort in someone else. When I was breaking, when I was grieving, he was with her — letting her in, letting her comfort him when it was all I wanted to do."

I shook my head, taking a quick drink before I ran my hands back through my hair. It was frizzy and sticky, not used to the Florida humidity.

"And I know that's ridiculous, because look at me. Look what I've done with you. I've done the same thing, betrayed him the same way, but—"

"It's not the same."

"It's not," I agreed. "At least, it doesn't feel like it to me. I mean, maybe it is. Maybe we're both going to hell."

Reese chuckled at that. "Don't worry. I'll build us a big mansion there before you two arrive. We can all live happily ever after."

I tried to smile, but failed, reaching for my drink, instead.

We were both quiet for a bit, listening as the thunder got closer, a few flashes of lightning illuminating the bar now and then. After a while, Reese turned to me, pulling my hands off the bar and into his lap. I had no choice but to meet his eyes then, and when I did, I found just as much pain and sorrow in his as I knew existed in mine.

Maybe that was where our love was born, mine and Reese's — between the lines of our scars.

"One thing I love about your heart is that it continues to love, even when it's bruised and beaten. You have always been the girl who loves, Charlie. You loved me when I was a stupid, bored, depressed teenager," he said, smiling. "And you love your husband still, even when he has hurt you. It's okay that you still love him. It's not what most others would do, and that's what makes it amazing."

He paused, his grip tightening on my hands.

"But, it's also okay to let him go, if that's what your heart is telling you. Just because you've given him so much of your life, so much of your heart, does not mean he is entitled to the rest of it. You deserve to be happy, *truly* happy, whether it's with him or me or some lucky bastard you haven't met yet, or hell, even without any man at all." Reese smiled. "But, what I want you to know is what he did to you, it is not a reflection of who you are. It does not mean you weren't good enough, or pretty enough, or sexy enough, or interesting enough," he said. "You are all of those things and more, Charlie. You are the most sensational woman I have ever known. And your worth is not defined by him."

My eyes bubbled with tears, and I watched Reese through them, his features morphing as his words settled in my bloodstream along with the alcohol. I hadn't even said that I'd felt those things — that I'd felt *less than* after what Cameron had done — but Reese had heard me, anyway. He'd known the whisperings in my heart before I'd even heard them, myself.

And it was then that I realized that no matter which direction I went, no matter which man I chose, both would exist in me forever. They were valves in my heart, and I could not beat on without both of them present in some way.

One tear slipped free, and I laughed, pulling my hands from Reese's and swiping them over my face. "Ugh, I'm sorry. I'm a mess."

"Yes, you are. But, you're the prettiest damn mess I've ever seen."

I shoved his shoulder, and he laughed, catching my hand in his and lifting it to his lips. He pressed a kiss to my knuckles just as the rain started to fall, soft at first, but quickly turning to a downpour. Reese peered up at the roof before he gazed back at the beach, and his eyes found mine with a mischievous smile.

"Come on."

He tugged on my hand, pulling me from my barstool, but I held onto the bar with my free hand.

"Wait, where are you going?"

"Just come on."

"We haven't paid."

He huffed, tapping on the bar to get our bartender's attention. "Can you add our drinks to my room tab, Leila?"

She nodded, but I still hadn't moved. I just stared at him, at where he held my hand in his.

"Damn it, Tadpole, stop being so stubborn and just trust me."

KANDI STEINER

I laughed, my hand still gripping the bar until he tugged me forward again. I stumbled into him, and Reese steadied me before jogging toward the beach. I couldn't protest before we were out from the cover of the bar, the rain soaking through our clothes, and Reese just kept running.

He pulled me by the hand until our feet touched the ocean, and then he stopped, and I ran right into him, crashing into his chest. But Reese caught me effortlessly, the rain pouring down loud and chaotic around us as he pulled me into him.

"I'm getting soaked!" I screamed over the rain, laughing as Reese wrapped his arms around me.

"Exactly!" He smiled, shaking his head fast and hard, spraying me with even more water. "Let it wash it all away. Let it take every thought, every doubt, every anxiety — consider the rain your spin cycle, Tadpole."

He gripped one hand then, spinning me in the sand as I laughed and laughed, the rain flying off me as I twirled. Thunder clapped around us, and Reese pulled me back into him, my hands landing on the wet t-shirt that stuck to his chest.

Lightning flashed, and his lashes dripped as he watched me, eyes searching mine under the warm Florida rain. There were a million questions in his eyes, most not meant to be answered, and I was thankful he didn't whisper even a single one out loud. Instead, he framed my face with his hands, his fingers sliding between the wet tendrils of my hair, and then he leaned in, and he kissed me.

He kissed my lips the very same way the rain kissed my skin — with gentle ease and purpose. He wanted to wash away the confusion, the pain, and with every kiss he took more and more of each. I wrapped my arms around his neck,

145

pulling him into me more, our chests pressed together as the rain poured down.

I didn't know what would happen next, but in that moment, he was all that I saw. *We* were all that I felt. He rained down on me, and I drowned in his love, lungs adapting to breathe under water.

"Take me somewhere," I moaned into his lips as he gripped my ass through the wet fabric of my dress.

Reese groaned, kissing me harder before he broke contact and searched the beach for an escape. We were the only ones that I could see, everyone else inside and sheltered from the rain. When he spotted a lifeguard stand, he tugged me toward it, and we sprinted through the rain again.

He stopped every now and then to kiss me, his hands fisting in my hair or tangling in the straps of my dress, and once we were under the cover of the stand, he pressed me against the wood, his lips on a hot trail from my neck to the swell of my breasts.

"Someone will see us," I breathed.

"I don't give a fuck."

I giggled, looking around us as he lifted the hem of my skirt long enough to peel my soaked panties down my thighs. I couldn't see anyone watching — not on the beach and not in any of the bars or hotels behind us. It was dark, only the lightning revealing us with each flash, but the stand only provided so much shelter. If someone wanted to see us, they could.

Still, when my panties hit the sand and Reese ran a hot hand up the inside of my thigh, his fingers sliding just between my lips, I realized I didn't give a fuck, either.

Let them watch.

He didn't enter me this time, just slid his fingers between my lips, groaning with appreciation at the wetness he found. It was a different wet than the rain — silkier, hotter, born from desire for him instead of from the clouds.

Reese kissed me hard again as he tore at the buttons of his shorts. He pulled them down just enough to free himself of his briefs, too, and then he lifted me.

My ankles wrapped around his backside, hands clawing his shoulder for any kind of grip, and we both moaned in unison when he slid inside me — hard and fast and mercilessly. He hit me deep, withdrawing just an inch before he plowed in even more, and I ran my nails down his back, desperate to feel him, to make him feel me.

Reese made love to me under the cover of rain, the thunder colliding with our sighs and moans for the soundtrack of the night. Every sigh was a flash of lightning, every kiss a burst of wind, and every time we touched, I felt the storm surge inside me, forever reminding me of the half of my heart that belonged to Reese.

The rain washed away the pain, just like Reese said. It washed away the confusion, the hurt, the scars and the questions. I laughed and loved, leaving all the *what ifs* behind, reveling in the feel of the water on my skin.

Yes, the rain took all that had weighed on me that weekend, but in turn, it revealed the sinner who lived beneath that weight. Everything I felt was wrong, every kiss was a sin, every touch a transgression. And I couldn't even find it in me to pray for forgiveness.

I would take whatever punishment would come for my crime, because the truth was as clear as the sky once the rain subsided.

I wasn't sorry at all.

And I didn't want to quit Reese Walker.

chapter eleven

CAMERON

Charlie thought I cheated on her.

She wasn't the only one. I wasn't naïve enough to think word hadn't spread around the office, and perhaps around the town — seeing as how Reid's Energy Solutions was so involved in the community. I imagined even Charlie's father knew, though he'd never confront me. Maxwell Reid knew more than he should about everyone who worked for him, but he was a man of respect and privacy.

Everyone thought they knew the real story, and I hadn't even tried to correct them. I hadn't even tried to explain the truth to Charlie, because in my mind, none of it mattered.

I had still hurt her, no matter what the circumstances actually were. *That* was what mattered, and that was what I'd always told myself.

But Patrick had a different theory.

He wanted me to tell Charlie the truth — all of it — every single detail of what happened between me and Natalia. It was uncomfortable enough for me to even talk to him about her, let alone to Charlie. Just the thought of it made me want to jump in front of a bus.

"She deserves to know the truth," Patrick had said at our session that Friday. It was the day after Charlie left for the conference. The day after she left to spend an entire weekend with *him*. "Let her be the one to decide if the truth makes a difference in how she feels or not."

In a way, I understood what he meant. Perhaps Charlie would see it differently, and maybe she would actually forgive me — but *I* would never forgive me. That was the truth of it. No matter how anyone else saw it or what they believed, I had still hurt my wife. I'd betrayed her trust. I'd broken my vows.

There was no excuse for that. No valid one, anyway.

Still, I replayed the words I'd say to Charlie as I put the finishing touches on my project for the weekend. I hoped it would show her my love, what my hands had built, and that my words would bring clarity to a time we never discussed.

I built her an aviary.

Charlie had let Jane go free, but I knew in her heart that it killed her. I knew she missed Jane and Edward both, and that our house had felt a bit empty since they'd gone.

Charlie was a woman of simple pleasures — she loved her books, her garden, her birds, and, for reasons unknown, me. I couldn't bring Jane or Edward back, but I could give her new birds to love, and a new place to find peace in our home.

I'd thought of just getting her two Budgies again, but I knew I could never replace Jane and Edward.

So, instead, I'd built a large aviary downstairs in our sun room.

It took up half the room now, the other half housing a bright couch, matching chair, and glass table Charlie had picked out when we first bought the house. I'd started building the aviary the second Charlie left on Thursday, forgoing work on both Thursday and Friday to spend the time I needed to complete it before she got home. Perks of not taking vacation time in years was that I had plenty to spare, and thankfully, my boss hadn't questioned my frequent use of it recently.

Maybe he knew Charlie was cheating on me, too.

Regardless, I'd spent the entire weekend bringing my vision for the aviary to life, and I couldn't wait for Charlie to see it. It was just as grand as I'd imagined, spanning from floor to ceiling, the welding wire stretching over the rustic metal framing I'd selected to give it a modern feel.

There was a small hammock inside, one Charlie could lie or sit in as her birds flew around her, and the sun shone through the glass ceiling of that room in such a way that I knew would bring a smile to Charlie's face every morning. I'd filled the aviary with plush greenery and branches for the birds, as well as several nest boxes, and the last and final touch had been to get her very first birds.

Two Bengalese finches.

They twittered around me as I set up the last perch inside the aviary, and when it was complete, I sat in the hammock, watching them flit around from branch to branch in their new home.

I read when researching the aviary that keeping a single pet finch happy and healthy was nearly impossible. They thrived in pairs or groups, always needing the love and company of another to keep them satisfied.

I could relate.

The thought of losing Charlie was one I never liked to dwell on, but it was impossible to avoid that weekend. I knew she was with Reese, on a beach, in another state, far, *far* away from me. I could only hope that our weekend together was still fresh in her mind, that she believed the words I'd said to her, that she felt my love the way I'd always felt hers.

But I also knew there was a part of her that would never trust me again, part of her that had forgiven me, but would never forget what I did.

And so, with our new birds chirping in the background, I focused again on what I had to tell Charlie when she got home.

I didn't want to relive that time in my life, and I definitely never wanted to discuss that day, but I had no choice. Patrick was right. Charlie deserved the truth, and more than that, she deserved to know what I had been thinking, what I'd been feeling.

Charlie thought I cheated on her, but I didn't.

Natalia Aleppo had been a partner of mine for years. We worked our first project together when I was in my second year at Reid's Energy Solutions, and from the very first moment I met her, I liked her.

But not in any way a married man wasn't allowed to like a woman.

I thought she was intelligent, and well-spoken. I liked that I could depend on her to pull her side of a project, that she could speak to a crowded conference room of people and articulate our ideas while I stood silent in the corner with the numbers and figures. She was the face of our team, I was the machine in the back. I liked it that way.

Natalia was always professional with me, always nothing but sweet and friendly. She and Charlie met many times, and she'd always treated Charlie with respect, too.

But after we lost the boys, when depression took me under, something in Natalia changed.

I liked to think of her as a predator, and me her prey, one she watched carefully from a distance until the exact right time to pounce. But I couldn't blame her for everything, not when I was equally as guilty. I may not have ever slept with her, but I had leaned on her — I had let her in when I should have been talking to Charlie, and to this day, I didn't know why.

She was just there, that's what I had told Patrick, anyway. When we were working long nights at the office, when I was trying to give Charlie space to heal while I dealt with the loss of our children on my own, Natalia was right there. She was asking questions, bringing me coffee, rubbing my shoulders, telling me it was all going to be okay.

And I should have told her to stop.

I should have told her no well before I did, should have seen the warning signs, should have admitted to myself that the way she looked at me had changed. But I didn't. Not until that very night when she let herself inside my office after hours and closed the door behind her.

I could still close my eyes and see the smile on her red lips as the door latched closed, hear the click of her heels on my floor as she crossed to my desk, feel the pressure of her fingers on my shoulders as she climbed into my lap. She didn't give me a chance to stop her, to argue, to even *realize* what was happening until her legs were spread over me, her skirt bunching at her hips, panties pressing to the zipper of my pants.

"I'm looking for trouble," she'd whispered, grinding her hips against mine.

But as she'd leaned in to kiss me, I'd stopped her, gripping her wrists hard and peeling her off me.

"I'm not."

She'd pouted, tilting her head to the side. "She doesn't have to know. Just... let me make you feel good, Cameron. You deserve to feel good."

Charlie was all I'd seen in that moment, she was all I cared about, and I didn't for one split second give in to Natalia, not even when the carnal urges inside me screamed for me to let go.

I told her to get off me.

I told her to leave.

But none of that mattered, because it was too late.

Charlie walked in. She saw Natalia in my lap. She saw the skirt around her hips, smelled Natalia's perfume on my shirt. I'd chased her down, begged her to listen to me, to hear me out, but once we'd gotten home, I knew in my heart there was nothing I could say.

It didn't matter if I hadn't slept with her, everything Charlie had seen had still been true.

Another woman had sat in my lap, with her bare thighs against me, with her arms around my neck, and I hadn't pushed her off. I hadn't stood and knocked her to the ground. I hadn't told her no, not fast enough, anyway. Not with enough conviction.

And I'd let that woman in.

I'd talked to her about my fears, about my pain, about the very loss my wife was dealing with on her own. I'd stayed late at work because I enjoyed being in Natalia's company, and I'd told her things I'd never once told Charlie. The more I told her, the more I opened up to her, the more I liked her. And even if I hadn't acted on it, I couldn't deny that I hadn't felt the energy change around us. I felt the pull, I felt the want, I felt the desire.

If we never acted on it, it was innocent, right? That's what I had told myself, it was what I'd convinced myself was true.

And *that* was why I couldn't tell Charlie I hadn't cheated on her. Because in the only way that mattered to me, I had. There had been many women who'd shared my bed before I met Charlie, but she'd been the only one I let inside my heart. For me, that was what real intimacy was. It was talking late into the night, sharing scars. Until Natalia, Charlie was the only one I'd ever done that with.

I may not have been guilty of the crime she imagined, but I was still guilty, nonetheless. And I'd never been a man to beg for a forgiveness I didn't deserve.

Still, I agreed with Patrick that Charlie deserved to know the truth — if for no other reason than that I'd always been honest with her. I didn't expect her to forgive me, or for it to change anything between us. I didn't expect it to be enough to make her stay.

I just expected more of myself, and I would tell her the truth, no matter how hard it would be.

One of the finches jumped to a new branch, the other following quickly before they both went up in flight again, shaking me from my thoughts. I watched them fly high and then low, and I smiled.

Charlie would love them.

I remembered her anger when she set Jane free, when she accused me of trying to buy a bird to mask the pain she'd felt from Jeremiah losing his house at school, but that wasn't the truth at all. Me building her a library or helping her in the garden or buying her new birds wasn't me trying to *buy* her love.

It was just me showing mine.

The one thing my piece of shit father had taught me was that actions spoke louder than words.

He told my mother he loved her, but he beat her within an inch of her life too many times to count. And then, one night, he just didn't stop.

Words meant nothing to me.

I loved Charlie, and I could say it all day long but it wouldn't matter. So, I showed her I loved her by listening to her, by understanding what makes her happy, what brings her joy, and doing those things for her. If I knew she was tired and dreading cleaning the house, I'd do it before she got home. If I knew she was stressed out from school, I'd take her to get a new book.

And if I knew my wife like I believed I did, I knew she missed her birds.

I knew it killed her inside that she lost them.

I only hoped this new aviary and her new friends inside it would bring back a little joy to this house for Charlie. Because whether she felt it anymore or not, this was our home.

And I was hell bent on keeping it that way.

I heard a car pull into our drive, followed closely by the sound of two doors shutting.

She was back.

Steeling a breath, I checked those final touches I'd added to the aviary and made my way out, shutting the door carefully behind me so our new finches wouldn't escape. Then, I made my way to the front door, checking my appearance in our foyer mirror.

I looked as tired as I felt.

My eyes were heavy, just like my heart, and my hair was a little longer than I'd let it grow in quite some time. I needed to shave, but I hadn't had the chance — not with the aviary being my main priority.

I was still dressed in the casual workout shorts and t-shirt I'd worked in all day, a welcome change from the coat and jeans I'd been wearing for months. Spring was finally starting to greet us in Pennsylvania, and I'd opened our windows to let in the warm air. It was only in the sixties, but to us, that was a heat wave.

I ran one hand back through my hair, trying to tame the mess, and then I let out a breath and opened the front door.

No oxygen came after that last breath.

I just stood there, right inside my front door, holding onto that breath as my heart beat loud and slow in my ears. I heard each thump like a war drum, my eyes zeroed in on the target, my hands curling into fists at my side.

It was one thing to know Charlie had been unfaithful to me, and it was one thing to know another man had touched her. Those were both facts that I knew to be true.

I understood that my wife was not just mine anymore, but it was one thing to simply know that in the back of my mind.

It was another thing entirely to see it.

Reese stood at the bottom of my driveway, leaning against his car with Charlie in his arms. His lips were on hers, one hand in her hair while the other gripped her lower back, and seeing him touching her poked a bear I didn't even realized existed inside me.

And that bear woke up like one angry, territorial son of a bitch.

My nose flared, nails biting into my palms where my fists clenched at my side, and I tried to be rational. I tried to force myself to stay in my house, to wait for her, to not let what I saw affect me.

But it was like stepping on a rattlesnake and expecting it not to strike.

A throaty growl ripped from my throat, one I'd never let loose before, one that was born from a primal instinct I couldn't contain. I flew from the porch and down the driveway, steam rolling off me like a freight train on a cold night, and the last thing I saw was Charlie spinning in his arms, her eyes wide when she saw me, and Reese stepped in front of her, meeting me first.

"You slimy fucking bastard!" I shoved Reese hard and he stumbled back, but his chest met mine in the next instant, his gritting teeth just inches from mine. "How dare you touch my wife, in my driveway, in my *home*." I shoved him again, faintly registering Charlie's screams for me to stop in the background. "Have some fucking respect."

"For who?" Reese challenged, bumping my chest with his. The force pushed me back, but I bowed up in the next instant, ready to fight. "For *you*? The only person I see here who deserves any respect is Charlie, and trust me, she always gets it from me."

He smirked with that last line, insinuating he gives Charlie much more than his respect, and that same primal growl ripped through me before I launched at him.

Reese fought me off, but not before I socked his jaw, catching his lip with my knuckle and busting it wide open.

"Cameron, stop! Please, *please*, stop!"

Charlie's little hands were on my arms, and I shrugged her off, gearing up to punch Reese again when she wiggled her way between us.

"I said STOP!"

She shoved my chest hard, and though her strength was no match for mine, I backed off, my eyes finding hers as I took four steps back toward the house.

She was crying, her eyes wet and tears staining her cheeks. I watched her struggle to catch her breath, her words still coming, though they were deaf to my ringing ears.

My gaze found the man behind her — the enemy — and every muscle in my body tensed again.

"Reese, leave." Charlie turned to him, shoving him toward his car.

"I'm not leaving you here with him like that."

"I said *leave*, damn it, Reese."

Reese's jaw flexed, like leaving her killed him, like *I* would ever do anything to hurt her. He was mental. He was fucking deranged.

I wanted to kill him.

"Fine," he growled. "But you call me if he lays even one finger on you."

"If you don't get the fuck away from my wife—" I started, charging toward him again, but Charlie screamed for me to stop, shoving Reese toward the car with more fervor.

It took every ounce of willpower I had left inside me to stand rooted to that spot in our yard as he finally climbed inside and backed out of our drive, and it wasn't until he peeled away that Charlie turned on me.

"What the hell is wrong with you?"

"What's wrong with *me*?"

"Yes, you! You tried to fight him!"

I gaped at her, throwing my hands up toward where Reese had stood.

"He had his fucking hands on you, Charlie. He was *kissing* you! I'm trying here, okay? I'm trying to..." I shook my head, running my hands back through my hair. I didn't even have words. "How could I see him kissing you and not lose my fucking shit? *How*, Charlie?"

"Not so fun on the other side of it, is it?"

Her words slammed into me like an anvil, pinning me to the spot where I stood, crushing my lungs with the weight of them.

Two more tears slipped from Charlie's eyes and she swiped them away, shaking her head. Her gaze fell to the ground between us, her arms folding over her middle, and in that moment, I'd never felt further from my wife.

We were just feet from each other, and yet we existed on different planets.

I didn't even know who she was, anymore.

And she was right. I had been on the other side. She'd had to see another woman in my lap, half naked, with her hands on me.

Her words were proof that though she'd forgiven me, she'd never forget.

I couldn't believe I was stupid enough to think telling her the truth would change that.

My eyes closed on a breath, and I scrubbed my hands down my face before letting them fall against my thighs. I looked anywhere but at Charlie, and all I knew in that moment was that I couldn't go back inside that house with her. Not yet.

"I'm going for a walk."

I started for the road, and Charlie didn't move, letting me pass her as a long sigh left her lips. The blood and adrenaline that had rushed through me settled when my feet hit the blacktop, and I clenched my jaw, fighting against my own tears that were threatening to fall.

"It's going to get cold soon," she called behind her.

"I'll be fine."

And though I'd omitted telling her the whole truth about Natalia, that last sentence was the first lie I'd ever said outright to my wife.

I would be a lot of things that night, and in the next few weeks, and for the rest of my life, should I lose her.

But "fine" was not one of them.

Not even close.

CHARLIE

I'm not sure how long I stood at the edge of our driveway before I dragged my suitcase inside. It was long enough for dusk to settle in, for my bare arms to get chills, and for me to be able to look as far as I could down the road and not see Cameron.

The tiny bit of joy I'd managed to find the last night of the conference with Reese had vanished the moment we pulled into my neighborhood, and as if I thought that sick feeling that had rested in the pit of my stomach couldn't get any worse, Cameron had walked outside.

He'd seen us. Together. And I knew the kind of pain that came with that sight.

I couldn't believe he'd tried to fight Reese, and yet, I didn't blame him. Maybe if I had been a stronger woman the day I'd walked in on him and Natalia, I would have tried to fight her, too. Maybe if I were the me who existed now, the woman who wasn't okay with just numbly floating through her life and her marriage, perhaps then I would have pulled that woman off my husband by her long, blonde hair.

Perhaps I wouldn't have stayed.

No, I couldn't blame Cameron for reacting the way he did, and I couldn't blame myself for him storming off the way he did, either. Maybe it's what we both needed — space, distance.

I didn't want to hurt Cameron, and yet it seemed I didn't know how to stop.

I sighed once I was in the house, dropping my purse and suitcase at the door and kicking off my shoes. All I wanted was a hot bath and a glass of wine, and time alone.

Time to think. Time to process.

I abandoned my phone on the table in the foyer, too, knowing Reese would likely text or call soon. I wanted time away from him as much as I did away from Cameron. So, I left the phone, making my way to the kitchen to pour some wine, but I didn't make it five steps before I stopped dead in my tracks.

Jane.

She was the first thought in my mind when I heard the chirps, but I recognized quickly that they weren't hers. I knew her songs, just like I knew Edward's, and the little tweets coming from our sun room were nothing like them.

They were a bit lighter, softer, sweeter.

I tiptoed toward the source of the sound, turning on lights as I slowly crossed our dining room. When I flipped on the switch that lit our sunroom, I gasped, hands flying to cover my mouth.

The beautiful, bright patio furniture I'd picked out for that room, the set that once took up most of the space inside it, had been slid over to the far right. And to the left, taking up half the room now, was the absolute last thing I expected to find.

An aviary.

Shiny, new welding wire stretched over beautiful stone, creating a home for lush greenery, bright perches and flowers to match, beautiful ficus trees, and the main attraction — two beautiful, happy, chirping finches.

I stood outside the aviary, watching them jump from perch to tree branch before they'd take flight and find a new place to land. They seemed to stick together like glue, the smallest one guiding the slightly larger one, and it was all I could do to just stare at them in wonder.

The smaller one was mostly white, it's belly fluffy and bright as snow, with misshapen little patches of light brown dotting its head and back. It was small enough that I knew it would fit easily in the palm of my hand, just by sight alone, and I assumed from the way its mate followed that she was a girl.

The other, larger one — the one I presumed to be a male — had an entirely black head, with his feathers spiraling down into a sort of owl-striped white and black pattern from his lower back to his tail. When his partner hopped off her perch and took flight again, he quickly joined, and before I could stop it, I laughed.

My eyes were wet as I finally stepped inside the aviary, closing the door carefully behind me as I took in the scenery. It had been decorated with so much care, with attention to detail, from the colors of the flowers — the way they matched those of the hammock cover — to the trees, the way they grew in the corners and spread outward from their pots toward the center of the aviary. It was dark now, but I knew the sun would shine in on the aviary and cast beautiful shadows over the stone.

In the corner, next to the hammock, was a small, softly running waterfall that would offer clean water to our new friends.

And right beside it was a photo of Jane and Edward.

I fell into the hammock, shaking my head in wonder.

Cameron had built me an aviary.

I didn't know why I was shocked, or even surprised in the slightest, because it was exactly something he would do. It was classic Cameron, to take his hands and build something he believed would bring me joy.

Not only had he been working so hard to give me the words I needed to hear, to let me inside his guarded heart and mind, but he had also spent his entire weekend building me an aviary.

It was the most selfless act, the most caring and thoughtful way to show me his love.

And with that realization, I choked on a sob, surrendering to my tears as the birds took flight again.

I watched them for a while before I buried my face in my hands, letting my palms absorb my cries. Everything hurt — the pain in my chest, the hole in my heart, the love I felt for both men, and more than anything, the love they had for me.

I'd never understood how love could hurt before, how it could be the knife between your ribs. It wasn't until that exact moment that I realized love hurts more than anything, because it's all we want, and yet it never comes easy.

Minutes turned to hours in that aviary as my tears dried on my face, and I watched my new friends fly, listening to their songs until they both settled into the same nest together. They cuddled tight and snug, their chirps softening, and with me still sitting in the hammock, they fell asleep together.

It wasn't too long after they'd fallen asleep that I heard the front door creak open, and I stood, making my way out of the aviary as quietly as I could. I rounded the corner of our sunroom just in time to watch Cameron lock the door behind him, and when he turned back around, I nearly fell to my knees.

He looked miserable.

His eyes were bloodshot, rimmed with shadows, and his shoulders sagged with what felt like the weight of the universe. He swallowed when he met my gaze, but no words came. I searched him for some hint of drunkenness, but found nothing. He'd drowned in his suffering instead of a bottle, and somehow, it made me feel worse that he was sober.

"You built this..." I whispered after a moment, my hand sweeping back toward the aviary. "You built this for me?"

Cameron's eyes flicked to the sunroom before they found mine again. "I did."

I smiled, though tears built in my eyes again. I couldn't believe there were any left.

"It's *beautiful*, Cameron. I... I don't have words."

"I hoped it would make you happy," he said.

"It has."

Cameron watched me then, something between a smile and a grimace crossing his face before he hung his head, shaking it slightly.

"I'm going to bed," he said after a moment, crossing to our stairs. I stared as he climbed the first few steps before I moved to follow him.

"Wait," I called, and he paused, though he didn't turn to face me. "Maybe we should talk... about what happened."

Cameron looked over his shoulder, offering only his profile, and that was enough for me to see the broken man I'd made out of my husband.

"I'm sorry, Charlie. I wanted to talk, before... but I can't now. Not tonight. I'm sorry."

I took a few steps up. "Can you at least try?"

Cameron shook his head again, but didn't answer, climbing the rest of the stairs with his silence answering me, instead. I stood there on the step third from the bottom and listened as he shut the door — the one to the guest bedroom, not our own.

My hands gripped the railing tight as I lowered myself to the stairs, leaning my back against the wood and gazing into the sunroom from where I sat. I could see just the corner of the aviary from that angle, but I could still imagine how the birds looked inside it, snuggled into their nest together, a team already.

I decided then to name them after Scarlett and Rhett, from *Gone With the Wind*.

They were the only ones who slept in our house that night.

chapter twelve

REESE

The Friday after the conference, I finally got time alone with Charlie again.

"This is so nice," Charlie said, carefully sitting down on the blanket I'd just laid out for us.

She tilted her head up toward the sun, the rays of it casting her face in a warm glow as she peeled off her light scarf and extended her legs. They were bare under her flowy skirt, one that was modest, cut under the knees. But she hiked it up a little, getting some sun on her thighs, and I couldn't help but stare as I took a seat next to her.

"I'm just glad I could steal you away," I said, opening the reusable bag I'd packed for us that morning.

She glanced at me, her eyes softening. "Me, too."

It was a beautiful day, a sneak peek of what spring would be like once it was in full swing in Pennsylvania. The sun was warm, though it was chilly in the shade, so I packed a picnic for Charlie and me and convinced her to eat outside with me.

It'd been too long since I held her.

Five days shouldn't feel like forever, but with her, it always did. I knew she was going home to Cameron every night, and while hearing that he was barely talking to her should have made me feel better, it didn't. Regardless of how he used his time, he still got to have every night with her, while I only had the minutes I managed to steal her away at school.

Blake living with me made it nearly impossible to see Charlie after school.

And though we spent as much time as we could together while we were at Westchester, there wasn't much time to go around. We'd get to school early when we could, have our coffee together and talk, and then we'd see each other at lunch — but even then, we were surrounded by other teachers.

Yesterday, I'd scouted the campus until I found a sunny spot behind the music center — one no one would walk by unless they were cutting behind the school, which wouldn't make sense. It was shorter to go the front way, and the back didn't have any sidewalks or paths to walk. It was just a little sunny hill with a few trees lining the fence.

It wasn't much, but it could be ours.

I only unpacked the grapes before I couldn't resist touching Charlie any longer.

Popping the top on them, I offered a red one to her, and once it was in her mouth, I pulled her into me. She giggled, adjusting herself until she was comfortable in my grasp, and then, we both sighed.

I'd seen her. We'd had a little time together. But it wasn't the same as this — having her in my arms, in a place no one else existed, with no one else watching.

"How's this?"

She sighed again, folding her arms over where mine held her. "Perfect."

"Yeah?"

Charlie leaned a little to the left, just so she could tilt her eyes up to meet mine. "Yeah. It's nice to get outside, to be away from everyone." She shrugged. "Especially since being at home isn't exactly easy right now, either."

I kissed her nose, holding her in my arms as I balanced my chin on her head. She picked up another grape and her eReader, and I held her as she read, letting my mind wander.

I knew she was having a rough week.

She was still going home to Cameron every night, but from what she'd told me, they barely talked. He was more of the man he'd been when I first showed up, and while that worked in my favor, it seemed to kill Charlie.

Which, in turn, killed me.

I didn't know how to help her. Sometimes I'd let her talk about him, about how she was feeling, and pretend it didn't feel like she was dragging a rusty blade down my back. Most of the time, I'd tell her I was sorry and that it would all be okay, all the while secretly wishing Cameron would continue to be a dumb ass.

Charlie was sticking to her word, giving him the time she'd promised, and he was wasting it.

I wasn't surprised.

It couldn't have felt good, seeing Charlie in my arms that day we'd come home from the conference. I remembered what it felt like the night I saw him kiss her at her parents' house after we'd had dinner, and that was only my first week back in town.

But I wasn't sorry, and I refused to back off to give him the comfort and time he wanted. Just like he wasn't going down without a fight, neither was I.

"How are the birds?" I asked after a while.

Charlie put her eReader away, sitting up to face me. "They're so sweet. I love them. They remind me a lot of Jane and Edward, but they have their own personalities." She chuckled. "I'll say this — Scarlett is even more feisty than Jane was, and she's definitely the leader. Wherever she goes, Rhett follows."

I smiled, though it hurt. She was happy — those birds made her happy — but I hadn't given them to her. They'd been a gift from Cameron, along with an entire aviary.

I couldn't do things like that for her.

Not yet.

But, one day, I vowed that I would. I'd build her the house of her dreams, and fill it with whatever she wanted — books, birds, baby grand pianos. Hell, if she wanted a moat, I'd dig it myself — just to make her feel like the queen she was in my eyes.

"Are you ready to eat?"

She nodded. "I'm starved."

Smiling, I dug through the bag, pulling out the sandwiches I'd made us. I passed one over to Charlie, and she laughed as soon as she unwrapped it.

"Stop it! Is this a Fluffernutter?"

"What else do you have at a picnic?" I asked incredulously.

Her eyes were wide as she unwrapped the rest of it, giggling as the white marshmallow goo dripped onto her fingers. "Oh, my God. I'm so excited. I haven't had one of these since I was a kid."

"Well, what are you waiting for?"

I unwrapped mine as she took her first bite, and as soon as she did, her eyes rolled back until she closed them completely, a sated moan leaving her lips.

"Ohmahgawd," she said around the mouthful. "Thish ish heaven."

It was my turn to laugh.

I took my own first bite just as she smacked her lips together. "It's stickier than I remember."

Digging into the bag, I pulled out another old favorite — a little plastic bottle of red Kool-Aid.

Her eyes lit up again, and she snatched it out of my hands eagerly.

"I feel ten again!"

"But with bigger boobs."

She laughed, almost spitting out her first sip. When she wiped her mouth with the back of her hand, a grin was left behind it.

"Best picnic ever."

"I'm glad I could make you smile. I just wish I could see you more."

Her eyes softened then, and that very smile I was thankful for slipped away.

She took another bite, an easy silence falling between us. And I knew in that moment, she was thinking about him.

It was killing her, being torn between the two of us, and I hated that I couldn't take that pain away. He'd asked her for more time, and she was giving it to him. All I could do was hold her hand through it, and remind her that — if she chose me — happiness was less than a month away.

So, I reached over for her eReader, pulling back up the book she'd been reading, and with a mouth full of Fluffernutter, I picked up with the top line.

Charlie laughed, swatting at my leg, but then she leaned into me, her head resting on my shoulder as I continued reading in a more serious tone.

And that's how easy it was.

We just sat there in the sun, eating sandwiches and reading together, and it felt like everything was right in the world. Charlie was my home, and I was hers. It was that simple, even though the world we lived in seemed so chaotic.

As long as we were together, it didn't matter what we did.

I just hoped we'd actually be together in the end.

CHARLIE

That Sunday, I took advantage of the nice weather and spent the day in my garden.

The flowers and plants we had adorning the front of our house were beautiful, and I loved the way they drew eyes to our home, but it was my garden in the *back* that was my pride and joy. Only Cameron and I got to enjoy it, along with our close family and friends, and that was what made me love it even more.

It was like our own little treasure, reserved for our guests and ourselves. We didn't need to show it off, and for that reason, I could do whatever I wanted back there.

Our back garden expanded throughout the yard, but my favorite part was the little corner near our sunroom. It was where our patio furniture sat, complete with a fire pit that we loved to use in the summer, and it was where I got the most creative with my plants.

In the winter, I watched most of my garden die, knowing only half of it would return once the weather was warmer. Most of it, I'd have to replant, but I didn't mind. That was what I loved most about gardening — it was a never-ending task.

My garden always needed me, no matter what season it was. Whether it was for sowing, clearing weeds, watering, or just being there to enjoy its beauty, was necessary for the garden, just as it was necessary for my soul.

Though spring was still far from being in full bloom, I spent that Sunday clearing away the dead plants and flowers, tilling the soil, and using the compost we'd saved to enhance the soil. I still wasn't sure exactly what I wanted to plant for spring and summer, but I had ideas, and I knew that no matter what I chose, the soil needed to be primped and primed.

My mind was free to wander as my hands worked, and as always, it seemed to drift back and forth easily from Reese to Cameron. There was so much to look at and do in the garden that, thankfully, my thoughts couldn't run too deep. But like a shallow creek, they filtered through me soft and quiet, an ever-present hum within me.

Cameron had pulled back into himself.

After coming home to the aviary, I thought he would open up to me again. I thought he would let me in, continue the connection we'd managed to find during our weekend getaway. But he'd been hurt by seeing me with Reese — and though I couldn't blame him for that, I also didn't see it as an excuse.

I had to see him with Natalia, after all, and I'd survived.

But Cameron wasn't like me. It was hard enough for him to talk at all, and just when he was opening up, he'd seen me in the arms of another man.

I knew it killed him, and that killed me.

But where he receded like the tide, Reese came crashing in to fill the void like the biggest wave.

Though we didn't have much time together, the time we did, he took full advantage of. I smiled as I spread more compost over the soil, recalling our picnic on Friday at Westchester. It was something so simple, so easy, and yet it had made me feel like I was on top of the world. The warmth of the sun on our skin, the taste of childhood favorite foods, the sound of his voice as he read my book out loud — it was perfect. It was a glimpse of what our life could be like, in the future, and I clung to that glimpse like the last vine that stopped me from falling into an abyss.

As much as I loved the way I felt with Reese, I still couldn't get over the fact that Cameron had built me an aviary. I couldn't let go of the fact that he was seeing a therapist — which he was with right now. He hadn't spoken much to me since the conference, but I knew just by looking at him that he *wanted* to.

And so, my heart remained severed. Because how could I turn my back on him when he still had time, when I'd promised him I'd wait?

As if my thoughts were calling to him, the sliding glass door connected to our sunroom opened, and Cameron stepped out onto our patio with a smile on his face.

"I had a feeling I'd find you here," he said, eyeing where I was working with the soil. "The weather is perfect today."

I leaned back on my heels, looking up at him from where I was on my knees in the garden. His smile was genuine, the first one I'd seen him wear in a week, and I returned it.

"It'll get cold again, but spring is teasing us."

"As it often does in Pennsylvania," he said. Then, he dropped to his knees in front of me, rolling up the sleeves of his long-sleeve shirt. "Can I help?"

"I'd love that."

He picked up where I'd left off, digging into our compost with his bare hands where I had my gloves for protection. He never was afraid of getting dirty — it was something I'd always loved about him.

I watched him for a moment longer before leaning forward to help, and a silence fell over us, though it wasn't the comfortable one that I was used to. Now, it was strained, riddled with unsaid words that hung between us like lasers that would singe our skin if we touched them. Every now and then, I glanced up to watch him work, but I never knew what to say.

Words were becoming as hard for me as they were for him.

"How was your session with Patrick?" I managed after a while.

Cameron kept his eyes on his hands, and I watched my own, trying to relieve the tension.

"It was fine."

Fine.

I swallowed, thinking of how complicated my relationship with that word was now. It was how I'd described my state of being for so long, what I'd told people when they asked how I was — or how Cameron and I were. But fine didn't mean everything was okay. It meant I didn't want to talk about how things really were.

It meant I was surviving. I was breathing. But that was all.

"That's good," I said.

Cameron nodded, glancing at me just as I came across an ugly, thick weed buried deep under where I would plant new flowers soon. I leaned back on my heels, grabbing my farmer's knife.

"It's hard," he said, voice soft as I started working at the weed. "Talking to him. Sometimes. He just... he likes to talk about my dad."

I stilled, the knife hovering under the weed. I stared at it before pulling up gently, freeing part of it.

"I can imagine," I said. "We never talk about him. Not since we were in college, that one time, when you told me what happened."

Cameron scratched his jaw, marking it with soil as he did. "Yeah. But it's good, even when it's hard. I have a lot of... *feelings* toward my dad, I guess. That I never knew about. Or rather, that I never dived into." He cleared his throat. "I think he's part of the reason I have such a hard time talking."

I yanked at the weed, my heart in my throat. I could sense it, something big building with Cameron's every sentence.

"I could see that."

I tried to give him his space to feel out his next words. He seemed frustrated, like the words were right within sight but blurred by a glass he couldn't break through.

"The night you came home from the conference, there was something I wanted to tell you. But, it's not easy to talk about."

The sun slipped behind a cloud then, making me shiver with the chill of the shade.

"And I want to tell you, but you just have to know that—"
"*Shit!*"

I dropped the knife, that hand coming up to press hard into the palm I'd just slashed with it trying to cut the last of the stubborn weed. Blood poured through my glove, and I cringed against the pain.

"Oh, shit," I said again, this time more resigned than panicked.

Cameron was already on his feet and pulling me up from my knees. He carefully rushed me inside and straight to our kitchen sink, peeling off my glove and running water over the cut. I watched the clear liquid turn red as he rinsed me, the sight of blood always making my head spin.

I gripped the counter.

"It's deep," Cameron said, and I just nodded. "We should go to the hospital. I think you need stitches."

I held onto the counter with my free hand, holding the injured one under the water as Cameron slipped away to grab our first-aid kit. He dried my hand when he returned, wrapping it in gauze and checking that it wasn't too tight before leading me to the front door.

"I'll grab you a light jacket from upstairs. Here," he said, swiping his keys from the table in our foyer. "Let me start the car first, get it warmed up."

"It's nice out," I reminded him. "I'll be fine."

"Well, we don't know how long this will take. Let me at least get the jacket."

He was already three steps up when I called his name.

"You were going to say something," I said, nodding toward the garden. "Outside."

Cameron swallowed, offering me a small smile. "It's okay, it can wait. Let's get you fixed up first, okay?"

My stomach sank, but the stinging pain in my hand echoed Cameron's sentiment. I nodded, and within five minutes, we were in the car and on our way to the hospital.

I held onto his promise that we'd talk later, but when we were back home, my hand stitched up and well on its way to healing, no words came.

They didn't come the day after, either.

Or the day after that.

As Cameron slipped back into his silence, I slipped back into just being *fine* when I was at home.

And the only time I felt happiness was when I was at Westchester.

With Reese.

CAMERON

The night that fell after Charlie cut her hand, I dreamed about my father.

He was standing over my mom's lifeless body, a snarl in his lip as he shook his head at me.

"I told you you were worthless," he sneered. *"She will move on. She will be fine without you — happier, even. She doesn't want you. Just like we didn't."*

That same scene, those same words, played on repeat. Over and over he said them, and over and over I tried to shake myself from the nightmare. I couldn't wake up, though I knew I was dreaming. I was aware of my body, of where I laid in the bed next to Charlie, of where her body touched mine.

But I couldn't wake up.

Not until hours into the night, when the nightmare faded with the sound of our heat kicking on, and I bolted upright in bed.

Sweat poured off every inch of me, and my breaths were erratic, like I'd just sprinted up and down our stairs for hours. I glanced at Charlie, but she was unfazed, a soft smile on her face as she slept peacefully.

And though I saw her, I saw him, too.

I heard him.

I heard the words I always knew to be true.

The next day, I cancelled the rest of my week's sessions with Patrick.

I had nothing else left to say.

chapter Thirteen

REESE

"Are you sure you don't want anything to eat?" I asked Charlie the following Wednesday evening.

We had stayed late after school to work with the students who would play at the end-of-the-year gala, and at the very mention of food, Charlie visibly turned green.

"Definitely sure."

I chuckled, but couldn't hide my frown as she stacked up the last of the leftover packets we'd handed out that evening. We'd had this on the calendar for weeks, ever since Mr. Henderson gave us the task, but Charlie had come down with food poisoning after lunch. I told her we could move the meeting, but she refused, saying it would be too difficult to get everyone together at a different date and time with such short notice.

She'd been a champ throughout the evening, and no one would have known she was ill if they hadn't outright asked her. But now that the last students were gone and it was just the two of us, her fatigue and weakness had caught up to her.

She dropped the packets on my desk, the wind from the fall sweeping her hair back.

"I also do *not* want to drive right now," she said, checking the time on her watch. "But it's almost nine. I told Cameron I wouldn't be later than seven."

"He'll survive," I answered. Crossing the room to where she stood, I took her hand in mine, tugging her toward the door. "Come with me."

"I really need to go."

"Twenty minutes isn't going to kill anyone," I said, and when she glanced for her phone that had been abandoned on my desk all evening, I shook my head. "And no phone. Just twenty minutes, and I promise I'll let you go."

Charlie sighed, but nodded, following me down the hall to the library. It was dark inside, but lit just enough to see by the lights from the hall that I didn't turn on any others. I led Charlie to the couch in the front study section, pulling her into my arms once I was seated against the left armrest.

Another sigh left her lips as I wrapped my arms around her, kissing her hair and rocking her gently.

"Better?"

"Yes," she breathed. "It's so quiet. And dark. And there are no... *smells*. Except for old books, which I can handle."

I chuckled, sweeping her hair off her forehead. "I told you to stay away from that tuna casserole in the teachers' lounge."

She forced a smile, but it was weak, and it fell just as quickly as it'd come. I just squeezed her tighter, glad I could be there for her when she wasn't feeling well — glad I could hold her without anyone around again, even if just for twenty minutes.

"I wish we could stay here tonight," she whispered after a moment.

I sighed, running my hand through her hair. "I know, I do, too." Then, I paused, a new idea sprouting to life. "But hey, close your eyes."

"They're already closed."

I chuckled. "Okay, mine too." I wrapped her tighter in my arms, leaning my mouth down to whisper in her ear. "Now, imagine we're not at Westchester. Imagine we're at home — at *our* home. We're sitting on our couch, in our living room, after a long day at work. I'm holding you while we watch the fire, and you're telling me about your day, and I'm kissing your neck as I listen to every word."

I creaked an eyelid open long enough to see her smiling before I closed it again.

"What are we wearing?"

"Oh, that's easy. Nothing."

She chuckled. "I have a feeling if that were the case, we wouldn't be just *talking*."

My body responded to the insinuation, and I inhaled a stiff breath, adjusting myself in my pants.

"I wish you didn't feel like you had to throw up every time you moved right now, because now I'm picturing a very different scene."

At that, she laughed. "Sorry."

"Oh, don't apologize, I'll make use of this visualization later."

Charlie shook her head. "I wish we could..." Her voice faded off, growing softer. "I wish I could go home with you, that I could make you feel good tonight."

I sighed, kissing her hair. "I know. Me, too."

Charlie said it was past nine when she'd checked the time, which meant Blake would be wondering where I was, too. I didn't have to look at my phone in my pocket to know it was filled with missed texts and calls from her.

"Maybe we could say we got locked in," I tried.

"I need to go home," she said softly, stiffening in my arms with her next words. "And you do, too."

I rocked her again. "I know."

I hated that we couldn't stay, that we couldn't have that night — *one* night — with just the two of us. It'd been too long, and I wanted more time alone with her. The moments I was able to steal were never enough.

"Have you told her about me yet?" Charlie asked. "About us?"

My stomach knotted, knowing Charlie had to feel the same way about me going home to Blake as I did her going home to Cameron.

"We've talked about this, Charlie. It's complicated."

"Uncomplicate it."

She sat up in my arms, her pale lips downturned as she waited for my answer.

I hated that I put that there — that frown — because in any other situation, I would have done whatever it took to make it disappear. But I wasn't being a chum when I said it was complicated. It was — more so than I could even explain.

Nothing was black and white in the world we'd found ourselves in.

"Look," I said, framing her face with my hand. "Every night, Blake comes home with more news about her father. And every night, it gets worse. The only thing she wants to hear from me right now is that it's all going to be okay, regardless of what happens with her dad, and I can't give her that assurance by telling her about us."

"So, you lie to her for her own good," Charlie deadpanned.

"That's not what I mean."

"That's what it sounds like."

"Please, Charlie," I begged. "Try to understand. I know it's hard, but can you just put yourself in her shoes? Imagine your own father was passing away slowly before your eyes, and the one and only comfort you had was that there was a friend waiting for you at home every night."

"I get that," she said, pushing herself up off the couch. She was slow, weak from losing so many fluids, but she waved me off when I tried to help her. "I do. But she doesn't think you're just her friend." She turned to face me. "And I need you, too."

"Right now, a friend is all I'm being to her. I swear. We haven't so much as kissed. We sleep in the same bed, but that's all." I reached for Charlie's hand, and she let me hold it as I begged her to believe me. "And you've got me."

"During school hours."

I frowned. "Come on, Charlie. Don't be like that."

"Whatever. It's fine," she said quickly, crossing the room. She was already in the hall before I was off the couch. "I should probably get going. She'll be home soon, and Graham and Christina flew into town tonight. I should make sure they're all settled in at Mom and Dad's."

"Charlie," I tried, catching up to her. I offered to hold her as she walked, but she shook me off.

"No, seriously. It's fine. It is what it is, right?"

We rounded into my classroom, and she bolted to my desk, clicking the power button on her phone to turn it back on from where she'd powered it down before our meeting. The screen lit up as it came back to life, and I tugged on her hand, pulling her into me again.

She huffed when I put my arms around her, but I took her chin between my thumb and index finger, forcing her to look at me.

"Do you not understand that I also wish we could be together after school hours? I wish I could come over to your house, or you to mine, or better yet — that we could go completely away from here. But, Blake isn't the only issue, here."

She swallowed. "Don't bring Cameron into this. Not right now."

"How can I not? Look," I said, stepping more into her. "It's complicated. The whole fucking thing. But remember what it felt like when you came to me that night, when we first touched under that fort?"

Her face softened at that, and I took the wiggle room she gave me to slide in more.

"And at the conference? In the rain, and afterward, in my room..."

Charlie closed her eyes. "Yes, I remember."

"I need you to hold onto that, to those memories, just like I do. Remember how it feels when we get alone, when we have our time."

"I ruined our time tonight," she added softly, eyes fluttering open. "Stupid body."

I chuckled. "You can't help being sick. I'm just glad I could be here to take care of you and, hopefully, make you feel a little better."

"You did help," she said, though she sighed again. "I hope I don't get you sick."

"Don't worry about me. Stomach of steel," I said, hitting my stomach with a closed fist like King Kong. I bent to kiss

Charlie in the next instant and she smiled against my lips, laughing a little as she pushed me away.

"You're ridiculous," she said, still smiling, but her face went ash white when she picked up her phone from my desk. "Oh, my God."

"What?"

"Oh, my God," she repeated, frantically typing out something on her phone. "It's Christina. Something happened on their flight over. She's in the hospital." Charlie shook her head, still glued to her phone as she blindly felt for her purse and keys. "Shit, everyone's been calling and texting me. Mom, Dad, Graham, Cameron. They've been there two hours now."

Her face twisted, tears pooling in her eyes, and her hands shook when she finally found her keys.

"Hey," I said, pulling her to a stop before she could bolt out the door. "Take a minute, breathe, it's okay. Come here."

"I have to go."

"I know," I said, hugging her anyway. "I know. Please, just take three deep breaths for me. You're not going to help anyone by getting in an accident trying to speed over there."

"I don't know what happened. I don't know if she's okay, if the baby..." She choked. "Oh, *God,* the baby, Reese."

"Charlie," I said again, pulling back until I could see her. I held her trembling body in my arms, smoothing my hands over her shoulders. "Breathe."

She blew out a breath, shaking her head like I was crazy, but then she inhaled long and deep, letting the next breath out slower. I breathed with her, and after her trembling stopped, she opened her eyes again.

"Better?" I asked.

She nodded, though worry still painted her face. "I have to get to them."

"I know. Drive safe, okay? I mean it. And text me once you know more. Hey," I said when she started breathing faster again. "It's going to be okay. You hear me? It'll all be okay."

She nodded, eyes finding mine again. "Can you come with me? Please. I just... can you come, too?"

I swallowed, chest aching with the way she watched me.

"I want to, Charlie. I do. But, Blake..."

Her breaths stopped altogether, mouth flattening, and she stepped back from my hold. "Right."

"She'll be home soon, and I just..." I tried to explain, but I could see by Charlie's expression that there was nothing I could say. "It's better this way. You need to be with your family right now. How would you explain it to your parents, if I showed up with you tonight?"

"You've been a part of our family since you were a kid," she countered.

"Yes, but what are you going to tell them? That you were with me all night at school, that we stayed long after everyone else left? Or that you had already left, but you called me first instead of rushing to the hospital once you turned your phone on?" I shook my head. "Graham will call and tell me soon, and I'll come to the hospital then. We were supposed to meet up tomorrow evening. He'll call me, Charlie," I said again, making her look at me. "And I promise, I will come."

She let out a long breath, nodding, though I knew she hated the truth of the situation as much as I did.

"Okay," she said after a moment. "I have to go."

"Text me," I told her as we walked out to her car — well, as *I* walked, and she practically sprinted. I held her door open for her as she climbed inside, holding it open until she promised. "Let me know you made it okay."

"I'll try."

"Charlie."

She sighed. "I will. And I'll drive safe."

"It's going to be okay," I repeated.

Charlie tried to smile, but it fell short, and as soon as I closed her door, she backed out of the parking lot and peeled off down the road.

CHARLIE

By the time I made it to the hospital, I was sicker than I'd been all day.

Food poisoning I could handle, but driving across town to the hospital where my brother and his wife were, where my sister-in-law and future niece or nephew were in trouble, where my entire family waited without knowing where I'd been or why I wasn't there — *that* was too much.

I couldn't even relieve the pressure by getting physically sick. I just had to sit and drive, cursing the speed limit and other cars around me as I tried to breathe through the horrible twist in my stomach.

Cameron was waiting outside when I arrived, his hands in the pockets of his work slacks, dress shirt undone a few buttons at the top. His eyes were worn and tired, his brows pinched together as I rushed toward him. I started in a speed walk that eventually turned into a jog, and by the time I reached him, I didn't realize I'd been full on sprinting until I crashed into his chest.

"Oh, Cameron," I cried as he wrapped his arms around me, the familiar smell of his cologne comforting me more than I could have imagined it ever would. "I'm so sorry. I had my phone turned off, and I didn't know, and I rushed here as fast as I could and—"

"Shhh, it's okay."

Cameron rubbed my lower back with one hand, the other smoothing over my hair as I shook my head against his chest.

"No, no I should have been here. Is she okay?" I asked, pulling back enough to look up at him. "Christina? Is she okay? Is the baby okay?"

"They're both fine," Cameron said, and a sigh of relief rushed through me, making me even weaker in his arms. He held on tighter. "It's DVT."

"DVT?" I repeated, and he nodded, smoothing his hand over my lower back again.

I was familiar with the term from my own pregnancy, the acronym short for Deep Vein Thrombosis. We'd been warned of the risk when we were trying to decide if we could fly for a trip on spring break when I was pregnant. We'd stayed local, just to be safe.

"The doctor said Christina likely sat in the same position too long on the flight," Cameron continued, "which caused a blood clot in her left leg. She didn't even realize it until they landed and she tried walking on it. The pain got worse the farther she went, so Graham brought her here. But, she's okay. They've got her on blood thinners and a few other cautionary medicines and they've got fluids going through her."

"And the baby—"

"Is fine," Cameron said quickly. "Heartbeat is strong, no stress. They want to keep them here for a while, just to monitor everything and make sure her clot clears up and that they can hopefully prevent it from happening again."

I blew out a hard breath, running my hands back through my hair. "Oh, thank God. Are Mom and Dad here?"

Cameron nodded.

"I've got to call Mr. Henderson," I said, ripping my phone from my pocket. "Tell him I'm not coming in tomorrow."

"It's okay. I already got in touch with him."

I blinked, thumb hovering over Mr. Henderson's contact in my phone as I looked back up at Cameron. "You did?"

"I did. I told him the situation and he said to take your time coming back, he'll get you a sub for the rest of the week." Cameron squeezed my hip where he held me. "And he sends his prayers."

"Okay," I said, relieved. "Well, next, we'll need rooms nearby. I'll ask the front desk here what they recommend and get us set up for the next couple of nights, at least."

"I got us all suites here at the hotel connected to the hospital. It's just a short tram ride away, takes less than five minutes, and we're all on the same floor. Me and you, Graham, and I got your parents a room, too."

I stared at Cameron, my heart squeezing like a sponge under my tight ribcage. "The birds," I said. "They'll need someone to feed them and give them water, and the cage, it has to be cleaned every other night."

"Baby," Cameron said, pulling me closer. He framed my face with his hands, running his right thumb along my jaw line. "It's handled. I got it all covered, okay?"

My throat was thick with emotion, and all I could do was nod. It was more than Cameron had said to me in the two weeks since I'd been home from the conference, and every word out of his mouth was as comforting as his hug. He'd handled everything, because that's what Cameron did — it was who he was.

"Now, the one who needs you most right now is your brother. He's had one hell of a night, and I remember what that felt like," he said, swallowing. "Being a father-to-be for the first time is already scary as hell, and to have something like this happen, it's hell on Earth. So, go freshen up in the restroom, take a few breaths, and I'll meet you at the room with a coffee. Okay?"

Tears were flooding my eyes again, but they didn't fall. I forced a breath to hold them back, squeezing Cameron's forearms as he let me go. "Okay. Thank you, Cam."

He smiled, tucking his hands back in his pockets as I took a breath and headed into the hospital.

I rushed through the halls, asking nurses along the way to make sure I was headed in the right direction. All the while, my mind swirled with thoughts of Cameron.

He didn't even ask where I was.

And, what was worse, was he likely already knew.

After two weeks of barely any conversation, of absolutely no love shared in our bed, I assumed he'd given up. I assumed he was finished, just waiting out the time I'd promised him, knowing what would happen at the end of it.

But he was here, in a time I needed him most. He already had everything handled. He knew exactly what I would need, and he took care of it — *before* I even got to the hospital.

He was here.

And Reese wasn't.

But now wasn't the time to think about any of that.

Dad was the first one I saw once I'd made it to the room, after I'd done as Cameron suggested and made a stop by the restroom. I started in on my story telling him why I was late, but he shook his head and swept me into a bear hug.

"No need for all that. You're here now."

"Is Graham inside?"

Dad nodded, and his eyes looked just as tired as Cameron's had. "They just asked us to leave for the evening so Christina could get some rest. He's saying his goodbyes to her now, though truth be told, I'm surprised she convinced him to leave, at all. I think the only reason he was okay with it is because he didn't sleep much last night, either, knowing they'd be flying."

"Charlie! Oh, Charlie, you made it."

I heard Mom's voice before I saw her, and I turned just in time to catch her hug.

"Hey, Mom. You okay?"

She pulled back with a sniffle, but a smile, nonetheless. "I'm better now that you're here, too. Did Cameron find you?"

"He did," I answered. "I think he was going to grab some coffee and head back this way."

"Bless his heart. He's done so much for all of us tonight."

My heart squeezed again, and I opened my mouth to respond when the door to Christina's room opened behind me.

I turned, finding my brother there, and he looked worst of all.

Graham had always been a larger version of myself — same dark hair, same dark eyes, and same knock-off version of our mother's nose. Where I was petite, he was just over six foot and shaped more like Dad with his broad shoulders.

I hadn't seen my brother cry since he broke his arm in tenth grade, but his eyes were red and puffy, his expression long and sad as he forced a smile.

"Hey, Sis."

"Graham," I whispered, pulling him into a hug and holding him there. "I'm so sorry."

"It's okay. Both my girls are okay."

I pulled back then, eyes wide. "*Both* girls?"

Graham nodded. "They did an ultrasound to make sure she was okay, and they didn't know we hadn't had our appointment yet. The doctor said, 'Her heartbeat is strong and steady.'" Graham choked out a laugh. "I think I blacked out for a second."

I laughed with him, squeezing his arms. "A baby girl. Congratulations, big bro."

"Thank you. Do you want to say hi?" He pointed to the door behind him.

"No, no. Let them rest. I'll see Christina first thing in the morning."

Mom and Dad were down the hall at the nurses' station, talking with someone behind the desk. Graham watched them for a moment before walking me away from Christina's door.

"Where were you tonight?"

I swallowed, avoiding his eyes as I picked a piece of lint off my shirt.

It was from Reese's blanket.

"I had a meeting at school," I said. "I turned my phone off so it wouldn't interrupt."

"This late?"

I nodded. "Yeah. Well, I mean, it ended a while ago, but we had to clean up and everything. As soon as I turned my phone on, I came straight here."

Graham watched me closely, one brow raised just a bit. I knew he didn't believe me, but thankfully, he didn't push.

"Well, I'm glad you made it. It's been hell, Charlie." He shook his head, crossing his arms over his chest as his eyes found Christina's door behind me. "When I explained her symptoms, they rushed her back here so quick. I couldn't come at first. And I..." He blew a breath through his lips. "I was a mess. I thought I was going to lose them both. I know that sounds dramatic, but it was all I could think. And I blamed myself, even though I didn't know what was wrong. It had to be my fault. I had to give myself the blame so I had something to focus on other than the fact that my wife and child were behind closed doors with their care in the hands of complete strangers."

I offered Graham a sympathetic smile, reaching out to squeeze his arm. "I can't even imagine. But they're both okay now, and you didn't do anything wrong."

"It's just crazy, you know? I haven't even met her, my daughter, and she's already my entire world."

That spot inside my chest for Jeremiah and Derrick singed to life, the ache strong and present, and I pressed a cold hand over that spot as I nodded.

"Trust me. I get it."

Graham's eyes found mine then, and he frowned, reaching out to pull me into a hug.

"I know you do. I'm sorry, I know turning on your phone to all those messages must have been hard."

"It was," I admitted. "But I'm okay. Don't worry about me. The only thing I want you to worry about is finding a way to get some sleep tonight."

Graham laughed, letting me go. "Yeah, well, I'm going to try," he said. "It'll be a little bit easier, thanks to Cameron. He got us all rooms right here at the hospital hotel, so I won't be far from Christina."

"He told me," I said, and as if on cue, I heard Cameron's laugh from down the hall.

He was there with Mom and Dad, making everyone laugh over something he'd said — even Mom. Her face was still spotted with mascara, but she was laughing and holding onto Dad's arm, staring at Cameron like he was the only source of relief in this entire building.

"He just stepped right up and started handling everything when he got here," Graham said, and my eyes stayed on Cameron down the hall as he spoke. "I mean, Mom was a mess. Dad, all he could do was try to keep Mom from having an all-out anxiety attack. I wasn't good for anything but hounding the doctors for more information. But Cameron? He made the calls, brought us coffee and water, made us eat dinner." Graham shrugged. "He took care of us. *All* of us."

"It's because we're his family," I whispered, more to myself than to my brother. "We're the only one he's got, you know?"

I turned to Graham then and he nodded, his hand finding my shoulder as we both looked down the hall again.

"He's a good man, Charlie."

Cameron's eyes found mine then, like he could sense me watching him, and he smiled, holding up the coffee he'd brought me just enough for me to see. He looked so right, standing there with my family, like it was a picture he'd been painted into long before the sketch was even drawn.

I just smiled back, still rubbing that ache in my chest — one that stung for more than one reason, now.

"Yeah," I said to Graham. "He really is."

chapter fourteen

CHARLIE

The next two days flew by and dragged all at once.

Christina was in great spirits, mostly just irritated that she couldn't eat pizza and chocolate like she wanted to, and Mom and Dad were taking care of fussing over her enough for the entire hospital. Graham was getting rest like he needed to, and my unborn niece was just as happy as she could be — or so the tests said.

Cameron and I had stayed at the hospital hotel for two nights, but had decided to check out on Friday. We both wanted to get home to our own bed, and I wanted to get back to Scarlett and Rhett. They were new to our home, only being there a couple weeks, and I didn't want to confuse them by being gone so much.

"Hey," Cameron said, his shoulder shaking me from my daze next to Christina's bed. She and I had turned on a movie when everyone else left to go get lunch, but I'd started daydreaming a quarter way through it.

"Hey, yourself."

"Brought you coffee," he said, handing me a steaming cup from my favorite shop in Pittsburgh. "We passed right by on the way home."

"No, you didn't."

I knew where all the shops were in town, and there wasn't one even close to where they'd eaten lunch or on the way back to the hospital.

"Okay, fine. We didn't."

I smiled, taking a sip of the warm, sweet mocha before settling back in my chair. I glanced over at Christina, who'd fallen asleep.

"I bet she's so ready to get out of here," I said softly. "Poor girl. Came down here to be with Mom and Dad and take some time off her feet, ended up in the hospital."

"At least she's still off her feet here."

"Yeah, but the food is way worse."

Cameron squeezed my shoulder, laughing quietly. "That's very true."

I looked up at him then, the coffee still warming my hands, and for a moment I just stared at him. He'd stepped up so much at the hospital, being whatever he needed to be for my parents, for Graham, for me. He took care of running any errands we had, phone calls, paperwork — all of it. Whatever he could do to make our lives easier, it was already done before we even knew to ask.

"Have I thanked you yet," I asked, "for everything you've done this week?"

"Many times," he said, mirroring my smile.

"Well, thank you, again. I know it's all meant so much to Mom and Dad, and to my brother." I paused. "And to me."

Cameron's cheeks tinged just the slightest shade of red. "I'm not doing anything special. Just trying to make it all a bit easier." His smile fell a little as he rubbed my shoulder. "Hey, listen... I was thinking, tonight when we get home, maybe we could—"

Cameron's voice was drowned out under the sound of loud laughter as the door to Christina's room swung open, and Christina bolted upright, her eyes wild as they landed on her husband.

Mine were just as wild when they landed on Reese.

"Oh, sorry, babe. Did we wake you?"

"I think you woke the whole hospital," she said, but she was smiling, her black eyes warm at the sight of Graham. "Is this Reese?"

Reese's eyes flicked to mine before he crossed the room with a wide smile, holding out his hand for Christina. "So nice to finally meet you. I've heard so much about you over the years."

"Well, I wish we could have met under better circumstances," she said, smoothing her hand over her hair once Reese stepped back. "I'm a mess right now."

"You look beautiful," Graham argued, leaning in to kiss her forehead before taking the seat next to her.

Reese stood with his hands in his pockets, and his eyes found mine with a crease resting between his brows.

"Hey Charlie," he said. "Cameron."

He didn't even look at Cameron when he said his name, and Cameron barely nodded in response to the greeting. My brother watched the whole exchange curiously, and his eyes locked with mine, more questions there than I had answers for.

I cleared my throat.

"So, are you hanging out here for a while with us, Reese?" Christina asked.

"I don't want to be in your hair too long," he said with a smile. "Just wanted to come by and meet you, and give this guy some shit." He wrapped his forearm around Graham's neck and knuckled his head.

Graham shoved him off, laughing. "Yeah, trust me, babe. No one wants to put up with Reese Walker longer than a few hours."

"Sorry," a voice said through our laughter, and my heart kicked up into my throat at the sight of Blake swinging inside the room. "I didn't like any of the flowers they had down there at the shop. I mean seriously, not *one* bouquet with roses? They're, like, the most universal flower." She shook her head, leaning up on her toes to kiss Reese's cheek.

I gritted my teeth.

"Oh! Hi, Christina. I'm Blake, Reese's girlfriend," she said, leaning in to hug Christina. The flowers she held smacked against the back of Christina's bed and tangled up in her IV wire, but Blake was oblivious. "It's so nice to meet you."

"You, too," Christina said, but I could tell by looking at her that she was a bit overwhelmed now, and once Mom and Dad barreled in the room, her anxiety showed even more.

The volume in the room rose exponentially, everyone talking over each other and laughing, but I just stared at where Blake hung on Reese's arm.

He watched me, our eyes connecting long enough for me to lower my brows in question.

What is she doing here?

But he couldn't answer, and judging by the way his tail was tucked between his legs, I guessed he wouldn't have an answer I'd like even if he could.

This was my family, *our* family — the same one he couldn't come with me to see the night I got the call. But now, here he was.

With her.

"Oh, Charlie," Graham said, talking loud so he could be heard over where Mom, Dad, and Blake were laughing by the door. "Reese and I were thinking of taking a drive later out to the old park we used to all play. You know, take a little trip down memory lane. Want to come?"

I just stared at Reese, trying to calm myself down. I knew he wouldn't have brought Blake if he had a choice, but in that moment, I couldn't rationalize, and I couldn't make excuses for him.

I was pissed.

Cameron seemed to pick up on my energy, because he squeezed my shoulder, offering my brother a smile. "Charlie and I were actually just about to head out. We're going to go home for the night, check on the birds, catch up on a few things."

"Oh, of course," Graham said, and yet again, he watched me with curious eyes. "We'll see you guys Monday for dinner? As long as the doctors still agree to let Christina go that day, that is."

"Yeah, we'll see you then," I answered sharply, jumping up out of my chair. I needed out of the room, away from Blake, away from Reese.

I quickly kissed Christina's cheek and hugged my brother and parents, carefully maneuvering the room so that I could avoid Blake and Reese. Cameron followed behind me, staying in the room longer than I did to say the more proper goodbyes and accept gratitude from my family for all he'd done that week. I waited outside the door, arms crossed, nose flaring like a dragon.

"Charlie," Reese said, joining me in the hall. "Please, don't leave. We can go."

I just stared at him.

"Come on, don't be mad. I didn't mean to..."

"Bring your girlfriend to my sister-in-law's hospital room?" I finished, my voice low but menacing. "Huh. Wonder how it happened, then."

Reese's expression flattened, but he didn't have time to offer an excuse before Cameron joined us in the hall. He put an arm around my shoulder, turning me toward the exit.

"Ready?" he asked, his eyes hard on Reese.

I just nodded, not leaning into him but not leaning away, either, as he walked us out of the hospital. I didn't look back at Reese even once.

"You okay?" Cameron asked once we made it to the parking lot. We'd driven separately, since I'd been late on Wednesday, and I dug through my purse for my keys with shaky hands.

"I'm fine. I'll see you at home?" I said, but I didn't wait for an answer before I yanked open my door and climbed inside. I couldn't look at Cameron, and I couldn't take the way he was looking at me.

I peeled out of the parking lot before Cameron even got in his car, and I took the long way home.

—

REESE

All I could do was curse under my breath as I watched Charlie go.

Cameron had his arm around her, and though she didn't exactly lean into his touch, she still looked comforted by the way he held her. And that murdered me.

I blew out a frustrated breath, making my way back inside the crowded hospital room with Blake's eyes on me like lasers. She smiled a little at my return, though I could see the questions she wasn't asking me.

She had insisted on coming when I got the call from Graham. I tried everything I could to get her to stay, to let me go on my own, but she was like a bull once her mind was made up. There was no reasoning with her, not without telling her the *real* reason why I didn't want her to be here.

"Everything okay?" she asked me, her voice low where we stood off to the side. Graham was by Christina's bed, the two of them in conversation with his parents.

"Yeah. Thanks for the flowers, that was nice of you."

She smiled, glancing at the vase, but she found me with questions still spinning behind her big, blue eyes.

"Charlie seemed upset that we were here."

"She's not," I assured her. "They're just tired, been through a lot in the last two days. I think they both needed rest."

"Sure," Blake said, nodding, but I knew she was biting her tongue. "You two are close, huh?"

I didn't answer. I was smart enough to see that trap before my big foot stepped right into it.

"How come you never mentioned her before? Back in the city?"

I cleared my throat. "We didn't keep in touch when I left. There was nothing to say."

"Oh," she said, forcing a smile. "Well, that's nice that you were able to pick right back up when you came back to town."

"Mm-hmm."

Blake glanced around, running a hand back through her hair as a shiver ran down her back. "I've had enough of hospitals. They're so sad," she said, voice soft. "I'm sure Graham is glad you could come." She paused. "I know I've been so happy that I have you to come home to after everything going on with my dad."

I blew out a breath, opening one arm for her to hug me. She leaned in, nuzzling her cheek against my chest.

"I know. You've been through a lot lately. Are you sure you want to be here?"

She nodded. "Yes, it's nice to get away from my own thoughts for a while." Her breath was hot on my neck as she peered up at me. "I'm just so thankful for you being here for me, Reese — for everything. Just like how I was there for you when... when everything happened. I just, I'll never be able to thank you enough. I know you understand more than anyone."

My throat was tight then, and suddenly the hospital room was too small to take an adequate breath.

She was still staring at me when Graham joined us, and I let out a breath of relief as low as I could, releasing her from my grip.

"Hey, you ready to go?" Graham asked me.

"Yep," I answered, looking back at Blake. "We're going to go out to the old park for a while, shoot basketball and catch up. You going to be okay here?"

Blake didn't look happy at our conversation being cut short, but she nodded. "Of course. I'm sure there's something I can help with around here."

"Okay. I'll be back soon."

I kissed her temple before zipping out of the room like it was on fire, and Graham followed. He chuckled when he caught up with me, glancing back over his shoulder before meeting me with a raised brow.

"Blake is... something."

I smirked. "That she is."

"Her and Charlie have beef?"

I stopped short when we reached the set of double doors that led out to the elevators. "What?"

"Charlie was looking at her weird, like an enemy. And my sister doesn't have any of those. Do they not like each other?"

I feigned nonchalance, opening the door for us and pushing the elevator button once we were through. "They've only met once before. I think Charlie was just tired."

"Yeah," Graham said, watching me closely. "Could be. Were you with her the other night?"

A flush ran over my face before I could cool it, and I couldn't even answer. I just avoided Graham's stare as we stepped onto the elevator.

"At the school event," he clarified once the doors closed behind us. "She said she had a meeting. Were you there, too?"

I cleared my throat. "Uh, yeah. It was for the end-of-the-year gala thing. We're both up for awards."

"Nice," Graham said, but I still felt him watching me. "It ran late."

"That's Westchester," I said, trying to laugh. "You remember how intense they are about school functions, don't you?"

At that, Graham seemed to lighten up a bit. "God, do I. I wanted so badly to go to a normal school like you and Mallory."

He chuckled, but all the color drained from me at the sound of my sister's name.

"Shit, I'm sorry, Reese."

"No, no, don't be," I assured him as we stepped off the elevator. "It's not like I can't talk about her."

KANDI STEINER

That should have been a true statement, but it was a bold-face lie — one I was too ashamed to admit to anyone out loud.

"Has your game gotten any better since you left Pennsylvania or am I about to run circles around you like usual?" I teased when we pushed through the doors to the parking lot, trying to change the subject.

"*Please,*" he said with a scoff. "We both know you were better with the girls and your stupid piano, I was better with everything else."

We continued talking shit the rest of the way to the car, and it seemed all questions about Charlie and my family had been left behind us — at least, for now.

For the next few hours, we played basketball and caught up, and just like I'd felt with Charlie, a little piece of home clicked back into place having Graham back in Mount Lebanon.

But in the back of my mind, his sister was all I could think about.

I knew that across town she was stewing over me showing up at the hospital with Blake. I had to explain what happened, and I couldn't talk to her until I saw her back at school — and that was a full weekend away.

Ever since I moved to Pennsylvania, weekends were my worst enemy. They were days away from Charlie — days she spent with *him*. And right now, I knew she felt betrayed. She was pissed, and she had every right to be.

But I'd make it right when I saw her. I had to.

All I could do was tick down the minutes until Monday.

chapter fifteen

CHARLIE

Late that night, I sat in the aviary with Scarlett and Rhett, feeling as numb as a hand without circulation.

I sipped on hot chamomile tea, watching the birds sleep, hoping the combination would somehow lull me into a sleep that night, too. My thoughts were loud, and none of them made any sense. It was a constant cycle of absolute nonsense, twirling and twirling, taking me down in a heartbreaking wind tunnel of truth.

Somewhere on the ride home, with the windows down, the warm May air whipping through my hair, I realized that it wasn't that I was mad at Reese.

It was that I was jealous of Blake.

That realization had sucker punched me, the truth of it stealing my breath away. I was jealous of a woman I barely knew, because she got to go home to Reese every night. He swore to me they weren't doing anything, that he was being strictly a friend to her now, but the fact was that she was still in his bed every night.

And I wasn't stupid enough to think they didn't touch.

That made my stomach roll, the thought of it, and I imagined it was only a muted form of what Reese must have felt every night I left school to go home to Cameron.

Cameron. My husband. The man who had shown me more than ever this past week that he loved me truly, wholeheartedly, in a way far different than Reese. It was different in the sense that it was comfortable and dependent, steadfast like a river with a never-ending source.

I was with him all week, and yet I'd also thought of Reese that entire time.

When did I become this person?

Even when I was quiet and reserved, when I didn't have many true friends, I was always proud of who I was. I was a daughter, a friend, a teacher, a wife. I was honest and true, sweet and kind, always thinking of others before myself.

But this year had changed me.

The new year had snapped me from one person to another, from old Charlie to new, and they sat on opposite sides of the spectrum. Where I used to place others before me, I now only thought of myself. I *wanted* things — truly wanted them — and I took them instead of waiting or asking. I acted first, thought later. I hurt those around me without realizing it, or maybe I *did* realize it, and I just didn't care.

It was like staring in the mirror and seeing a completely different person, like a bad dream I couldn't wake from.

I couldn't go back to the woman I was before. I didn't even know who she was anymore.

I also didn't know what — or who — was the catalyst that sent me from old Charlie to new.

Was it Reese? Did he wake me up, change me, ignite an old burning flame when he came back into town?

Was it Cameron? Did we hit our breaking point, one coming all along? Was it his lack of care, his years of apathy, that somehow transitioned me from one point to another?

Or was it me?

Was it a quiet giant within my soul, one that had been sleeping, waiting, hoping it wouldn't have to emerge? Was it the real me, the one who'd always been there, only just freed from her chains?

The answers never came, not with the chamomile and not as the minutes ticked by, taking me later into Friday night.

"I brought you more hot water," Cameron said, shaking me from my thoughts as he entered the aviary.

He held his hand out for my cup, pouring it full with steaming water from the tea pot in his hand before he sat it on the table beside me.

I was seated in the hammock, folded into it like it was a chair instead of lying down flat, and I swung back and forth lightly, pushing off the ground with my bare toes.

Cameron dunked my old tea bag in the new hot water, handing me the cup before grabbing one of the small stools from the corner. He sat it down right in front of where I was on the hammock, folding his hands between his legs with his elbows balanced on his knees as I steeped the tea.

"I have wondered about the thoughts inside that beautiful mind of yours for the last few months," Cameron said, his eyes bouncing between mine. "It's maddening, knowing there is so much that troubles you, and yet not knowing *what*." He paused. "This must be how you have felt with me our entire relationship."

I traced the lip of my tea cup with my finger. "If it makes you feel any better, *I* don't even know what's going on up here," I said, tapping my temple.

Cameron reached forward, taking my tea cup from my hands and sitting it on the table next to the pot. He wrapped my hands in his then, covering my cold knuckles with his warm palms.

"There's something I need to talk to you about."

I squeezed my eyes shut. "Not tonight, okay? It's been a long day, and I—"

"No, I have to say it tonight," Cameron insisted, squeezing my hands. "This has waited long enough."

There was an urgency in his voice, mirrored in his soft caramel eyes, and that tone had my heart accelerating before I even knew the subject on his mind.

"What is it?"

Cameron swallowed, his eyes dropping to where his hands held mine before they resurfaced. "We need to talk about Natalia."

And with just the sound of her name off his lips, my stomach dropped, landing somewhere below the hammock.

"Cameron, please," I tried, shaking my head. She was the absolute last thing I wanted to talk about in that moment.

But he squeezed my hands, smoothing his thumbs over my knuckles.

"I know it hurts," he said. "Trust me, I know. But, we never talked about her, about what happened — what *really* happened — and with everything..." His voice trailed off, and he swallowed hard, his eyes on mine. "I just have to tell you this, okay? You need to know the truth."

"I know the truth," I told him, pulling my hands from his. I crossed my arms over my middle, sitting farther back in the hammock. "I *saw* the truth, remember?"

A flash of red struck behind my eyes — her red nails, red lips, red bottom of her heels. I could still see Natalia straddling my husband like it was happening right here and now in the aviary.

"You saw only part of it, and the part you saw told the wrong story."

I cocked one brow, honestly curious. It was the first time Cameron had talked about what happened, other than the night he simply apologized and asked me to forgive him. He hadn't stuck up for himself, hadn't offered any excuses or lies.

Why now?

Cameron took a long breath, scrubbing his hands back through his hair before he clasped them together between his knees again. His eyes were on those hands as he began to speak.

"Natalia and I have worked together for a long time... for years."

"I know," I deadpanned.

Cameron's lips pressed together, a frustrated breath sounding through his nose, but he continued.

"I respect her. She's intelligent, driven, and she always balanced me out well. When we worked on projects, I was the numbers guy, and she was the presentation. She was the closer."

Another flash of her in his lap, her long blonde hair, her skirt around her hips.

"Everything between us was strictly professional, Charlie. I need you to understand and believe that. There were never any lines crossed, not even so much as an innocent flirt between us. Not until the boys died."

My emotions were too sensitive, like an exposed nerve, and just that sentence leaving his mouth pricked my eyes. I sniffed, crossing my arms tighter and looking away.

"Something changed in her, then. It felt almost like I was her... her prey. She hunted me, looking for opportunities to get inside my head, to comfort me, to make me happy when I wasn't. She tried to find a way in. And I'm ashamed to say that sometimes, on the weak days," he said, his voice trailing. "I let her."

I shook my head. "Yeah. I caught that."

"I'm so sorry I did that," Cameron said, reaching for my hands again. I let him peel them away from my middle, but they were limp in his grasp. "I'm sorry I let her comfort me, that I let her be the one I leaned on. I know I've told you before that I thought I was doing the right thing by giving you space, by letting you heal on your own time, but I was wrong. I see that now. I should have been there for you, and I should have opened up to you about how I was feeling, too. I failed you in that," he admitted, voice breaking as he squeezed my hands tighter. "But I swear to you, on everything that I am, I did not sleep with her, Charlie. Not once."

My heart leapt into my throat, the beat of it strong enough to block my next breath.

"You didn't?"

He shook his head. "I never even kissed her."

My mouth fell open, heart dropping back into my chest before it took off in a full gallop. I shook my head, searching his eyes for a sign of him lying, but I came up empty.

"No," I said, still shaking my head. "No, I saw her. I saw her skirt... and she was straddling you, and..." I tried to remember if his hands were on her. Were they grabbing her hips? Were they in her hair? But I couldn't remember.

Maybe they were on the chair. Maybe he wasn't touching her at all.

"You saw her sitting on me," he agreed. "She had come into my office right before you, and she straddled me like that before I could even register what she was doing. It was late, we were the only ones there, and I guess she thought it was the right time to pounce. She told me she was looking for trouble," Cameron said, shrugging. "And I told her to get off me. But it was too late, because before she could even argue with me, you walked in."

Suddenly, his hands were too warm, the aviary too small, and I ripped away from his grasp before jumping up to stand. Cameron remained seated as I paced, waking Scarlett and Rhett with my quick movements.

"This doesn't make any sense," I said, running a hand through my hair. "Why didn't you tell me this? Why wouldn't you say anything until now?"

"I didn't think it mattered."

"You didn't think it *mattered?*" I repeated. "You didn't think it was worth it to mention to me that what I've thought for the past four years was completely wrong? That you never cheated on me like I thought you did?"

"But I did," he said. "In a way, in the only way that matters. Sex is just that — sex. To me, that was never true intimacy. At least, not until I met you. Sex has only been more with *you*. So, no, I didn't have sex with her." Cameron swallowed. "But what I *did* do was worse. I leaned on her. I let her in, I gave her access to my thoughts and feelings. So when I chased you down that night to plead my case, and I saw your tears, I knew there was nothing I could say that could make you feel any better. I couldn't defend my actions, because I'd hurt you. I'd betrayed you. You looked at me like a piece of shit that night, Charlie, and I was."

"But that was because I thought you slept with her!"

"I know," Cameron said, finally standing, too. "I see that now. Talking to Patrick, he helped me see that even if I still feel guilty for what I've done, even if I feel like there is no difference in what I did and what you thought, that I still owed you the truth." Cameron shook his head. "He said you needed to have all the facts, and that it was *your* decision whether it was the same or not."

Black invaded my vision, the same nauseous feeling from Wednesday's food poisoning stint creeping up on me. I moved back to the hammock, flopping down in it as I tried to steady my breaths.

"I can't believe this," I whispered, shaking my head. "You never slept with her."

Cameron dropped to his knees in front of me, taking my hand in his. He pressed a kiss to my knuckle before holding my gaze.

"Charlie, you are the only woman I have ever loved, and I would never dream of touching another woman the way I touch you. You are my wife," he reminded me, and my heart cracked with the word. "I made vows to you, and though I may have broken some of those along the way, I would never break the most sacred one. I am yours and only yours," he promised. "And I'm sorry I ever made you doubt that."

I couldn't cry, couldn't scream, couldn't do anything but sit there in his grasp and stare at the man I thought I knew. Shame seeped through me like dark ink, tattooing me with the truth.

Cameron had never cheated on me.

He stared at me, lifting my fingers to his lips every now and then, and all I could do was stare back. The guilt I'd felt over Reese before was nothing compared to the kind I felt now. Because before, at least a little bit anyway, I felt justified. An eye for an eye, a heart for a heart. I wasn't doing anything to Cameron that he hadn't done to me.

But I had been wrong.

My husband had never betrayed me, not the way I had him, and now that the truth was laid out in front of me, I felt more lost than I ever had before.

"We should try to get some sleep," Cameron said after a while. "I know this is a lot to process. Just... let me hold you tonight, okay? And if you have any questions for me in the morning, I'll answer them. No matter what they are."

His words were muffled, like we were on an airplane or like I was half asleep. I think I nodded, though I couldn't be sure, and the next thing I knew, we were climbing the stairs together.

We both crawled into bed, and Cameron leaned over to turn out the light before he pulled me into his chest. He ran his fingers through my hair, his other hand resting easily on my hip, and I could already sense how much lighter he felt now that he'd gotten everything off his chest.

But it was the law of physics. That weight had been transferred, landing on my shoulders instead. And though it didn't make any sense whatsoever, it was under that pressure where I finally drifted off to the best sleep I'd had in months.

CAMERON

I held Charlie close all that night, listening to her sleep, knowing I would not. But for once, I wasn't scared of being alone with my thoughts.

I could distinctly recall the chapter breaks in my life.

I knew where each one began, where each one ended, and what each new chapter had held for me. There was the chapter that ended when my father killed my mother, when he went to jail, and the one that began next as I moved in with my grandparents. There was the chapter that ended with me getting the scholarship to Garrick, and the one that began that first day of orientation.

There was the chapter that ended my sophomore year on a night I slept with one of five girls I'd had that week. I left her room early in the morning, swearing to myself that I was done with that lifestyle. I couldn't even see another chapter in sight, I just knew this was the end of one for me. I knew the meaningless sex wasn't what I wanted — not anymore.

The next chapter brought me Charlie, and nothing was the same again.

The chapters with her were my favorite.

There was the one where we said we loved each other, and the one where I asked and she said yes. There was the one where we bought a house together, and the one where she started her dream job. There was the one where she became pregnant with our children, and sadly, the one when we lost them.

And even though the chapters after that were the hardest ones I'd lived, they were still some of my favorites — because Charlie was in them.

I realized during my time talking with Patrick that my life had been split into two — before Charlie, and after Charlie. I was a different man in each part, and I knew that if there were to be a third section where I existed without her again, I'd be a different man then, too.

It was the absolute last thing I wanted, to live life without her as my wife, but I had to come to terms with the fact that it might be reality soon. The next chapter in my life could be the worst one, and I had to prepare.

After tonight, all my cards were on the table.

I'd laid everything out — my heart, my truth, my vows. She knew how I felt, she'd seen inside my heart, and now, finally, she knew the truth about what happened.

But, was it enough?

I didn't know.

I was fighting against a rip tide, clinging to survival, but I was growing weary. Time was running out, and I knew I was down to my last chance to prove I was the man she loved.

And the man she deserved, too.

Next Friday was the end-of-the-year gala at Westchester, and the following day was when we would break ground on the house we were building for Jeremiah's family.

That day would also mark two months.

So, I held Charlie a little tighter that night, kissing her as softly as I could so as not to wake her. In my heart, I couldn't imagine a life where she wasn't mine, but in my mind, I had to paint the picture, anyway.

Prepare for the worst, fight for the best. That was my motto.

Because I *would* fight for her — until the very end, I would fight. But if her happiness laid in the arms of another man in the end, I would lay down my gloves, and I would walk away for her. I loved her enough to do that, even if it would kill me in the process.

With one last, long breath, I pushed out the negative thoughts haunting me just for one night. For that one night,

I would hold her, and listen to her heart beats, and feel her skin against mine.

For that one night, I would cherish my wife as if I wouldn't get to keep her.

And before I fell asleep, I'd pray that I actually would.

chapter sixteen

REESE

Every song sounded wrong.

It was all I could focus on, though I tried hard not to, as the night I'd waited for all week spread out like a missed opportunity before my very eyes. It seemed like everything had been working against me — Blake, the first part of the conference, and just when I'd brought her back to me, the hospital ordeal.

I'd been counting down the days until the gala, knowing it would be a chance for me to get Charlie alone again — except it hadn't. She'd been with Cameron all night, since the very first moment they walked in together, and I was going mad watching them.

I couldn't win, and time wasn't on my side, either.

Tomorrow marked two months.

Two months since she'd promised that time to Cameron, two months since I'd agreed to wait on the sideline, to give him a chance to fight. But I was done waiting.

And every song sounded wrong.

The one that played when I walked inside the beautifully decorated gala hall, Blake hanging on my arm, had been too fast and shrill. The one that filtered through the speakers when I excused myself to the bathroom to splash my face with water had been too low and ominous. The notes were all wrong, no matter what played, or who played it, and I realized music wasn't the same when I wasn't with Charlie.

Not anymore.

It was the end-of-the-year gala, a time for celebration, and a night when I would likely receive my first award as a teacher. And yet, I couldn't find it in me to even pretend to smile. Because all night long, I'd had to watch from a distance as Charlie danced with Cameron, as she swayed in his arms to the awful music that had no rhythm.

She was more stunning than usual that night, her long hair pinned up in a delicate bun of braids, with soft tendrils hanging down to frame her jaw. Her eyes were dark and shimmery like stardust, playing off the midnight blue of her long dress. I needed her in my arms like I needed my next breath, but Cameron had her — he held my oxygen in his hands.

I was going to pass out if I didn't get a gulp of air soon.

"They should be announcing award winners within the next half hour or so," Blake said, flipping through the program for the evening. "It says it's right after dessert, and they're cutting up the cake now."

I took a sip of my scotch, inhaling a stiff breath through my teeth at the burn. "Okay."

Blake frowned, dropping the program to squeeze my shoulder, instead. "You okay over there?"

"Just nervous," I lied.

I couldn't tear my eyes away from Charlie. She and Cameron were dancing near the stage, and at that precise moment, her head was thrown back in laughter, and Cameron was smirking like he'd just shared the dirtiest secret with her.

My fist tightened around my glass.

"Oh, don't be," Blake said, leaning in to kiss my cheek. "You're going to get it, and then we can celebrate tonight."

She smiled suggestively at me, rubbing my neck, but I just took another drink with my eyes on the dance floor.

"I'm going to run to the ladies' room," she said, standing. "Freshen up before the awards start. Need anything? Another drink?"

"I'm good," I told her, and as soon as she disappeared in the crowd, I pushed my way through it in the opposite direction — toward Charlie.

I drained the rest of my scotch on the way toward her, dropping my empty glass on a server's tray just as she noticed me heading her way. She shook her head almost imperceptibly, warning me to stop, but it wasn't physically possible now. My feet were moving too fast, my heart beating steady along with them, and I wouldn't stop until I had her in my arms.

Cameron followed her gaze just as I reached them, and his eyes hardened at the sight of me, his arms tightening around Charlie.

"Mind if I cut in?" I asked him, forcing my most charming smile as I held my hand out.

There were others around us watching, including Mr. Henderson and his wife, and Cameron glanced at them with a forced smile of his own as he took a step back from Charlie, offering me her hand.

"Of course not," he said, loud enough for those around us to hear. "I'll refresh our drinks."

But before he stepped away, Cameron clapped his hand hard on my shoulder, squeezing with enough force to make me wince as he leaned in.

"Keep your fucking hands to yourself, Walker."

"Well, I've got to put my hands on her to dance with her, don't I, Cam?"

I smiled even wider, clapping his shoulder in return before I ripped away from his hold and pulled Charlie into my arms. I watched as she and Cameron exchanged a look, and once he'd gone, her eyes found mine.

"Hi," I said, the first real smile of the evening settling on my lips.

Her brows pinched together at first, but then they smoothed, and she shook her head with a small smile of her own.

"Hi."

"You look incredible tonight," I said, shaking my head slowly as I took her in. She was even more glammed up than I'd realized from afar, from her makeup to the pearls that rested around her neck. "I mean seriously, how can you blame me for going crazy wanting to hold you in my arms when you look like that?"

"I'm with Cam tonight," she reminded me, as if I didn't already know. "Everyone here knows us, Reese. It's... we have to be careful."

"What does it matter?" I asked. "Tomorrow marks two months. Everyone is about to know, anyway."

Charlie's eyes fell to my tie, and she swallowed.

"Right?" I asked her, tilting her chin up.

She didn't answer.

"Charlie. Tomorrow is—"

"I know what tomorrow is," she hissed, glancing over my shoulder. "Okay? I know. But everything is just... complicated right now."

"What does that mean? What's complicated now that wasn't exactly that same way last time I held you?"

"Oh, you mean two nights before you brought Blake to my sister-in-law's hospital room?"

I pressed my lips flat. "I didn't have a choice. And you left as soon as we got there, anyway."

"I wonder why," she snapped back.

"I'm sorry, okay?" I said, wanting so badly to pull her into me. But there were eyes everywhere, and I had to settle for enough room for Jesus between us as we swayed. "I didn't want her to come, but she invited herself, and I couldn't tell her *not* to come. She had just come home from seeing her dad in the hospital, and he's *dying*, Charlie. He's dying. I'm the only thing she has to hold onto and I just couldn't tell her to sit home alone that day we came to the hospital."

Words were flying out my mouth, but none of them seemed to make Charlie any happier.

"I know you're mad at me, but she's temporary — just like your situation with Cameron. We're going to get past this," I told her. "All we have to do is make it through tomorrow, and everything will be different."

Charlie wouldn't look at me, her lip pinned between her teeth as her eyes skated everywhere but up to mine.

"A lot has changed since then..."

The blood drained from my face, my heart thumping loud in my ears as I tried to keep us dancing. "What the hell does that mean? Are you... are you saying you might stay with him?"

Her eyes snapped up to mine, but she didn't have a chance to answer before Mr. Henderson's voice spoke over the fading end of the song.

"Let's hear a big round of applause for our band this evening, The Ravendoors," he said, the room breaking into applause as Charlie pulled back from me to clap with them.

My jaw was clenched, my hands clapping a little too hard as I tried to focus on the stage, all the while watching Charlie. I was losing her, or maybe I already had, and I couldn't let her go back to her table with Cameron — not yet.

"If you'll all make your way back to your seats, we'll be starting the award ceremony shortly. But, before we do, I'd like to thank our sponsors for the evening..."

Mr. Henderson continued, the dance floor clearing as everyone found their seats, but before Charlie could make her way back to her table, I grabbed her wrist and tugged her in the opposite direction.

"What are you doing?" she whisper-yelled.

But I didn't answer. It was all I could do to smile at people as we passed, putting on whatever show I still had to give. I didn't care what anyone thought. I had to have her alone.

The gala was hosted on the top floor of one of the hotels downtown, and I pulled Charlie through the doors that led to the rooftop garden. Mr. Henderson's voice was muffled as soon as the door closed behind us, and we were the only ones outside, everyone else already back at their tables to await the ceremony.

"We can't be out here," Charlie said, pulling her wrist free. "They're about to do the awards."

"I don't care."

I grabbed her hands in mine, pulling her behind one of the large trees that the garden lights hung from. It was a bit chilly that evening, though the days had brought spring on in full force. Charlie shivered once we were blocked from the view of the ballroom, and I stripped off my tuxedo jacket, wrapping it around her shoulders.

"Reese, we have to go back inside."

"Not yet," I argued. "Not until you tell me what's going on."

Charlie pressed her fingers to her temple. "Please, Reese. Let's talk about this later. I don't feel well, and—"

"It's been two months," I interrupted, waiting until she looked at me to say my next sentence. "Just tell him goodbye. Tell him it's over."

Charlie looked so small in that moment, wrapped in my jacket, her breath escaping her painted lips in little puffs of white. Her brows drew inward, her arms crossing over one another as she looked down at my shoes.

"Damn it, Charlie, tell him it's over. Tell him the truth!"

"What, like you've told Blake?" she shot back, her eyes hard on mine again.

"I'll tell her right now. Tonight. You want me to go get her and bring her out here? Because I will. I'll do it." I started for the door, but Charlie stopped me, pressing one tiny hand into my chest.

"Don't be stupid," she whispered.

"I'm not, I'm being serious." I held her small arms in my hands, catching her gaze with mine. "I will tell her right now, Charlie. I want you. I want to be with *you*."

Her lip quivered, but she looked up at the lights above us to force a calming breath. I let her capture it, watching the emotions wash across her face. I wanted to kiss her more than I could say, more than I wanted almost anything in the world — other than to hear her say she loved me, that she chose me, that it was all over and we could be together.

"I want to be with you," I repeated, stepping into her.

I slid one hand into her hair, and she leaned into the touch with a sigh. I wished I could hold her like that forever, that I could have her in my hands that way and know I didn't have to memorize the feel of her because there was no guarantee I'd touch her like that again.

I dropped my forehead to hers, our lips just inches apart, and I breathed in her scent before I asked the only question that mattered.

"Do you want to be with me?"

Charlie's face twisted, her hands reaching out to fist in my dress shirt, and I heard the sound of my own heart crack when she spoke again.

"I don't know."

"You don't know?" I asked, pulling back from her. I searched her eyes, confusion sinking into me right along with the overwhelming urge to jump off the roof. "You don't *know*?"

"I don't know!" she said louder, pushing away from me. She turned, pacing toward the city with her thumbnail in between her teeth, and I stared at the silhouette of her against those lights like I was in the middle of a bad dream.

"You do know," I argued. "You know, Charlie. You love me. I know you do. You *love* me, damn it."

"I do!" she turned, her hands outstretched toward me as tears flooded her eyes. "But, I love him, too. And I just... I can't... this is all too much. Everything I thought, it's all just... it's a *mess*. My whole life is upside down and I can't see or make sense of anything."

Her words stumbled into each other, they fell out of her mouth so fast, and her breaths were as unsteady as the heartbeat under my ribs.

"I need to sit down," she said, one hand finding her head as she wobbled forward for the bench. "I need to think. I need time."

"You've *had* time, Charlie," I reminded her, grabbing her hand to help her sit. I took the place next to her, folding her hands in mine. "I know you love us both, I get it, but you don't love him like you love me. I'm the one for you," I said as she shook her head, tears pooling in her eyes again. "I'm the one for you and you know it."

"Please, Reese."

"Tell him. Tell him tonight."

"I don't feel well. Please, can we just—"

"Damn it, Charlie," I said, and in the next instant, my lips were on hers, hard and needy and bursting with the urgency I felt in every inch of my being. I wrapped her in my arms as she melted into me, her tears falling to slip between our lips. She was crying because she knew the truth, because she knew it was me, and she didn't want to hurt Cameron. I knew it, but I couldn't wait any longer.

I had to have her now.

"Tell me you love me," I begged her, my hands framing her face as I kissed her again. "But only if it's true."

"I love you," she whispered, her face breaking with the admission. "I always have. You brought me back to life, Reese."

She kissed me between her words, shaking her head like I was stupid to even question her love at all.

"I have never felt the way I feel with you with anyone else in my entire life. Saying I love you isn't enough to really

226

say how I feel about you. I cherish you, I want you, I can't imagine having to live without you."

"Then *be* with me."

Her face warped with emotion again, but before she could say another word, her eyes shot open wide at something behind me.

"I knew it."

A chill raced down my spine, dread covering me like a cool mist as I turned to find Blake standing behind me.

"I fucking *knew* it!" She threw her drink at me, splattering me with wine as I dodged the glass. It shattered somewhere behind Charlie as she hid behind me. "Is this why you won't touch me, why you won't so much as *kiss* me?"

"Blake, I can explain."

"You can explain why you're making out with a married woman while your girlfriend is in the other room?!" she challenged, laughing. "Oh, please, do tell."

"I love her," I said. Charlie squeezed my arm, but I kept going. "I'm sorry, Blake. But I do."

"And what about me?" Blake cried.

I just stared at her, a foreign ache in my heart surging at the sight of her crying. I never wanted to hurt her. I never wanted her to find out like this. But I couldn't take it back, now, and I wouldn't even if I could.

"Fuck you, Reese Walker," she spat, and she turned on her heels, knocking straight into Cameron on her way back inside.

He held an award in his hand.

"Cam," Charlie gasped, stepping out from behind me. She looked from him to me and back again, her mouth open with words stuck just inside.

Cameron's brows were low over his eyes, his mouth in a flat line as he glanced between the two of us. He shook his head, a sardonic laugh slipping from his lips as he let his head fall back, his eyes cast up toward the sky. He slid one hand into his pocket, the other still holding the gold apple award, and he took his time bringing his gaze back to Charlie. When it was there, the hurt in his eyes was enough to feel like a knife between my own ribs, but I couldn't find it in me to care.

"You won teacher of the year," he said, his voice flat. "They just announced it. Congratulations."

And with that, he set the award on a bench, turned, and stormed off in the same direction Blake had.

Charlie lunged forward, her voice strained with emotion. "Cam!"

"Let him go," I told her, wrapping her in my arms, but she shoved me away, stumbling over her heels in the process.

Then, she ran to the nearest tree, doubling over just in time to vomit at its base.

"Shit." I rushed to her, holding her steady as she lost her dinner in the bushes. "It's okay. I've got you, it's okay."

"Stop!" she managed, throwing up again as soon as the word was out of her mouth. She shoved me away, wiping her mouth with the back of her wrist as she stood. "Can't you see we're monsters? Look at us!" Charlie was screaming now, her eyes wild. "We've hurt people we love. We've *killed* them, without even caring, without even feeling so much as a tinge of guilt."

"We love each other," I reminded her, stepping into her space. I just needed to hold her again, I needed to pull her into me, feel her heartbeat against my own. "Yes, it's messy, but it won't be forever. This is just a means to an end, and—"

Charlie held up her hand, shaking her head with her eyes squeezed shut.

"Just let me take you home."

"I'll get a cab."

She started for the door, yanking her wrist away when I reached for her.

"Charlie, don't. Please. Don't walk away from me."

She spun, desperation written in every feature as she begged me. "I need time, Reese. Space. Sleep. I just... I need to fucking *think*." She cried, her hands falling to her thighs in exasperation. "Please, for the love of *God*, just give me one night."

Every cell in my body ached with the need to hold her. I debated kidnapping her then, throwing her over my shoulder and stealing her away like a caveman claiming his property.

But Charlie wasn't mine.

And I knew more than anything in that moment that I'd be lucky if I ever got to say she was.

I threw my hands up, swallowing my pride along with the need to be with her in that moment. "Whatever you need, Charlie," I promised her. "I will give it to you. Tonight, tomorrow, for the rest of our lives, should I get the chance."

Her eyes flicked between mine, and she sniffed, nodding just once before she turned her back on me.

And then she was gone.

chapter seventeen

CHARLIE

There was a secret place I went that no one knew about. It was just five blocks from my house, just a left, a right, three streets past a stop sign and one more left turn. That's where my spot was, and no one knew about it — not Cameron, not Reese, not my parents — no one but me.

This place was not a beautiful waterfall or a breathtaking view of the city. It was not a quiet place, nor was it a place for contemplative thinking. For all intents and purposes, I was the last person you'd expect to find in such a place, but it was my favorite one to go to on days like this — days when I needed time with myself.

It was the morning after the gala, and though it was the last place most would expect to find me, my spot was where I went.

Because this place, my spot, it was loud and full of laughter. It was a snapshot of time for so many, a little memory they'd hold onto, or perhaps one they'd forget. It housed secrets and stories, heartbreak and triumph, and joy for people of all ages.

To the average man or woman driving by, it was just a park. It was just a swing set and a jungle gym, a few picnic tables, and a statue. It was just some trees and flowers, just a place to take children, a place to keep them occupied and entertained for a short while.

But for me, that park was where I'd walk when I was pregnant with Jeremiah and Derrick.

It was where I'd sit on the same bench almost every day and imagine what it would be like to watch them play there. It was where I'd talk to them, where I'd tell them about their family, about me, about Cameron, about the town they would live in and the house they would call a home. It was where I'd close my eyes and feel the breeze in my hair, the sun on my skin, wondering which beautiful day that summer would deliver me my baby boys.

After they passed, I still came to the park.

I would sit on the same bench, though not as often as before, and I'd try to recount that joy I'd felt before. I'd watch other children play, wondering if they would have been friends with Jeremiah and Derrick, and I'd observe the parents, wondering if they would have talked to me if I had the boys by my side.

To most of the people there, I was invisible — just a lonely woman on a park bench with her head in the clouds. They likely thought I was on my lunch break, or just passing by on my way home. None of them knew that was my place, that they were just visitors, but I knew.

That park was where I first talked to my sons, the ones whom I lost, the ones whom I would never forget. It was where I talked to them after they were gone, praying they'd hear how much I missed them, and how much I loved them still.

And it was where I talked to the new baby, the one who grew inside me now, along with the hope I had that he or she would get the chance to live.

I watched a little boy wobbling his way up the stairs to one of the smaller slides, his tongue sticking out of his little mouth as he focused on his balance. The man I assumed to be his father watched him from a bench across from me, a small smirk on his face, and I found myself staring at him just as much as the boy as I rubbed my still-flat belly.

Soon, it would be round, full of life, just like it had been once before. And the little peanut that existed inside me now would grow to a peach and then to a cantaloupe and a watermelon, too. I would talk to my baby during each stage of growth, feel how he or she changed within me, and on a date yet to be determined, I would hold that baby in my arms. I would kiss their nose, their feet, their tiny little hands, and standing there beside me would be a proud, smiling man just like the one that sat across the park from me.

I just didn't know which man that would be.

For the first time since Mallory moved away when I was just sixteen, I found myself wishing I had a friend. I wanted someone to dump my thoughts and feelings on, someone who could tell me how to detangle the absolute mess that my life had become.

I'd been so mad when Mallory moved away, so hurt by being left behind, that I'd never gotten close with anyone like that again. I had my books and my schoolwork, my parents and my volunteering — that was all enough for me. I didn't need friends to go out and party with, or a bunch of girlfriends to have over for wine and movies. And when I met Cameron, *he* became my best friend.

After that, I decided I didn't need anyone else.

But here I was, painted into a damp, dark corner with no one to help me out of it but myself.

There was only one person I could think of who would let me share my load with them, who would take my secrets to the grave as their own, and who would give me the tough love I needed — and that was Graham.

That's why he was the first person I ever told about my spot, and the first person I ever invited to meet me there.

I saw him when he first pulled in, all alone in Mom's car that she'd been letting him borrow since he and Christina got into town. They were leaving in a few days, and other than the hospital and one family dinner night, I'd barely seen him. Asking him to come sit at a park with me while I told him what a shit human I'd become wasn't exactly my idea of brother/sister bonding, but it was what I needed.

And I knew Graham would always be there for me when I asked.

His eyes swept over the park, confusion on his face until I lifted a hand to wave from where I sat. He smiled then, tucking his hands in the pockets of his shorts as he made his way over.

I slid to the left side of the bench, making room for him to sit, and once he did, he let out a long breath of air.

"I gotta say, this is the last place I expected when you said you wanted me to meet you somewhere," he said, looking up at the trees. "Looks like I can't get coffee *or* booze for whatever conversation we're about to have, huh?"

I chuckled. "Nope. Just fresh air and the sweet sound of children screaming."

"Guess I should get used to that last one, huh?"

I smiled, tucking a strand of wind-blown hair behind my ear. "That you should, big brother."

"At least it's beautiful outside today," he said, gazing out over the park.

It was a gorgeous day, spring finally blessing Pennsylvania one slow day at a time. Cold fronts still whipped through, but the sun was shining more, the temperatures peeking into the sixties and seventies. I was glad to be out of the house without a coat on, with the sun on my skin as it shone through the trees.

"How's Christina?"

Graham kicked back more on the bench, crossing his ankles in front of us while his arms rested outstretched on the back. "She's great, back to her normal, hormonal self — if there is such a thing. Mom's doting on her, which she loves, and she's had more pizza since we got home from the hospital than she did the entire time wc were dating, I'm pretty sure."

"Sounds like the life to me," I said, squinting against a ray of sunshine peeking through the trees as I glanced at Graham. He looked so happy there on that park bench, watching the same little boy I was watching before. I wondered if he was thinking what I had the first time I'd been to the park, if he was picturing his life as a father.

"No kidding. But, I have a feeling you didn't ask me to come here to talk about Christina," he said, still watching the playground. "So, go ahead, little sis. Spill."

I chewed my thumbnail, almost laughing at how easy he made it sound. "I don't even know where to start."

"Dad always says the beginning is a good place to start."

"Yeah, well, Dad would have a heart attack if I told him the beginning of this story — or any part of it, for that matter."

Graham looked over at me, but I couldn't meet his eyes. And I was glad I kept my gaze in my lap when the next words left his mouth.

"You're having an affair."

My thumb dropped from my mouth, and I gawked at my brother, at the calm, cool way he sat there and stared at me after what he'd just said.

"With Reese, right?"

My jaw dropped farther.

"It's okay," Graham said. "Seriously, save the time being ashamed or embarrassed or whatever and just talk to me. From the second I got into town, I've known something was eating you up from the inside, and as soon as I saw you and Reese in the same room together, I knew what it was."

"*How*?" I asked when I finally found my voice again. "How did you know?"

Graham uncrossed his ankles, sitting up a bit. "Well, first of all, you both basically shit bricks when you saw each other. Secondly, Cameron looked like he wanted to murder Reese and you left immediately when Blake came into the room. And thirdly, you've had a crush on Reese since you were eight," he said easily. "Honestly, when I found out he was back after all that time? I was worried how it would affect you."

I shook my head, crossing my arms over my middle. "I never knew you knew I liked him."

Graham scoffed. "Oh, come on. *Everyone* knew — Reese included. And he liked you, too." Graham cracked his neck. "He just knew I'd kill him if he touched my baby sister."

I smiled, shoving his shoulder, but then an awkward silence fell between us.

"Cameron knows," I said. "About me and Reese. I tried to leave him, and he asked me to give him the same time I'd given Reese. He asked for two months." I swallowed, looking back at Graham. "Today marks the end of that time."

"Wow," Graham said. "I can't believe he didn't murder Reese when he found out, but I'm not shocked he didn't let you go right away."

I tilted my head in question, and Graham looked at me like I was the stupid one for not seeing what he'd seen.

"Come on, Sis. I've never seen anyone love a woman the way Cameron loves you. It's fierce, like a fire, and I can't imagine any scenario where he bows out without putting up a fight."

"Yeah, well," I said, eyes finding a girl on the swing set. "He fought, alright. And just like I felt when Reese first got inside my head, I have no idea which way is up anymore."

Graham was silent a moment, watching the same girl on the swing.

"So, are you supposed to make some sort of decision today?"

I nodded.

"Jesus…" Graham breathed. "Cameron I could see that from, but I'm surprised Reese waited around."

"You're not the only one. And honestly, I think it's been driving him insane. I think knowing I'm with Cameron makes him crazy, so when he does get me alone, he gets so desperate for me that he loses himself."

"That's Reese, though, isn't it?" Graham said. "If Cameron's love for you is a fire, then Reese's passion for anything he desires in life is a bomb. It's intense, all-encompassing, and, sometimes — most times — out of his control. I mean, here is this guy who has wanted you for years, who lost his family and any semblance of home he ever knew, and he comes back to find you here married. But you let him in, you gave him a glimpse of what life could be like if you were together." Graham shrugged. "I bet he's clinging to that. And honestly, Charlie, from what he's told me about his life after his family passed, I bet it's the only ray of light he has to hold onto."

I shut my eyes tight, letting out a long, tired breath. "There's more."

"*More*?"

I nodded, folding my hands over my stomach. "I'm pregnant."

At that, Graham popped to sit up straight, turning to face me. "You're... oh my God, Sis."

Tears pricked my eyes. "I know."

"That's amazing," he quickly said. "Are you... happy?"

I nodded more intensely, smiling through a laugh that could have been mistaken for a cry. "I'm so, *so* happy. But also terrified."

"Because you don't know who the dad is."

Graham sighed, running a hand through his dark hair before sitting back on the bench again. We sat there in silence, listening to the wind rustle through the trees, both of us lost in our thoughts.

"Look, I'm not the best at advice," Graham said after a moment. "Hell, I'm about to be a dad and I can't even make a pancake without burning it."

I chuckled.

"But the one thing I know after hearing what you just told me is that you can't let the fact that you don't know who that baby belongs to affect your decision today."

"How?" I asked. "How could I possibly not let it affect me?"

"Regardless of which one you choose to be with, or if you choose to be completely on your own without either one of them, that baby is going to be born, and it's going to live, and it's going to have the happiest life any baby has ever had because you're its mother."

I smiled, rubbing my belly as my brother searched my eyes.

"And if you do decide to be with Cameron, or with Reese, I know without a doubt that both men would step up and be a great father right alongside you."

"But what if I choose the man who isn't the baby's father," I counteracted. "What then?"

"If you're upfront with the man you choose, then they will have that decision to make, just like you had this one. And, if it's the right man, then he won't give a damn."

I sighed, blinking away the tears. "I can't believe this is my life. I can't believe this is me, Charlie Pierce, sitting on a park bench telling her brother she had an affair and is pregnant with a baby whose dad can't be determined."

"Yet," Graham said. "Can't be determined yet. But you can take a test, Charlie. And you'll know one day. And until then, you need to focus on what you want — on who you want. Which man do you see the rest of your life with?" He tapped my nose. "That's what you need to figure out."

I shook my head, my heart aching with the tear in it stretching longer and wider. "I can't believe you didn't berate me when I told you. I can't believe you didn't call me a cheating floozie."

"Well, no one says floozie," he said, and I laughed, shoving his shoulder again. "But also, you're my sister, and we all make mistakes. I'm not judging you, I'm just here to listen. And to hopefully help a little."

I sank down on the bench, resting the back of my head on the top of it as I stretched my legs out in front of me. It had to be a dream. It couldn't possibly be my life I was talking about.

It couldn't possibly be Charlie Pierce who was having an affair, who had to choose which man to be with and which one to break, who was pregnant by one of those men — who didn't know which one.

But it was. I was living in what would have been a nightmare to me only months before, an unthinkable nightmare, and it was my reality now whether it was just as terrifying or not.

I rubbed my stomach, picturing a little boy who looked like Cameron, his same wide smile and sharp-edged nose. Would he play soccer, or hockey, like his dad? Would he be afraid to use his words, or would we bring him up in a loving home that showed him he could always be open and honest and communicate?

Or what if it was a girl, one who looked just like Reese — her eyes bright green, her hair long, curly, and unruly just like his. Would she play an instrument, possibly the piano, like him? Would she brighten up the world with her laughter and love? Would she be a little trouble maker, one who eventually grew to teach — just like her parents?

I smiled, still rubbing my stomach, loving both of those possibilities. I could never know which would come true, which child I would give birth to, but there was one decision I could make. There was one path in my life that I would set forth, that I would make happen — all by a choice I would make by the end of this day.

I still loved them both, Cameron and Reese, and I felt as torn between the two of them as I had before I'd even given in to Reese, at all. Maybe it was even more so, now that Cameron had opened up and let me in, now that I'd had a snapshot of what my life could be like with Reese.

How was it possible that they both loved me, that they both wanted me, desired me? They wanted me *so much* that they put themselves through what I imagined to be the most torturous months of their lives, knowing when I was with the other, still waiting for me, for my choice.

But, Cameron had stormed away from me last night, and we hadn't spoken since. I hoped to see him later at the groundbreaking of Jeremiah's new house, but I couldn't be sure. And I had pushed Reese away, begging him for space, for time, only to discover this morning that my suspicion of being pregnant was true.

Would either of them even have me now? Now that there was more at stake, that there was an unborn baby with an unknown father... could they love me still?

Graham's hand on mine brought me back to the park, and I sighed, squeezing his in return.

"So, did I?" he asked. "Did I help at all?"

I nodded, a slight smile on my lips before it fell away. "You did, big bro. You did."

But the truth covered us there on that bench like a hot, weighted blanket — one too heavy to ignore.

I could talk to as many people as I wanted, and I could torture myself with thoughts and memories, with my "what ifs" and "almosts," but I still had a decision to make.

I still had a heart to break.

And no one could help me now.

chapter eighteen

REESE

T he morning of Charlie's decision, I sat on my couch with Blake, staring at my hands while she stared at me.

It had been a long night. I'd figured after the gala, Blake would have packed up her things and left. But instead, she was waiting for me when I got home with a bottle of gin and about a million questions. Neither of us had slept more than a few hours, and those hours had been spent tossing and turning through fitful dreams.

I couldn't guess what hers were about, though I imagined her father and I both were present. In mine, though, it was Charlie. It was only Charlie, just like it had been since I'd shown back up in Mount Lebanon.

In my dreams, it always came back to us. No matter how bad the fight, or how long the distance, or how persistent her husband was — she was always mine in the end. I'd dreamed of this day so many times in the past two months, and every time, it ended with her in my arms.

I just couldn't imagine another option, another way for the day to turn out. Charlie was meant to be mine since we were kids. We were born for one another, destined to find a home in the other, and I couldn't picture a world where we didn't work out. It had to be us.

It always had been.

But, my heart still broke for the woman sitting beside me, the woman who had also been a home for me at one time. She was a temporary home, one I took advantage of and moved away from too easily. She'd given me all of her heart, all of her trust, and I hadn't known what to do with it because it wasn't what I wanted.

There was no excuse to be made. I had treated her poorly, and it had hurt her.

Every now and then, when her eyes would drift to the far side of the room, I would look up at her. I would trace the edges of her slender face, marvel over the brightness of her hair, and remember a time when seeing those things was the only joy in my life. It wasn't difficult to close my eyes and remember the darkness, the depression, the long, drunken nights and even more painful mornings where she was my only saving grace.

Blake had put me before herself in every way possible when my family had passed, and she'd shown me the first love of my life. She'd loved me when I was completely unlovable, when most of my friends walked away. She'd helped me stand when I was weak, when I had no will to even crawl, and I would be eternally thankful to her for that.

I'd told her that, over and over, all night long. I did love her, I always would, but not in the way I loved Charlie. It was just that simple — but though it was easy for me to say, it was torture for her to hear. That's why she couldn't let it go, why she couldn't leave, why all her bags were packed and in her car and yet still, she sat there, on my couch, unable to move.

Blake cleared her throat, dragging her gaze back to me, which always led to mine falling back to my hands or the floor.

"Any sane person would have left by now," she said. "And yet I'm still sitting here, waiting for something. I don't know what."

I just swallowed. There were no words for me to say — none that hadn't already been said.

"I'm sure I already know the answer to this," Blake continued, squaring her shoulders to face me fully. "But I need to ask, anyway. I need to hear you say it."

I lifted my eyes to hers, giving her the respect she deserved in that moment. It hurt to look at her when I knew I was the cause of the pain she endured, but I needed to take it. I needed to accept what I'd done.

"If it came down to it, and you had to choose between us... between me and Charlie... who would you choose?"

She asked it as if it were a hypothetical question, a scenario we'd never be in, but we were already living it. We were already at that apex, at the point where she was asking me to choose her, to be with her, and we both knew I couldn't.

Charlie was the woman my heart beat for, and I couldn't change that any easier than I could change how the moon revolved around the Earth. It would always be true, no matter the time, no matter the distance, no matter the circumstance.

I shook my head, knowing Blake already knew the answer just like she said she did.

"No, damn it, Reese," she said, voice louder now. "I need to hear you say it."

I sniffed, looking down at my shoes before I found her gaze again. The way her blue eyes bore into mine, begging me to prove her instinct wrong, killed me — especially when I knew I wouldn't.

"It's Charlie," I whispered. "I'm sorry, Blake... but it always has been."

Her eyelids fluttered at my words, her eyes glossing, but she sniffed back her emotion and pulled her long hair over her shoulder as she ripped her gaze away.

For a while she just sat there, and I watched her while she looked around the house, as if she was deconstructing every dream she'd had for what would happen inside those walls. Maybe she saw herself moving here permanently, saw us building a home and eventually a family. Maybe she really hadn't seen this coming, hadn't felt how distant I'd been since she'd arrived, how different it had been from when we were in New York together.

It was like watching an entire kingdom crumble in her eyes, and I was the one holding the hammer that took down the first wall.

Finally, Blake stood, snatching her keys off the coffee table and crossing her arms as she looked down at me.

"Let me ask you this last question," she said, her voice soft but steady. "If she doesn't pick you, would you want me then?"

I grimaced, stomach turning with even the thought of it.

"There's no right answer to that question."

"I didn't ask if there was a right answer," she said. "I asked what *your* answer is. If she doesn't pick you," she repeated, this time waiting until my eyes found hers again before she finished. "Would you ever want me, Reese?"

There had been many times in my life when I'd recognized that I could sometimes be a shitty human. I'd broken many girls' hearts, pulled pranks that went too far, saw disappointment in both my mother and my father's eyes too many times to remember them all. But in that moment, with Blake looking at me like I was tossing her heart in a paper shredder right in front of her — that was the worst.

I didn't look away when I shook my head in answer, and the pain on her face when she registered the meaning was an image I'd never forget.

Blake closed her eyes, forcing a breath before the mixture of a laugh and a cry left her lips. She shook it off, running her hands back through her hair, and then her eyes found mine.

"Rot in hell, Reese Walker."

She turned on her heels, and I stood to watch her go, suddenly wishing I could reach out for her and comfort her. But how could I, how could I be the solvent when I was the poison, too?

Blake shoved through the front door, and when she did, she toppled right into Cameron.

He caught her before she fell, and she straightened herself, looking back at me once more with tears in her eyes before she shook her head and stormed toward her car. Cameron watched her with me until she whipped out of the driveway, and once the car was gone, he turned.

The husband of the woman I loved was on my doorstep, and there wasn't any doubt in my mind that I wouldn't like the reason he was there.

"We need to talk."

I stepped out onto the front porch, guard up and ready for whatever fight Cameron had brought with him.

"What do we need to talk about?"

Cameron nodded toward the door I still held. "Maybe I should come inside."

"Maybe not."

He laughed, shaking his head like my answer didn't surprise him. "Fine. Doesn't matter where it happens, but we need to talk about Charlie."

My shield dropped a little then. "Is she okay?"

Cameron walked over to lean against the wooden railing on my porch, crossing his arms over his chest. "She's fine. At least, she's as fine as she can be in the situation we've put her in."

"*I* didn't put her in any kind of situation," I defended. "You're the one who made her wait two months, to give you a chance or whatever."

"Like you wouldn't fight for her if you were in my shoes."

"I wouldn't have lost her in the first place."

Cameron's nose flared at that, his jaw tight, and I would have bet money that he was two seconds away from charging me. But instead, he blew out a long breath, gazing out over my front yard.

"I didn't come here to fight you," he said, his voice resigned.

And as much as I hated the man, I felt a little sorry for him in that moment. I never considered how he felt, how it would be to see his wife with another man, to know he was losing her to him.

If I was being honest, I didn't care because he'd betrayed her first — not just with turning his back on her after their children passed, but by cheating on her, too. Still, I knew what it felt like to fuck up and then have to stare at the consequences of those decisions as they unfolded.

"So, why did you come, then?"

Cameron squinted against the sun, still looking out over my yard and past it, off into the distance.

"You don't know me," he said first, his tone careful and calculated. "I know you think you do, but you don't. To you, it probably seems like I'm a selfish man, one who took his sweet, caring wife for granted. I bet you think I'm a man who never imagined she'd leave me, who didn't see any other man as a threat, who never once considered what it would be like to lose her. But, you're wrong."

I finally stepped onto the porch with Cameron, letting the screen door close behind me. I still kept my distance, though, standing tall against my house while he stayed against the railing.

"I always knew what I had with Charlie," he continued. "I always knew how special she was, from the very first moment I met her. It's why she was the first woman I let inside my head, inside my heart, and why I was scared every single day regardless of the fact that she swore she loved me. Because I'm fucked up," he admitted, those words riding out on a laugh. "I'm fucked up and I know it, and I can't for the life of me figure out how she managed to see through that and find a good man in me. Or why she married me, or stayed with me. But she did." He looked at me then. "Until you."

"I didn't change anything when I came into town, Cameron," I said. "I just gave her someone to talk to, someone who would actually listen. And I loved her the way she deserved to be loved. I let her see another life, one she could live, if she wanted to."

"That may be the way you see it," Cameron acknowledged. "But, I love her, too. And I've loved her in a way you haven't yet, in a way you can only imagine. I loved her on the hardest days of her life and some of the best ones, too. I loved her in the way you love someone you build a life with, the way you love someone you build a family with." He swallowed. "It doesn't matter if our boys didn't get the chance to live. We had a family, one we built together, and then we had to love each other through that loss, too."

"Except you abandoned her," I reminded him. "You left her to grieve on her own. You shut her out, and then, you cheated on her."

Cameron's eyes widened at that, shock flashing in them. He was surprised she'd told me, at least, that's what I guessed. And that only made me stand taller.

He clenched his jaw, looking back over the yard.

"Look, I didn't come here to defend myself, either — or to try to change your perception of me. You have your mind made up about the kind of man I am just like I have mine made up about you. But I do need you to understand me when I say that I love my wife," he said. His voice broke a little at the end, and he turned to face me, his eyes hard on mine. "And I will love her every day until I take my last breath, just like I vowed to eight years ago."

"And I've loved her since I was a teenager," I told him. "We can go tit for tat all day here, Cameron. You love her, I love her, we both think we deserve her over the other. You keep saying you didn't come here to fight, so just get to the point, already."

Cameron stood, uncrossing his arms. "The reason I reminded you that I love her, that I always will, is because I cannot pretend that there isn't a very large chance that my wife will not be mine anymore after today."

A cool breeze swept between us, like the Earth was listening, like it needed to cool the tension before it was too hot not to explode.

"Charlie could choose you," he said, and my heart thumped hard in my chest.

She could choose me.

God, I hoped she would.

"And if she does," he continued. "Then I will bow out gracefully. I will wish you both the best, pack my bags, and be gone. I won't bother her, I won't fight you, and I won't beg for more time. She gave me what I asked of her," he said. "And she knows her heart better than both of us. She knows what, and who, will make her happy." He shrugged. "And that's all I want. More than the breath in my own lungs, I want Charlie's happiness."

"As do I."

Cameron nodded, as if he didn't doubt me one bit. "Then, you'll understand why I came today. Because if she does choose you, Reese, then I need you to be everything she wants and desires in life. I need you to promise me, right here and now, that you will never intentionally hurt her, that you will always put her first, that you will listen to what she doesn't even say out loud. Charlie is so selfless, so kind and caring, that sometimes she forgets to love herself and put *her* first. I need you to be the man to do that. I need you to be the one who makes her laugh on the bad days, and the one who lets her cry on the worst, and—"

"So, be all the things you couldn't be?"

Cameron still had his mouth open, but his tangent died on his tongue. His jaw clenched with his eyes still on me, and he took another deep breath, shaking his head.

"I guess so," he said after a moment, his voice low. "Charlie deserves the greatest love of all time. I think that's one thing you and I can both agree on. So, I'm just saying, if you're the one she chooses..." He swallowed, like the possibility of it was enough to make him physically ill. It was the same for me.

"Love her like she deserves," I finished for him.

Cameron's eyes softened a little, and he nodded.

In that moment, we were just two men who understood each other, who were in very different shoes yet nearly the same. We recognized each other's battles, each other's wounds, and perhaps there was even a level of respect present on that porch where we stood.

As much as he irritated me, Cameron had put his pride aside to come to my house. He was being a man, coming to me as an opponent, seeing the worthiness in me and the possibility that he could lose to me.

And more than that, he was here for Charlie.

I could see that most of all. He loved Charlie enough to accept the fact that he could lose her, and if that was the case, that he would wish the best for her, even still.

I respected him, but I still didn't have to like him.

"Look," I said to Cameron. "I don't have much to say to you. Honestly, I just don't think you deserve Charlie and I never have — not since the moment I came back into town and saw a lifeless shell in the place of a girl who used to be full of so much light. And I'm not saying you stole all of that away," I clarified. "But, I do think you were part of it. And I want you to know if she chooses you, and you hurt her again, I will literally murder you."

Cameron chuffed, as if the possibility were ludicrous, but I narrowed my eyes more.

"I'm serious."

We stared at each other, each of us standing tall and square.

"But, if she chooses me, I promise you I will treat her right. I have never loved another the way I love Charlie, and I know I never will again. So, I will treat her like the air I'm lucky to breathe, and I'll show her every day how much she means to me. I will give her everything she wants and needs, and I will not lose her the way you did," I said, and Cameron swallowed, his demeanor breaking a little. "You have my word."

He stared at me, like he was looking for a sign of weakness, a glimpse of what could be a lie. I knew he found nothing when he simply nodded, making his way toward the stairs of the porch.

"Then I guess there's nothing left to say," he said, and he held out his hand for mine.

I took his hand in a firm grip, shaking it just twice.

"May the best man win," I said.

Cameron smirked, shaking his head as he pulled his hand away.

"The best man for her isn't even playing, Reese," he said, making his way down the stairs. "If he was, neither of us would stand a chance."

When Cameron pulled away, I watched him go, thinking over what he'd said. He didn't think either of us was the man for Charlie, that we deserved her, or that we were what she deserved.

But I knew better. I knew in my heart that I would make her happy — happier than she'd ever been, than she ever knew she could be.

Cameron was wrong.

And I swore to myself that if Charlie chose me, I would prove it.

chapter nineteen

CHARLIE

J ust like Reese promised me, he gave me space and time to think.

I knew it had to be killing him, sitting at home after what happened last night at the gala, not knowing what I was thinking.

Reese was so unlike Cameron in that respect. Communication was key for him, and he needed it from me to feel safe. Last night, I hadn't been able to give him anything.

I still wasn't sure I could.

But, whether I was ready or not, my decision had to be made. Not just because of the time I'd promised Cameron, but because it wasn't fair of me to have both of the men I love tangled up in this mess with me. They deserved to know where they stood, no matter where that was. They deserved my respect and my honesty.

But before I could be honest with them, I had to be honest with myself.

I rode with the radio off the entire drive down to Jeremiah's house. They were rebuilding it right on the same lot where his old one had stood, and today was the day they broke ground. All of the top associates of Reid's Energy Solutions would be there, including my father and my husband, and I'd get to see the light in Jeremiah's eyes as work began to bring his home back to life.

It should have been a happy day. It should have been a *perfect* day, one filled with only thankfulness and joy, but I'd lost the right to feel either of those emotions. The more I drove, the longer I sat in silence, the more I realized how uncomfortable I was in my own skin.

I just couldn't shake the disbelief, or the new reality I'd found myself in. I was a broken record, stuck on the same track, constantly repeating the phrase *how can this be?*

On top of not even knowing who I was anymore, I had to search within myself to find the answer — an answer that seemed to elude me as much as the night eludes the sun.

Where did my happiness lie — with the boy I loved as a child, one who brought me back to life, or with the man I married, one whom I built my current life with?

In my heart, I already knew the answer, though I was scared to say it out loud. And more than that, I wondered if I even deserved what made me happy, anymore. How had I allowed myself to be with both of them the way I had, to enjoy their company, their love, all the while knowing I would hurt one of them in the end?

There was a constant ache in my chest, weighing down like an anvil of guilt. I pressed my fingers into that ache as I drove, but no pressure could relieve it. Nothing would make it better, make me better, make *us* better until I owned up to my feelings and I made a decision.

And the first thing I needed to admit to myself was that though I was disappointed in my actions, they had all been made with my heart and soul. I had listened to myself, to what I wanted and needed in the moments when I took them.

There was a reason I was still able to sleep at night, and when I searched below that guilt, below that shame, I found the answer — I did truly believe I deserved to be happy.

I had flaws, just like any other woman, and mine had been displayed on the highest shelf over the past few months. I had let my natural state of selflessness and care be overshadowed by the selfish wants and needs I'd always ignored. I'd let the monster inside me break free, let her roam wild, taking what she wanted with little care to how it affected those around her.

But I was a good woman, a good wife, a good teacher and daughter and, soon, I would be a good mother, too.

As my own mother once told me, we all fall from time to time. We are all sinners. We all make mistakes. But today, I would right my wrongs, and I would make my choice, and I would accept the consequences as they came.

When I pulled into the lot where everyone else had parked, I could already see the crowd forming around the podium Reid's Energy Solutions had set up. There was just a lot of dirt behind it, and an entire row of shovels was propped against the workers' shed, hard hats hanging on each of them. I watched from the car as the people milled around, shaking hands and chatting, news crews setting up their cameras for the speech my father would make. And instead of getting out of the car, I called Reese.

"Charlie?"

"Hey," I breathed. It was the same sigh of relief from his end, that connection between us fixed just with one call.

"I didn't think you'd call..."

"I know, I'm sorry," I started, still staring out the windshield at everyone working before me. I spotted my Mom and Dad talking with the mayor first, and I knew Cameron had to be close. "Thank you, for giving me the time I asked for. The space."

"Can you come over?"

"Not yet," I answered. "I'm at the groundbreaking of Jeremiah's house. But... I'll come later. Tonight."

"Okay," he said, and I felt the questions hanging in the silence between us. He wanted to know my decision. He wanted to know everything I was thinking. But, I wasn't ready to voice the thoughts I had.

The truth was, I didn't trust them — not yet. There was something inside me holding back, keeping my words as prisoners along with my heart.

"I should go."

"Wait," he said. "Can you do something for me first?"

My eyes caught on Cameron across the yard, though his were locked on the woman he was talking to. She was flanked by a cameraman, her hand wrapped around a microphone as she spoke with Cameron, and I watched them as I answered Reese.

"Anything."

"Close your eyes," he said. "And I mean it, really close them."

I chuckled, doing as he said. "They're closed."

"Okay. Now, I want you to come away with me, just for one moment. I want you to lie under the sheets of that fort we built together. Remember the candles, the wine? Remember the warmth when you curled into me, when my arm was around you?"

I smiled, feeling the sunshine through my windshield as the same warmth I remembered in Reese's arms. "I remember."

"Remember how it felt the first time we kissed," he whispered. "The first time we *really* kissed, when we had each other after years and years of wanting. Do you remember how it felt to have my hands on you, to touch me, to have me as your own?"

It was easy to remember — so much so that I knew I'd never forget it, not as long as I lived. When he touched me for the first time, he washed me clean like an avalanche, leaving behind the same woman, yet one who was forever altered. I could still feel that charge of energy, that burst of heat, that overwhelming sensation of being *right*.

"I do," I answered.

"Do you remember the song?" he asked, and on cue, that soft melody that played in my dreams filtered through the speaker of my phone. I smiled, leaning my head back against the head rest, remembering him playing shirtless at his piano like it was happening right now.

"I remember it all," I told him, voice soft as I listened to the song playing. "Every second."

"That happiness you felt with me, Charlie," Reese said, his hands still working the keys. "It was real. It may not have been at the time you expected it, the time you felt was right. It may have even felt wrong. But the love I have for you is the kind that cannot be tamed, the kind that cannot be told what rules to follow or what lines to stay within. The love you have for me is the same."

I kept my eyes closed, smiling though tears pricked behind my lids. I felt his every word like a muscle under my own skin — they were strong, undeniable and true.

"I know what I'm asking isn't easy," he said. "Asking you to love me when you've promised to love another, it isn't fair. But Charlie, it is right. You and me? We are *right*. We may have missed an earlier opportunity, we may have led lives away from each other, but just like you said the night you came to me…"

"I'm the river," I finished for him.

"And I, the ocean. It all comes back to us in the end, Charlie. It always has, and it always will."

I choked on something between a laugh and a sob, finally letting my eyes flutter open.

"You don't need to say anything right now, okay? I'll wait here for you. I will wait as long as you ask me to."

I shook my head, that ache pinging to life in my chest. "I love you, Reese."

"I know," he said softly. "And I love you, Charlie. I always will."

I didn't say another word, just listened to the last of his song, the notes of it sounding through my soul. When the last one played, I closed my eyes again, imagining Reese at his piano. And as I ended the call, letting my phone fall in my lap, I pictured myself sitting there on top of it, too.

The sound of my car door opening made me jump, and my eyes shot open again, finding Cameron standing above me. His eyes fell to the phone in my lap before they found mine, and he forced a smile, holding his hand down for mine.

"We're about to get started," he said. "Jeremiah and his family are over talking to the news outlets now, but I thought you might want to see them before the speech."

"Yes." I wiped my cheeks, though they were dry, before grabbing my purse out of the passenger seat and taking Cameron's hand. "Yes, I want to see them."

Cameron helped me out of the car, closing the door behind me, and then we stood there together, strangers and lovers all at once.

"Are you okay?" he asked. "I know last night was... I'm sorry, for leaving the way I did, and for sleeping in the guest room. I figured you needed your space."

"I did. Thank you. And don't apologize," I added, shaking my head as I looked down at my little white sneakers in the dirt. "You have nothing to apologize for."

Cameron breathed out a laugh, grabbing my hands in his. "I have many things that fall under that category, actually. I think you and I both know that."

I smiled, but it fell quickly, my eyes still on the dirt beyond our hands.

"I have something for you."

Cameron pulled his hands away, reaching into his back pocket to reveal a long, slender, black velvet box. He held it in both hands like an offering, like I was his queen, and I traced the edges of that box before my eyes trailed up his arms to his face.

"What is it?"

He swallowed, searching my eyes with his own as he opened the box.

For a moment, I just looked at him — at my husband — my own face mirrored in the warm brown reflection of his eyes. The way he looked in that moment reminded me of a day long ago, a day when he was unusually quiet, when I wondered for hours what was on his mind. He'd had the same crease between his brows that day, the same slight tremble in his hands.

It was the day he proposed.

I let myself breathe in that memory a moment longer before I finally gazed down, and when I did, I gasped.

Inside the box was a small, gold bracelet.

It was dainty, the chain slender and light, and in the center of it rested four stones. The center ones were an emerald and a sapphire, the green and blue gems reflecting the sunlight above us as Cameron carefully removed the bracelet from the box. Those two stones were hugged by pearls on each end, and I stared at those pearls as Cameron held the bracelet carefully, signaling for me to hold out my wrist.

"I know today is a day that will change our lives," he said as I extended my hand forward, turning my wrist up. "And I also know your heart hurts today. I know *I* have hurt you, that I have failed you as a husband in so many ways, but I also know that *you* know I love you."

He clasped the bracelet, and I turned my palm down again, staring at where the gemstones rested across my petite wrist bones.

"The emerald is your birth stone," he said, holding my forearm in one hand as he used the other to point out the stones. "The sapphire is mine. And the pearls are for Jeremiah and Derrick."

My heart squeezed at the sound of their names coming from Cameron's lips, and though I knew it was unlikely, I swore I felt my newest child stir to life inside me, too.

"No matter what happens today, I want you to have us," he said, his voice tender and soft. "I want you to remember me, and them. I'm sorry I ever tried to make you forget, that I ever thought that would fix the hole left in your heart by their passing."

He tilted my chin up then, his knuckle resting there as he searched my eyes.

"I want you to stay, Charlie," he whispered, his voice breaking on my name. "*God,* do I want you to stay. But no matter what you decide today, I want you to know it's okay. I'm okay. As long as you're happy, as long as your life is what you want it to be, I will be happy, too."

"Cameron..."

"No, no, don't say anything," he pleaded. "Not yet. Please, just... if this is my last day to call you my own, let me have today."

My eyes welled with tears, and I stared at my husband through them, wishing I could comfort him. I wished I could take his pain and Reese's both. I wished I could go back and do *something,* anything, that might have prevented the pain from happening in the first place.

"I will be at home waiting for you tonight," he said after a moment. "No matter what the decision is, it's okay. Just... come home, and we will figure it out together."

I rolled my lips between my teeth, holding them there as I nodded.

Cameron smiled, his eyes flicking back and forth between mine, like he was taking in the way the sunshine looked reflected in them just one last time. Then, he let my hand go, stepping back and releasing the tension between us.

"Let's go talk to Jeremiah," he said, and he held out an arm to escort me.

I slipped my hand inside, wrapping it around his bicep, and together we walked in a sort of daze toward the crowd.

I spoke with Jeremiah and his family, talked to my parents, listened intently as my father gave a speech, and clapped loudly with the rest of the crowd as the first shovel was planted into the ground. I watched as my husband shook hands with the mayor and Jeremiah's parents, stared as he took photo after photo, and even smiled bright and confidently when I was asked to join.

I lived the day, and to anyone around me, it would have seemed like I was fine.

But inside, I was burning.

I was caught in the flames of the fire I had started, the one I'd wanted to warm me, now slowly killing me, instead. Both Cameron and Reese were my oxygen, but as much as they cleansed my lungs, they also fueled the fire. It was a deadly circle, a never-ending cycle of torture, and to stop it, I had to jump through the hottest part of the fire.

This was it.

My mind was made up, and my heart, too. Still, I knew I would feel the scars I was about to leave just as much as the man I'd mark them with.

Jane Austen once wrote that to love is to burn, and I never knew the true meaning of that until the very moment I singed my heart with the love I had for two men at once. I wasn't supposed to love them both, and some would say it wasn't possible, but I was living proof that it was.

Love had shown me a new side, one more painful than I could have ever imagined, and yet the promise of a beautiful, happy life lay just on the other side of the flames.

All that was left to do now was jump.

Left or right.

It was as simple as that, except it wasn't simple at all.

If I went left, the road would eventually lead me to the house on the east side of Mount Lebanon — to the man I promised my life to, the one I'd imagined building a family with, the one who'd done everything in his power to try to keep me.

If I went right, the road would take me to a house not so familiar — to the man I used to only know as a boy, the man who came back unannounced, the man I loved first, before I even knew what love was.

I'd spent the evening up on the Incline, watching the sun set over the city as I worked through what I had to do, and now I was back in my car, back on the road that I knew I'd always eventually drive on. The tears I'd fought back had finally come, and now, I was convinced I didn't have any more to shed. They were all dried on my face, inky lines of mascara marring each cheek like scars.

I was at the fork I knew I'd eventually get to all along, the decision I never wanted to make between two choices I never knew I had before two months ago.

The truth was simple.

I loved them both.

My heart was forever severed, destined to exist in two equal halves — one with each man.

One half of me would forever be with Cameron, with the man I'd vowed to let hold me as his own until our last breaths. One half of my heart belonged to his quiet, loving heart, to the home we'd built together, to the promises we'd made in our youth — the ones we'd solidified as we grew together.

The other half would always be with Reese, with the man who was never supposed to come back, the one who shook up my entire life when he did. One half of my heart belonged to his loud, passionate love, to the music we'd made, to the sins we'd committed knowing in our hearts they were right even when they felt wrong.

Yes, my heart was severed, and I accepted that as my new truth.

But one half beat stronger.

One half had the vein that ran deepest, the love that spoke loudest, and one half held my choice in silence well before I ever admitted it out loud.

The other half would always be a part of me, but in a softer way — a more subdued beating, a quieter presence, a different kind of life support.

A different kind of love.

My chest ached with the realization of what I had to do, of the words I had to say, the heart I had to break. Though the snow had cleared and spring was beginning to paint the earth green all around me, I still felt the harsh bite of winter nipping at my heels as I fled from it — from the cold, from the hurt, to a new beginning, to a new me.

Left or right.

It may not have been a simple choice, but I knew with every beat of my severed heart it was the right one.

So, I took a deep breath, let it out slowly, and turned the wheel.

chapter Twenty

CAMERON

In my heart, I always felt that Charlie would come back to me.

Even on the hardest days, on the days when I saw her in his arms, or watched her watching him from across the room, I still believed. That belief was solidified after our weekend away together, and given a little ray of hope again after I told her the truth about Natalia.

But that belief was like a small candle flame, and it had been snuffed last night after the gala.

It wasn't that I was accepting the fact that she would likely choose to be with Reese, but more that I was preparing for it. I spoke my peace with Reese, letting him know that if she were to choose him, he had better never treat her like less than a queen. I'd also given Charlie a little piece of me — of our family — to take with her, should Reese be her choice. And right now, I was packing up a bag with enough supplies to get me through a week, just in case she walked through that door and told me it wasn't me she loved anymore.

For all intents and purposes, I was ready.

But I knew I'd never be able to truly let her go.

I could pretend. I could smile for her, bow out and let them be, and try my best to move on with my life. Her happiness was all that mattered to me — and that was something I didn't have to pretend to believe. It was as true as my belief in God above, and even if it killed me, I would walk out of her life if she told me it would make her happier — that *he* would make her happier.

After last night, the likelihood that those would be the words she said to me was enough to knock me to my knees.

I'd asked for two months, and truth be told, I wasn't sure I'd done enough. Even with talking to Patrick, with digging through my dark caves to pull out whatever I could offer, with telling her the truth about Natalia, with reminding her about the life we'd built together — I didn't know if it was enough.

I'd let Reese get in my head. I'd let him shake me from telling her about Natalia the first time, let him get under my skin at the hospital and again after the gala last night. I should have taken Charlie home, should have spent the evening cherishing her — like it was my last night, or like it was the eve before our new life began.

But I didn't.

I was flawed, far from perfect, and though I'd done all that I felt I could, I looked back on the months that had passed with the overwhelming want to try again. I wished for a redo button, for an extra life, for a rewind and pause — but I couldn't have any of those things.

All I could do was trust that smothered belief deep down inside me that felt Charlie would come home to me.

I folded another shirt and tucked it into my suitcase, trying my best to keep my eyes off the clock in our bedroom. It was late, the sun had set hours ago, and I still hadn't heard from her.

Maybe she won't come home at all, I thought, but just as it crossed my mind, I heard the front door open and close downstairs.

And then, I felt her.

Charlie's presence always hit me the way I imagined a drug would hit an addict. Just being in her vicinity had my entire body alert, my senses locked in, my hands and eyes searching for her — wanting her, needing her.

My ears perked up as her feet hit the stairs, and I continued packing, listening to every step. She called my name somewhere down the hall, but I couldn't answer.

I thought I was ready.

I thought I could do this.

But I couldn't.

I heard her as much as I felt her step inside our bedroom, but I kept my back to her, stuffing ten pairs of socks into my bag.

She was here. She was standing in our bedroom, in a place where we made love, and I already knew by the energy rolling off of her what she had come to say.

Time was up.

I was too late.

This is where it ends.

CHARLIE

"Hey," I breathed, still leaning against the door frame that led into our bedroom.

Cameron's back was to me, his hands busy organizing the suitcase he had laid out on our bed. It was the same one he'd packed for our honeymoon, the same one he'd packed for our getaway trip back to Garrick.

He paused at the sound of my voice, turning just slightly, enough to offer me his profile. "Hey."

I'd never felt more like a stranger in my own home.

My hands shook as I crossed to sit on the bed across from where he was packing, and I folded them together once I sat, trying to calm my breaths.

For a while I just watched him as he went from his dresser to the suitcase, back to the closet and then to the suitcase again. Back and forth he went, packing, taking clothing I'd seen him wear for years and fold it away like it'd never be back in this house again.

I didn't know where to start.

That was the first thing I realized as I sat there watching him, seeing the pain etched on his face, knowing the tension that riddled his slumped shoulders, the same as it did mine. Where were the right words, the ones I needed to say to him? I'd searched for them the entire car ride over, and I'd come up empty-handed.

Maybe it was because there *were* no right words — not in a situation like this.

Cameron packed while I watched him in silence, finally zipping up the suitcase when everything was inside it. His eyes finally found mine then, the weight of them heavy and dark. He was out of other things to look at, to keep him busy, and now, it was time.

"You've been crying," he said, slowly rounding the bed.

I moved to the side, offering him room to sit beside me, but he just shook his head.

He didn't even want to sit next to me, and as he tucked his hands into his pockets, I realized his were shaking, too.

I swiped at the dried, mascara-streaked tears on my cheeks. It was no use, I wouldn't be able to get them off without makeup-remover, but I tried, anyway.

"I have so much I want to say," I whispered, looking up at him. "I'm not sure where to start."

Cameron looked so much older in that moment, like God was granting me a glimpse of what he would look like in ten years' time. I traced every crease that surrounded his eyes, the ones that outline his lips — though those were fewer. His dark eyes watched me like I held a gun, one pointed straight to his forehead, and he was just waiting for me to pull the trigger.

"My life feels like a carnival ride," I started. "So many violent twists and turns have happened over the last few months. If you would have told me this would have been my future, if you would have told me at Christmas that any of this would have happened, I would have laughed." I tried to smile, but couldn't manage. "I mean, it's just..."

I shook my head, the words not coming out right. Nothing felt right.

"Will you please just sit with me for a second?" I begged him, sliding over again. "Please?"

Cameron stared at the spot next to me like it was a trap, but he forced a breath and did as I asked.

"Thank you," I breathed, and my eyes fell to where my hands were folded in my lap as I tried again. "You and I, we have a love that I don't think many people ever experience. The day I married you, I knew I was the luckiest woman in the world to have a man who loved me as fiercely as you did. As you do," I corrected. "We were so *happy*, you know?"

I glanced back up at Cameron, and he was staring at my hands, too. He swallowed, waiting for me to continue.

"We built a life together, built this home together," I said, looking around our room. "We tried to build a family, too. And through all that, we were... perfect. Honestly, we were. And I'm not saying we always have to be perfect, because that's unrealistic to expect, but... what happened after..."

I ran one of my shaking hands through my hair, tugging it at the ends, as if I could pull the right words out by force.

"We messed up, Cameron," I said. "Both of us. I should have asked you for what I needed, I should have gone to see someone, to talk to someone, the way you've been talking to Patrick. And I should have asked you more about what happened with Natalia," I said.

"It doesn't matter," Cameron interrupted.

"It does," I argued. "It does, Cameron. I know you feel like you betrayed me, that confiding in her was wrong. And it was. You should have come to me." I swallowed, waiting for his eyes to meet mine again. "But to me, the real betrayal was that I thought you cheated on me. And though I know you didn't now, you still kept the truth from me. For *years*."

"I didn't want to make excuses. I—"

"I know," I said, holding up one hand to stop him. "And I understand, I really do. But you still let me sit in that hurt, in that embarrassment, for years. And you left me," I choked. "You may have stayed here, in this house, but you weren't really *here*. You weren't present. You didn't touch me the same, look at me the same, *love me* the same. The day I caught you with Natalia was the day you walked out on me. You checked out. And I had to grieve alone, rebuild alone."

Cameron's brows pulled together as tears filled my eyes. I couldn't believe I had any left.

"And then, Reese showed up."

Cameron shut his eyes at the sound of Reese's name, and when he opened them again, they fell to the floor at our feet.

"When I was a young girl, Reese was everything to me. He was my first crush, my first love, my first heartbreak. Seeing him again, it knocked the breath out of me. He was the one man in my life before you, Cameron, and I didn't know how to handle him coming back — *especially* when he saw right through me, like I was glass, like he knew every cell that made up who I was."

"Charlie, please..." Cameron said, standing.

"No, you need to hear this."

He didn't sit back down, but he did turn again, his eyes finding mine.

"I love him, Cameron. I do. And I know that hurts to hear me say," I said, feeling the pain of those words as much as Cameron seemed to.

His bottom lip trembled and he bit it hard, willing it to stop.

"And he saved me when he came back to town. He woke me up from the daze I'd been walking in, from the horrible life I was living, pretending it was enough. I was miserable, Cam. I was *dying*."

Cameron's jaw clenched.

Just as much as my life had been killing me, my words were doing the same to him, now.

"He showed me what life could be like with him, with a restart, with a new beginning. He brought passion back into my life, made me feel wanted again, needed, *desired*. And more than anything, he made me feel like I deserved to live a better life. He made me feel like I could be happy again — and that I deserved to be."

"You do deserve to be happy," Cameron said, his voice breaking. "And I'm sorry I didn't make you happy. I'm sorry I let that go, that I let *you* go. I will never forgive myself for abandoning you when you needed me most. I made a promise to you," he choked. "And I couldn't keep it. My word means nothing."

"Stop," I said, standing with him. I wrapped my arms around him, but he wouldn't hold me in return. He just stood like a statue in my grasp, his shoulders tense, two tears falling parallel to each other down each of his cheeks.

"I failed you," he whispered.

"You did," I said, my eyes searching his. "But I failed you, too."

Cameron shook his head.

"I did. Just as you leaned on Natalia, I let Reese in when I should have come to you, instead. We both betrayed each other, as much as that hurts to admit. We messed up. We did. And honestly, when you told me you wanted more time, a chance to win me back, I thought it was a waste. I thought I'd be counting down the days, wishing for it all to be over so I could leave once and for all."

Emotion surged through me, along with the realization that it didn't matter if the words were right or not, as long as they were from the heart.

"But, I stand here in front of you humbled and thankful that you begged me for that chance, that you didn't let me go, that you didn't give up on me," I said. "Because you opened my eyes to the one thing I'd somehow forgotten, the one thing I'd lost sight of."

Cameron's eyes flicked between mine, a flash of hope lighting them from the inside out.

"We have hurt each other, we have failed in so many ways," I said, grabbing his arms and placing them around me. I laced my own around his neck. "But you are my husband. You are the man I love, the man I promised forever to. Through thick and thin, for better or for worse. I love you, Cameron, with every fucked-up, shattered piece of my heart. And it is shattered," I told him. "And I am broken. But it's you who makes me whole. It's you who I cannot live without. And I'm sorry I ever made you doubt that, that I ever made you believe I could walk away from this, from us, from *you*."

"What are you saying?" Cameron asked, his hands trembling where they held me. "Do you... are you saying you choose me?"

I smiled, tears still blurring my vision as I nodded. "I choose you, Cameron."

He broke at my words, his arms crushing me in his grip as I leaned into him. He pulled back with his hands framing my face, his eyes searching mine like he didn't believe me.

"You choose me?"

"I choose you," I repeated. "Just like I did the night we made our vows, just like I should have done when we faced our first challenge. The truth is, you make me forget I even *have* a choice at all. Like the writer who cannot live without the reader, and the rose that cannot exist without the rain, I am bound to you, to your love, and I cannot go on without it."

Cameron blinked, a new set of tears racing down in the trail made by the first.

"It's you," I said. "It always has been, it always will be, and from this moment on, I will choose you. Every day, every minute, every second of my life." My voice broke as I cried, but I didn't fight against the emotion. "If you will let me, if you will choose me, too — then I am yours forever, and I will love you the same."

He laughed, pressing his lips to mine as he shook his head. "As if I have a choice. As if I ever did after the moment I first met you."

Cameron kissed me harder, his entire body surrounding me, arms pulling me close like he was afraid I'd disappear if he didn't root me to him.

"I can't explain how I feel right now," he said between kisses. "I believed in my heart that you would come home to me, but after last night, I knew nothing for sure. The longer I packed, the more I waited for you to come, the more I thought you wouldn't. I don't deserve you," he said, pulling back to frame my face again. His eyes flicked between mine. "But I will spend the rest of my life making you happy. I promise you that."

I wrapped my arms around him, resting my cheek on his shoulder as he squeezed me tight.

"I'm so sorry, Cameron," I whispered. "I'm sorry for hurting you, for walking out on you, for finding comfort in the arms of someone else. It's *me* who doesn't deserve you. But I want you, and I will do whatever I can to be the woman who does deserve your love."

Cameron pulled back, brows bending together. "What about Reese?"

My throat constricted at the thought of him, at the memory of his heart breaking in front of me just hours before.

"He will always be a part of my life," I said. "And he's broken. I hurt him, just as we have hurt each other."

"You told him already?"

I nodded. "And he understands. As much as he can, anyway."

Cameron let out a breath. "I just... I can't believe this. You're really here," he mused, tracing my jaw with his thumb. "You're really mine."

My stomach twisted as he leaned in to kiss me, and I pressed my hands to his chest to stop him.

"There's something else you should know," I whispered. "Before we go any further."

Cameron tensed, his chest tightening under my hands.

There was no easy way to say it, no tender way to drop such a heavy bomb.

"I'm pregnant."

Those two words sucked all the air out of the room, and neither Cameron nor I even struggled for a breath as he let me go. I felt ice water seep into my veins when his warmth was gone, when he took a step back, and it flooded my system altogether when his wide eyes disappeared from view as he turned his back on me.

"I just found out," I said, voice shaking as much as my hands. "And I... I don't know who..."

Bile rose in my throat as Cameron pressed his hands against our bedroom window, the same one I'd let Jane free from.

"It could be yours. Or it could be..."

"His," Cameron finished for me.

"I'm sorry," I whispered, so softly I wasn't sure he'd even heard me.

I sat back down on the bed, my hands finding my stomach, as if the child that grew inside it could somehow give me the strength I needed in that moment.

"I don't know how long yet," I continued. "I don't know when I... when it happened. But I'll go to the doctor soon, and when I do, I can ask about getting a test."

Cameron still stared out the window, his slow, steady breaths the only sound in the room.

"Please, say something," I begged him. "Anything."

I smoothed a hand over my stomach, comforting the little one growing inside. No matter what Cameron said, no matter what he chose next, I would be a mother to that baby. I would love him or her unconditionally, and give them the life they deserve. I would teach them, help them grow, love them on the good days and the hard days, too.

Even if I had to do it alone, I would raise that child.

Cameron was so still, I wondered if he'd gone into shock. I wondered if he was debating flinging our window open and jumping out of it, just as Jane had — only he wouldn't fly.

"Cameron?"

"I don't want it."

His words were a fist to my chest, my next breath stolen. They were loud and final, as sure and steady as a rushing rapid, and the waves of it took me under faster than I could blink.

He didn't want it.

If I wasn't already sitting down, I would have fallen to my knees.

I stared at his back, at the way it rose and fell with each easy breath he took, and the glimpse of hope and joy we'd lived in just moments before was stolen.

Here we were at the foot of another challenge, and he wouldn't face it with me. He wouldn't stay. He wouldn't love me through it.

Though, could I really ask him to? Was it fair of me to even ask that he love me and a child that may or may not be his, let alone to expect it?

I didn't even have to ask the question to know the answer.

I was a selfish woman, and I'd taken too much — from him, from Reese, from everyone around me. I couldn't undo what had happened, couldn't right this wrong, but one thing I knew for sure was that I would not walk away from my child.

No matter who the father was.

"I understand," I whispered after a moment, sniffing back the tears gathering in my eyes again. "I just wanted you to know, and now you do. I love you, Cameron, and I choose you. But I choose this baby, too. And I get why you wouldn't want it, I get why—"

"The test," he said, interrupting me as he slowly turned. His eyes found mine, his gaze fierce. "I don't want *the test*."

I blinked.

"I don't understand."

Cameron crossed the room, carefully lowering himself to his knees as he took my hands in his. He kissed my knuckles, his eyes on mine before he dropped my hands and placed his own over my belly.

"I want you, Charlie. I choose you today just the same as I chose you on our wedding day eight years ago. You are mine," he said. "And so is this child — regardless of its DNA."

There he was.

It was Cameron — *my* Cameron — who knelt before me with his hands on my stomach, welcoming the child within it as his own, whether it was or not. It was my husband, taking me for who I was — flaws and all. It was the man I chose, the man I would choose time and time again, in any lifetime, in any situation, reminding me before I even had the chance to forget why I really had no choice at all.

I folded my hands over his, smiling through my tears, and Cameron leaned up to press his lips to mine.

He kissed me like the horizon kisses the sun as it sets — tenderly, with the blinding promise that another day would come.

With that kiss, we sealed our choice. With that kiss, we shut the door on the past. And with that kiss, with my hands over his, and his over our child, we began a new chapter in our story — together.

And I knew this one would be brighter than the last.

chapter twenty-one

REESE

Three hours earlier

I wished I never quit smoking.

My body itched for the sweet relief of nicotine as I flicked the wheel of my lighter, on and off, watching as flame after flame was lit and then snuffed just as easily. At first, I'd counted each one, but I'd lost count somewhere around two hundred, and now I simply watched numbly as I rubbed my thumb raw on the lighter.

It wasn't that I was nervous. It was that I was impatient.

Right now, Charlie was likely across town, telling Cameron that their marriage was over. I knew when she got to me, she'd be a mess. She'd be crying, she'd be mourning the loss of him and what they built together, and all I wanted was to fast-forward to when she was in my arms. I wanted to hold her, to rock her, to assure her the choice she made was the right one.

I wanted to love her — without him — and I couldn't wait much longer.

I started counting the flames again, and somewhere around seventy-two, there was a knock at my door.

I jumped up like my couch was on fire, sprinting to the door and flinging it open in one fell swoop. And then she was there, on my porch, just like she had been the first night I'd had her as my own. She looked just as sad, her eyes just as dark, face just as long.

For a solid minute, I just held the door open, my eyes tracing every single feature. I wanted to remember that moment, the one right before she was mine. I took in her long, dark hair, the waves of it broken by the wind. My eyes traveled down her slim waist, catching on the jean shorts she wore, though it was cooling down now that the sun had set. She trembled a little as my eyes devoured her legs, trailing all the way back up slowly to connect with her brown irises, and then I held the door open wider.

"Come in."

She stepped in slowly, crossing her arms over her middle as another shiver traveled through her.

"Here," I said, reaching in the closet near my door for one of my hoodies. I ripped it from the hanger and passed it to her. "I'll get us some wine. White or red?"

Charlie pulled the hoodie over her head, letting it fall down to her mid-thigh. It swallowed her, and I loved her in it. There was something about the way she looked so small in my sweater, how something I wore so often felt brand new against her skin.

She didn't answer once the hoodie was on, just watched me with those same sad eyes. And I knew she was hurting, knew she was in pain for the choice she'd had to make, so I took the burden of any more decision-making off her shoulders.

"White," I said, and then I turned for the kitchen.

I was already lighter with her in my home, already riding the high that came from having her back. I was only gone a few minutes before I returned with two glasses and the bottle. I nodded toward the room where my piano waited, and Charlie wrapped her arms around herself, following me with her eyes on the floor.

"Hop up," I said, patting the top of the piano. I'd already put the lid down before she arrived, anticipating the night.

She climbed up slowly as I filled both of our glasses, and I handed one to her, holding mine up for a toast.

"To new beginnings," I said. "And to us."

We clinked our glasses together, my eyes watching her as she watched our glasses. I took the first drink, but Charlie just lowered hers again, the glass trembling slightly in her hand.

She wasn't ready to talk yet.

I could feel the pain without even touching her, without even holding her, and all I wanted was to make it go away. So, I set my glass next to her on the piano, took my seat, and floated my fingers over the keys.

I played nothing at first, just warming up, letting the smooth notes flow between us. Once Charlie took another sip of wine, I transitioned into the song I'd written for her — for us — the one I'd been saving for tonight.

It was a piece I'd started the night I'd come back into town, and the beginning was soft and slow. It took me back to the day she walked into the teachers' lounge, that old book in her hands. I saw her eyes when they first met mine, how empty they were, how I wasn't even sure she recognized me at all. That woman seemed so far away now from the Charlie who had come back to me. She was full of life again, full of love, and I wanted to continue making her happy — so much so that she'd spill over.

As the song progressed, the melody turned darker, emotional, for all the nights I longed to touch her, all the days I wished for her to be mine. I built up the crescendo gently, bringing the song to a grand, expressive and dramatic climax. It was the night we gave in, the night our worlds collided, our stars uniting under one universal sky. The melody only grew louder as I mirrored my emotions watching her with Cameron, knowing he was trying to win her back. My fingers flew over the keys, my eyes closed as I felt every note.

And then, everything ceased.

I kept my eyes closed during that pause, feeling the weight of that silence, of the past two months. Slowly, I brought the song back to life, filling the room with the same melodic notes that mirrored the beginning, only they were happier now — comfortable and sure. It was our coming together, making it through the storm.

The river meeting the ocean once more, just like it always would.

When I finished, the last notes floating from the piano, I carefully opened my eyes to find Charlie.

She was crying.

Her cries were silent, tears streaming down her cheeks and running toward each other at the apex of her chin before they fell to her lap. She held her wine glass, still full, her eyes on me, lips trembling.

"I named it, *Where the River Meets the Sea.*"

"It's beautiful," she whispered, but her tears still fell, one after the other.

I took her calves in my hands, pulling her closer to me as I looked up into her eyes. "I know you're feeling a lot right now," I said. "I know these past few months have been hard on you. And I know what you did tonight wasn't easy."

Her face crumpled at that, and she let her head drop, shaking it where it fell between her shoulders.

I squeezed her legs, smoothing my hands over the skin there. "It's okay. You don't have to talk right now. Come, let me hold you."

I slid my hand up to grab hers, but when I tugged, she pulled it away, still shaking her head.

"It's okay," I repeated. "We can talk tomorrow. Tonight, let's just be."

"I can't." Her voice was meek, muffled by her cries.

"I know," I said quickly. "I know you can't talk right now."

"No."

Charlie jumped up from the piano, abandoning her wine as she moved for my bay window. Her hands flew to her hair, her shoulders trembling.

"Charlie?" I asked, making my way toward her.

"Please, just, I need a minute."

"Okay." I held up my hands, and when she turned, I kept them there. Slowly, I stepped toward her, and the more I watched her face, the more it twisted with grief, the more my stomach knotted. "What's wrong?"

She cried more, shaking her head.

"He'll be okay," I tried. "I know it was hard. I can't imagine how you're feeling but I'm here. I'm right here," I told her. "Just let me hold you, let me take the pain away."

"It's not Cameron."

I paused, still holding my hands up. "What is it then?"

"I haven't gone to him," she whispered. "I haven't been home yet."

"Oh," I answered, confusion sweeping over me. "Well, did you want to talk before you go? Do you want me to go with you?"

Her bottom lip slipped between her teeth. "Reese..."

At the sound of my name, the coldest chill of my life swept over me in a rush.

It was the way she said it, the way her face crumpled as it tumbled from her lips, the way the syllable rolled off like an apology.

My confidence was zapped like a bug drawn to a false light, one designed to kill, and the truth settled in like the darkest death.

"It's him."

My voice broke with the words, with the way Charlie's hands flew to cover her mouth when I said them.

"It's him, isn't it? You're choosing him."

"Reese—"

She reached for me, her small hand wrapping around my forearm, and my instinct was to pull away. But once she touched me, I knew I couldn't.

I would never be able to.

"No," I said, shaking my head, my eyes searching hers. "Charlie, you can't. You can't choose him. It's us, it's always been us. I make you happy, can't you see? I love you. I *love* you. Don't you love me?"

"I do," she cried. "Reese, I love you so much it hurts."

"But you love him more?"

She pressed her lips together, squeezing her eyes shut just the same as she set more tears free.

Black invaded my vision, and I moved back to the piano bench, falling down into it harder than I intended. One hand braced on the keys, sounding a loud, abrasive collision of notes, and the other found my bouncing knee.

"He hurt you," I whispered. "He cheated on you, Charlie."

"He didn't."

I looked up, watching as she moved slowly toward me.

"He never slept with her."

My mouth fell open. "What? How..."

"I walked in when she was on top of him, but he had already told her to get off. She told him she wanted him, and he said no." Charlie shrugged. "Yes, he betrayed me. He found comfort in another woman when he should have come to me. But he never slept with her," she said. "It was me who cheated, Reese. And only me."

"But he still left you. He wasn't there when you needed him, when you were grieving."

"But I wasn't there for him either."

Charlie took the seat next to me, wrapping her hand around mine.

"Reese, Cameron hurt me. And I hurt him. Neither of us is perfect." She squeezed my hand. "But he's my husband. I made vows to him, the same as he made to me, and I can't turn my back on those vows at the first warning sign. Every couple has challenges they face — and those challenges either make or break them. Sometimes we run from our problems, and other times, we hold hands and go through them together."

"And you don't want to run."

"I can't," she said easily. "And I know if you were in my shoes, you wouldn't either."

I sat there as disbelief colored every inch of me, hitting me in different waves. One moment I was angry, the next I was in shock, and somewhere underneath it, maybe I knew it all along. Maybe I saw it coming.

"I love you," she whispered. "And I know you love me, too. But it's a different kind of love than the one I have with Cameron. You and I, we're friendship and forbidden want. We're late night music and talks. We're the kind of love that burns bright and fast, but fizzles out just the same. We're a comet — a shooting star. We can't last, Reese."

"No," I said, shaking my head.

"It's true, and you know it. We want each other, we always have. And when we have each other?" She laughed. "It's... explosive. Catastrophic, maybe. I've never felt passion like that, the way I have with you. But it was born out of years of want, years of being told no, and at the base of it all, you're looking for something that doesn't truly exist in me," she said. "The same way I looked to you for something I should have found in my husband."

My heart ached with her words, so much so that I doubled over.

"I remind you of home," she said. "I remind you of your family, of Mallory, of your parents. I remind you of your youth, of a simpler time when you had them, when you had *time* to figure everything out in your life. I'm a piece of your life before it hurt. But now, you're thirty-five, your family is gone, and no matter where you end up — whether it's here in Mount Lebanon or back in the city or somewhere completely different — no place or person will ever bring them back," she said, and her voice dropped lower with her next words. "Not even me. Not even as much as I wish I could."

Emotion pricked my eyes, and I blinked against it, the ache in my chest growing stronger with every second. Oxygen hurt just as much as not taking a breath at all.

It was true, every word she said, and the truth had never hurt so badly.

"You love me for who I used to be, for the wide-eyed, untouched girl I once was. But I'm a woman now. I have scars. Cameron was there when they were made, and though he may have lost his way just as I did, he has his own scars, too. We both have them, and we both slipped into this dark hole together." She paused, her hand sliding up from mine to grip my wrist. "We have to climb out just the same."

Her words faded off, and the suffocating silence of my house surrounded us. It was like a weighted cloud, dark and heavy, and I let it take me under its grasp.

She wasn't mine.

Charlie would never be mine.

It killed me — physically, I felt my heart cracking as it digested the truth. But what hurt more was that Charlie was right. I had come to Mount Lebanon searching for a home, and I'd found it in her.

But she couldn't be my home. She was already Cameron's.

The longer we sat there, the heavier my thoughts were, and I felt darkness slipping inside me like an old friend coming home. I tried to hold the door closed, to block it out, but it was no use.

I didn't realize how long I'd been silent until Charlie spoke again, her words muffled with a fresh wave of tears.

"I'm sorry, Reese," she said, breaking. "I'm so, *so*, sorry. I care for you so much, and it breaks my heart to break yours. I hope you'll forgive me, I hope one day—"

"Shhh."

I pulled her into me, wrapping my arms all the way around her as she broke in my arms. Her tears came harder, her shoulders shaking, and I smoothed a hand over her hair as I searched for the right words.

"Don't be sorry," I told her.

"I hurt you." Her voice was muffled in my chest, and I held her tighter. "I never wanted to hurt you. I never wanted to hurt anyone."

"I know. I know you didn't." I forced a breath, kissing her hair. "In another lifetime, it could have been us, couldn't it?"

Charlie sniffed, not answering, her hands fisting in my shirt.

"Maybe if I would have kissed you, if we would have stayed in touch. Maybe if I never would have left at all." My heart squeezed. "Maybe my family would still be alive, then, too."

Charlie pulled back, her eyes finding mine. We were both a mess, tears staining our faces, eyes red and puffy.

"You could never know," she whispered. "In this lifetime or any other, everything happens for a reason, Reese. Your heart will heal, and you'll find home again," she promised me, as if she could possibly know for sure. "It may not seem possible right now, but you will. And something tells me the home you find will be more than you ever imagined. More than you've ever had before."

She smiled then, a small, timid smile, and I returned it with as much energy as I could muster. Then, I pulled her into me again, allowing myself just a few moments more to hold her, to be with her, to pretend she was mine.

There's nothing okay about losing the person you love.

Nothing would help ease the pain — I knew that even in the very first stage of it. There would be nothing to make it go away, nothing to numb it at all. So, in that moment, with her still in my arms — I welcomed it. I lived in it like I had after my family passed, only this time, it was a little easier.

Because I knew in the end, she was happy.

I had been wrong about Cameron. That much I knew when he fought back, when he didn't let her go so easily. But then he'd shown me even more of who he was when he'd come to my house, when he'd told me he would bow out should she choose me. He wanted her happiness more than his own, and it was then that I realized he was a better man than I was — even if I hated admitting it.

He was fucked up, just like all of us, but he loved Charlie fiercely.

I knew he would treat her right, that he would mend what was broken, and that they would find happiness again together.

Perhaps that was what hurt the most.

Charlie was in no rush that night. She let me hold her as long as I needed to, and only when I stretched my arms and let her loose did she look at me, her eyes dry now, a soft smile on her lips.

"I will always love you," she whispered.

I mentally traced the gold flecks in her eyes, knowing I would forever see them in my dreams.

"As will I always love you."

I sealed that promise with one final kiss, one soft and sweet pressed to her lips.

And then, I let her go.

It was only in the exact moment that I let her walk out my door that I realized I truly did love her. Not in the selfish way I had since I was a kid, not in the empty way I had when I returned to Mount Lebanon looking for something to fill me again. I loved her in the true, genuine way.

Because I loved her enough to set her free.

In that moment, as much as my soul split open as she walked away, I put her happiness above my own. It was what Cameron had done from the start, what I wasn't sure I could ever do, and yet here I was.

And I was thankful for that love.

If it was all I had, that one chance to love someone that much, that wholly, to care for them more than I care for myself — then I was glad to have it.

Even if it didn't last.

It felt like an addict letting go of an addiction of sorts as Charlie pulled away, and I found myself already thinking of making amends. I owed a lot of people a lot of things after the way I'd been behaving — Blake an apology, Cameron one, too. I owed Charlie the respect and space to love her only from a distance, to never cross that line she'd redrawn between us. I owed it to my family to truly live again, to let them go, to somehow find a way to release the guilt I felt over their death.

And more than anything, I owed it to myself to build a new home — one that started with me — instead of trying to find it in someone else.

I knew the pain was far from over. I knew the race had just begun. I would spend months drowning in the bottle, in the memories, and a part of me knew I'd never fully let Charlie go.

But still, as her taillights disappeared from view, I found myself smiling.

My heart was broken, but it was still beating.

I could work with that.

The end

epilogue

CHARLIE

Eighteen months later

I'd never seen my parents' house covered in so much pink.

Pink streamers hung from the banisters, along with classy, delicate pink lights that dangled from rose gold wire. There were pink chairs at every pink tablecloth-covered table. The napkins that wrapped around the silverware were pink, along with the plates and glasses, and of course, the cake was pink, too — and covered with glitter. Mom had even had two kiddie pools put in, though it was only thirty degrees outside and just weeks from Christmas. Both were heated, with pink walls and lights to illuminate the water, and there were more balloons in the house than I remembered at my college graduation party.

It was Daisy's first birthday.

I scanned the entertainment room with a smile as I balanced a fresh pitcher of strawberry lemonade in one hand and a pack of wipes in the other. There were kids all over the house — some that I knew, most that my mother knew from other grandparents at the country club. Even Daisy's older cousin, Callie, was in attendance, along with my brother and

Christina. They sat at the edge of one of the pools, holding Callie's hand as she splashed around.

Mom was fussing with the plates on the table where the large cake was, talking eighty-miles-per-minute to the poor server assigned to that task. Dad was standing right next to Cameron, who sat in front of the smaller cake, the one Daisy would smash her face into.

And Daisy sat on his lap.

She was all smiles in her bright pink onesie and tutu, both just as glittery as the cake we were all about to eat. Her dark hair that had been present from the moment she was born curled over her ears, and her dark lashes brushed her cheeks with each giggle that slipped from her lips.

Her eyes were bright blue.

The doctor told us they wouldn't stay that way, but they had so far, and I loved those little blue eyes. They were the ones that looked up at me as Cameron and I cried in the hospital, and the ones that watched me curiously each night when I breast fed her. They were the eyes that watered when she stuck her little tongue on Cameron's lemon drop, the ones that lit up whenever we played peek-a-boo, and the ones that watched her cake now with the most mischievous smile right beneath them.

When Mom told me she wanted to plan Daisy's first birthday, I had nearly laughed. *"Why so early?"* I had asked. But then I realized her birthday was just a month away. My little girl had already been alive for one full year, and it just didn't seem possible.

So much had happened in that year.

Cameron had completely renovated the house after the dust settled last spring. My library had yet again been turned into a nursery, only this time, it had also been rebuilt

— downstairs, right next to Scarlett and Rhett. I spent many afternoons there as my belly rounded, and even more with baby Daisy in my lap as I rocked in the hammock and she stared up at the birds in wide-eyed wonder.

Work had slowed down for Cameron, too. He'd told his boss that he needed less work now that he had a family coming, and with my father behind him, his wish was granted. He still worked hard, and there were still overtime days, but they were few and far between.

Less time at the office left more time for us.

I started joining Cameron at his sessions with Patrick, realizing I had just as much to work through as Cameron did. We had individual and couple sessions both, and together, we worked toward a healthier relationship.

And by the grace of God, we fell in love again — *deeper* in love.

We spent hours in the garden, and full days in the aviary. We would talk until our throats were sore, and dance like we were just twenty again. We rebuilt the connection we had broken, earned back the trust we had lost, and more than anything, we started a new chapter together with more gusto than we'd ever written with before.

Watching him now from across the room as I sat the new pitcher down, it was hard to remember what we'd been through. We were so happy now, so blissfully happy, I couldn't remember what it had felt like to feel rejected by him. I couldn't remember the darkest days, the betrayal, the torture — for both of us.

Life had a way of doing that, of giving us brighter days that seemed to completely knock out the dark. I loved living in that new light with Cameron.

"I think everyone is here," Mom said, flitting by me in a hurry with an arm full of damp towels from the pools. "We should do the smash cake soon."

"Yes, Mom," I said on a chuckle, but I doubted she even heard with how fast she whizzed by.

I was in no rush to do the cake, or to open the presents, or send everyone home. My daughter was turning one, and all I wanted to do was take the day in. I watched Cameron as he whispered in Daisy's ear, her little hands wrapped around his fingers, and then he'd nibble at her neck and she'd giggle like it was the funniest thing in the entire world.

And I realized how much our life had changed once she'd come into it.

Graham and Christina had given birth to a healthy Callie just months before we did the same with Daisy, and once we were flung into life with a newborn, the days flew by. It was more than I could have ever imagined, living in my new world with Cameron. I had thought I was prepared, that anticipating the arrival of Jeremiah and Derrick had set me up for motherhood, but I had been wrong.

Being a parent was so much more than baby books and birthing classes.

It was late night groans over who would get up to change diapers. It was fits of laughter over each face she made, and fits of anger over each toy stepped on in the dark. It was pictures that didn't do real life justice, memories captured with eyes and cameras both. It was worry over if we were feeding her the right things and loving her the right way. It was tears of agony when she was sick, when all we wanted to do was take the pain for her, and it was tears of joy over her first word spoken.

Of course, her first word was "no."

She already knew what she wanted and what she didn't, and I loved that about her. Daisy inspired me already.

Yes, a lot of things had changed since Daisy joined our world, but some things remained the same.

Life at Westchester ticked on as usual, though I found myself more involved in after-school activities once I'd been awarded Teacher of the Year. Each new class that came in was a new challenge, the curriculum constantly adjusting to technological advancements, and the students seemed to be more and more prepared for school each year that I received them.

Once they left Kindergarten, I would see my students only every so often — except for Jeremiah. He found me at least a few times a week, either stopping by my classroom or joining me for lunch when I would sit in the cafeteria with the kids. He was moved into his new home just seven short months after we broke ground, and our connection was only solidified in that time. He'd always be like a son to me.

And with Westchester came another constant.

Reese.

At first, after everything that happened, Reese seemed to disappear from my life altogether. He was still at school, I knew, but never around me. Our paths never crossed, and for a while, I wondered if they ever would again.

I didn't tell him I was pregnant, not until my belly was round enough that I was telling everyone else. And I saw it in his eyes, the want to know, the curiosity if it was his child.

But he never asked me.

He stayed away, saying nothing to me other than a mumbled *congratulations* when I'd first told him. But something changed around six months into my pregnancy.

He went to Cameron.

To this day, I had no idea what happened during that conversation. I had no idea what was said, what was yelled or cursed, or what was agreed upon. All I knew was that one day Reese wasn't looking at me, and the next, he was at my parents' dinner table right across from me and Cameron.

Cameron and Reese weren't friends — not even close — but they existed in the same space together. It was more than I ever expected, especially once Daisy was born. Cameron invited Reese to our home to meet Daisy, and Reese had attended family functions with my parents and us just like he had before everything went down. We'd had game nights and dinners, fundraisers and lazy afternoons on Mom and Dad's porch over the summer.

And though Reese was around, he still kept a respectful distance from me, only speaking to me when Cameron could see us. He kept conversations light and easy, and though I thought it would never be possible, we'd found a sort of friendship.

A very strange, very nontraditional friendship.

I pulled a few wet naps from the pack, ready to make my way over to Cameron and Daisy when the front door swung open. A burst of cold rushed in, and Mom's high greeting was the first thing I heard.

"Reese! You made it!"

She pulled him into a hug, and I didn't see him fully until she'd flurried away again, spouting off directions for him to drop his present on the gift table. He shrugged off his coat first, handing it to the butler at the door, and once his gift was no longer in his hands, his eyes found me.

There was always a spark of something when Reese looked at me, and I knew for as long as I lived, it would exist.

It wasn't the same heat or passion I'd once felt, and it wasn't that first spark I remembered feeling as a girl — the one that rumbled up from deep in my tummy like a volcano of butterfly wings. No, it was more comfortable now, safe and dependent, like the feeling you get when you hear an old favorite song and still remember all the lyrics, or smell a candle that takes you back to a memory once forgotten.

Reese offered me a timid smile, tucking his hands in his pockets as he crossed the room to the table where I stood. I tidied up the drink station as he made his way over, and once he stood beside me, I returned his smile.

"I just wanted to drop off a gift for her," he said quickly. "But I won't stay."

"It's okay to stay."

"No, I don't want to intrude," he said, eyes skirting over to where Cameron held Daisy.

"Reese," I said, lowering my voice. "It's fine. Stay. We're about to do cake."

His eyes were still glued on my daughter, and he swallowed, nodding his head as he found my gaze. "Okay. If you're sure it's alright."

"It's fine."

Reese looked around at all the decorations then, his brows rising higher with each new area he took in.

"This is insane."

I barked out a laugh, shaking my head. "Yeah, well, that's my mother for you. I'm actually quite shocked you're surprised by the magnitude of a first birthday party."

"Oh, I knew it would be grand," he clarified. "I just didn't realize it'd be so..."

"Overwhelming?"

"Pink."

I laughed again, resting my free hand on my hip as the other still gripped the wet wipes I had ready to go for the smash cake. "Yeah, I wasn't expecting this much pink, either. I think Mom is still frustrated that we had such a gender-neutral theme in our nursery and the same at the shower. She's been dying to do *something* pink."

"I don't think I'll ever see the color the same again."

Reese's phone dinged from his pocket, and he pulled it out quickly, silencing the second notification.

"That the new girl?" I asked.

His face reddened, and he shook his head, but he was smiling. "Yeah. I asked if I could see her again."

"And?"

Reese typed out a message on his phone before tucking it away again. "She said yes."

"Yes?" I asked, excited. "That's good, right?"

"Honestly? I'm not sure. I don't know if I know what I'm doing anymore."

I laughed. "Yeah, well, none of us do. You'll figure it out. It's kind of like riding a bike. And you used to ride a *lot* of bikes back in the day."

He cocked a brow at me, pretending to be offended, but then he laughed, too. "I don't know. I guess we'll see."

We both smiled then, a comfortable silence falling over us. Reese's eyes fell to where my hand circled my belly, and he swallowed.

"You look great, by the way," he commented, shifting the conversation. "Feeling uncomfortable yet?"

I looked down at the basketball swelling under my sweater dress and smiled, resting my hand at the top.

"Not yet. I've been lucky in my pregnancies so far. Now the birth?" I shook my head. "I'll never be prepared for that torture."

Reese grinned. "And it's a boy this time?"

I nodded, and he whistled, his eyes growing wide as silver dollars.

"Better prepare yourself there, Tadpole. You think Daisy has been a handful... boys are the real trouble."

"Don't I know it," I agreed, and we both laughed, our gazes sweeping over the room before we both settled on Cameron and Daisy.

Cameron looked up at us, a flash of something crossing his face before he smiled, half waving at Reese. Reese waved back, tucking his hand in his pocket once more when he'd finished.

"She's sure beautiful," he whispered, his eyes on Daisy.

"She is. Dad will have his work cut out for him once she's not a little girl anymore."

Reese smiled again, but it slipped easily as we watched Daisy and my Dad playing patty cake. Her giggles could be heard over every other sound in the party. After a moment, I pulled my gaze to Reese again, watching his face warp as he watched her.

He'd never hid his emotions well, and I knew there were questions he'd never asked me, ones I had tried not to ask myself. But he was stronger than I was.

"She's his, Reese," I said softly.

He ripped his gaze from Daisy to me in a flash, his brows pinching together over his sharp nose.

"Cameron didn't want a paternity test," I said. "Not at first. And even after Daisy was born. But I know you've been wondering," I said. "And honestly, I had, too."

Reese swallowed, his jaw tense as he listened to the words I spoke. The party continued on around us, as if nothing was happening, but it felt like we were standing on our own little edge of the world.

"I asked him to take one a couple months ago," I explained. "He refused at first, but I begged him. I told him I needed to know, and I wouldn't tell him. I would look at the results and he'd be none the wiser. So, he agreed." I smiled, the same relief I'd felt that day rushing over me again. "And Daisy is his daughter."

Her laughter shrilled out over the party again, and Cameron looked to me, nodding to his watch next. Daisy was getting fussy, and he wanted to do the cake as much as Mom did, but I held up one finger, asking for a moment longer.

Reese just stood next to me with his eyes on the pink cups that lined the table.

"Does that make you sad?" I asked, but he quickly shook his head, before I'd even finished asking.

"No," he answered. "Not if it makes you happy."

"That's not what I asked, Reese."

He considered me then, his eyes finding Daisy before they drifted back to me.

"I think I knew even before you told me," he said. "I can just tell. They're one in the same, aren't they?" He shook his head. "Cameron is a great father, and I'm glad she has him."

I swallowed, reaching over to squeeze his forearm gently before I released it just the same. "Me, too."

"Charlie!" My mom called, snapping her fingers from beside Dad.

I laughed, holding up the wet naps to let them know I was on my way.

"Well, time to let my daughter shove cake up her nose," I said, but my eyes softened as they found Reese one last time. "Thank you for being here... for always being here."

Reese smiled, shrugging as if he had any other choice. "Get over there. Your family is waiting."

With one hand on my belly still, I carried the wipes over to where Cameron and Daisy sat, smiling as everyone lined up on the other side of the table with their phones and cameras at the ready. I smiled at Graham first, who held his daughter — the one who favored him just as my daughter favored me. Then, my eyes trailed over my parents, family friends, children whose eyes were as wide and open as their hearts at that age.

Finally, I found my husband, squeezing his shoulder where he sat below me. He smiled, kissing my belly, and our eyes stayed connected until my Mom started the countdown.

"Three... two... ONE!"

Together, Cameron and I gently guided Daisy's face to her cake. She was shocked at first, her little hands stretching out in front of her and her face scrunching up in surprise. But once her hands found the icing, the creamy stickiness of it gooping between her fingers, she grinned, then laughed, and then everyone was laughing, too.

We all watched with smiles on our faces as she played in the cake, and after she'd snapped enough photos, Mom slipped away to help coordinate the cutting of the larger cake, the one that would be distributed. Cameron squeezed my hand, both of us still watching Daisy.

And from across the room, I felt another pair of eyes watching, too.

Later that night, when the sugar highs were done and the presents all opened, Cameron and I loaded a sleeping Daisy into the car for the trip home. She woke up only long enough to call out for the birds when we got home, who she referred to as *Wet n Wet* since she couldn't say their full names. We let her sit in the hammock with us for a while until her eyes began to close again, and then Cameron took her upstairs, tucking her into her bed before joining me again.

"Tea?" he asked, dipping his head inside the aviary. I was watching Scarlett and Rhett settle into their nest for the night, and I only shook my head, reaching out a hand toward him to ask him to join me.

Cameron closed the cage door behind him, sliding into the hammock next to me, and I tucked in under his arm with a content sigh.

"What a day."

"You said it," he mirrored, his hand playing with my hair. "You tired?"

"Strangely, no."

"Me either. I think it's the time, you know," he said. "One year. She's already been alive for one year. It doesn't seem possible."

"It doesn't. But *God* am I glad she got the chance to live, that she is here with us today."

A long breath left Cameron's lungs, and he kissed my hair, the hand in his lap finding mine. He held it for a moment before his fingers slipped up to my wrist, tracing the birth stones of our sons that hung there on the same chain he'd given me almost two years ago.

"They're still here with us, too," he said softly. "They always will be."

I nodded, tucking tighter into his side, and for just one small moment, on my daughter's first birthday, I thought of my sons. I missed them, missed who they could have been, but I knew Cameron was right. They were always with us, and they always would be.

After a while, Cameron lifted my chin with his knuckle, his eyes searching mine.

"Have I told you today that I love you?"

I smiled, brushing my nose against his. "You have. Many times."

"Well," he said, lowering his lips to mine. He hovered there, and just before he kissed me, he said, "I hope you never get tired of hearing it."

He kissed me long and soft, his hand sweeping through my hair, and I smiled wider when he pulled away.

"I never could."

Cameron held me until the birds were fast asleep, and once they were, he led me into the kitchen, making us both a pot of tea as soft music played through the speakers. I smiled to myself when I realized the song, the same one we had danced to at our wedding, and Cameron pulled me into his arms as soon as the tea was made.

We danced slow and sweet, swaying to the melody of the song, and I closed my eyes, remembering how it felt to dance to that song for the very first time.

Back then I'd worn a white, lace dress, tonight I wore a nightgown.

Back then, Cameron held me tight, but tonight, he held me tighter.

And there in the middle of my kitchen, with my daughter upstairs sleeping and my unborn son dancing right along with me and Cameron, I realized every heartbreak and trial along our path had led us to this moment.

I wouldn't have changed a moment of that path, of our story — not the beautiful days nor the dark. Because I knew in my heart that without them, this moment wouldn't have been the same.

On the northeast side of Mount Lebanon, Pennsylvania, there was a house.

And now, finally, a home.

acknowledgments

I've said in the last couple of books that this part gets harder each time, and I'm here to tell you — that's still true.

There were SO MANY hands that went into the making of this duet, and I don't think there are words to truly explain how grateful I am to every single person who has been a part of this process. This was my most aggressive writing schedule, my most intense edit, and — in the end — my best work to date (in my opinion). That would not be true if it weren't for all the loving (and critical) people who held my hand in this journey.

Let me start by thanking you — the reader — whether you are a book blogger, a writer, or just someone who inhales books like oxygen, as Charlie would say. I know it was scary taking a chance on this duet. For some of you, angst and emotional romances scared the living hell out of you. For others, it was the horror of having to wait two weeks between installments. And, even if you did love angst and torture (like me), you still had to trust me to take you on a love triangle ride, knowing there was a possibility that your guy wouldn't win. I truly hope that no matter which "team" you were on, you were happy with the ending. And THANK YOU for trusting me and taking a chance on my duet. Your reviews and messages are what get me through the hard days.

I love you all so, so much.

To Staci Brillhart, thank you for putting up with me when I had a complete meltdown during the editing process of book one. I knew every critical thing you had for me was valid, but I still needed you to hug me while I spent hours and hours making those changes. You were always there to talk me through scenes and pet my hair when the days were long and I was tired. Because of you, book one is better than it ever could have been had you not been a part of this process. Thank you for being my friend always and my mentor as a bonus. I love you.

Karla Sorensen and Kathryn Andrews, both of you were also critical voices in this. As two ladies who LOATHE triangles and cheating, you helped me make this duet something more than just a series for the "angst-lovers." I appreciate all your guidance, your feedback, your words of encouragement and your suggestions. More than that, I appreciate your never-ending love and friendship. Thank you.

I have to send out a huge thank you to Brittainy C. Cherry, my forever ride or die. Thank you for cheering me on, for sharing the struggles with me along the way, and for making me laugh when my anxiety was threatening to pull me under. I truly can't think of a single other person in this world who understands me the way you do, and I value our friendship more than words can say. Friends who slay together... ;)

To all of my incredible beta readers: Kellee Fabre, Monique Boone, Sarah Green, Danielle Lagasse, Ashlei Davison, Jess Vogel, Maegan Abel, Trish QUEEN MINTNESS, and Sahar Bagheri — YOU. ARE. THE. TITS. I don't know if I'm aloud to write that in my acknowledgements, but I am, because it's my book and I said so. Seriously, WOW. What a ride we had this time around, #amiright? Not only did many of you read multiple versions of each book, but you also waited (maybe not so patiently) for more from me when I left you at the worst spots. I mean, readers think they had it rough with a two week wait — if they only knew your pain as you waited MONTHS. I cannot say how much you helped shape this duet. Thank you for all your time, feedback, and love. I have the BEST team.

And to Sasha Erramouspe, thank you for being my last minute "Charlie" reader who reviewed the manuscripts after all the beta changes were made. Your feedback was crucial and so, so appreciated. I just adore you. Thank you for your time and thoughtfulness on this project!

To my momma and my best friend, Sasha Whittington, I thank both of you for always being there and cheering me on with my writing. Even if you do it from a distance, you're always there pushing me to do better and reach higher. I think you both get more excited on release days than I do LOL. I love you both so much.

There is a whole team behind my books that really make them as successful as they can be, and I feel like just writing a thank you in here isn't enough. You all deserve medals. To Elaine York, my editor and formatter, thank you for making my words prettier and for bringing the feeling of this duet to life with the gorgeous formatting. I always love working with you, but this time around you were absolutely invaluable with how flexible you were timing-wise. To my agent, Flavia, thank you for hustling as hard as I do. It's so comforting and refreshing to know you have my back. Then, there's the team at Social Butterfly PR. Nina, Chanpreet, and Hilary, you ladies have made this duet release everything that it is. Thank you for your hard work, your loving messages, your support, and your guidance. And, last but not least, thank you to Lauren Perry of Perrywinkle Photography for, yet again, bringing my vision for the covers to life. Your work is amazing and I'm so happy I get to continue to work with you.

Thank you to my tribe, my peoples, and especially to the ones that dried my tears at the writing retreat in January. You guys were there with me through the most intense edit of my life, and it's thanks to you that I felt inspired and motivated enough to keep going.

I'd like to give a special shout out to Angie McKeon for pushing this duet SO HARD. Your love for it absolutely inspired others to take a chance on it, and that word-of-mouth love is invaluable. I can't thank you enough.

To #MysteryMan, I only wish I could tell you how much your support has meant to me. From rubbing my shoulders after long days of writing to checking in on my goals and pushing me on the days I felt like quitting, you have shown me what TRUE love and support looks like. You inspired me when you didn't even know it, and knowing you would be there for me whether this duet succeeded or failed miserably made it easier to keep going. I don't know what our future holds, but I do know that my life is forever changed for the better by having known you, and having been loved by you.

And of course, I have to thank Pocket. Because if I don't, she'll aggressively meow at me while I try to sleep and knock bottles of water off my nightstand onto my computer. So, meow meow, I love you, thanks for not judging me when I don't shower for days during writing deadlines.

other books

The Kings of the Ice Series
Meet Your Match
One Month with Vince Tanev: Tampa's Hotshot Rookie – twenty-four-seven access on and off the ice. The headline says it all, and my bosses are over the moon when the opportunity of a lifetime lands in my lap. Of course, they aren't aware that they're forcing me into proximity with the one man who grates on my last nerve.

Watch Your Mouth
My brother's teammates know not to touch me — but that doesn't stop me from daring Jaxson Brittain to be the first to break the rule.

The Red Zone Rivals Series
Fair Catch
As if being the only girl on the college football team wasn't hard enough, Coach had to go and assign my brother's best friend — and my number one enemy — as my roommate.

Blind Side
The hottest college football safety in the nation just asked me to be his fake girlfriend.
And I just asked him to take my virginity.

Quarterback Sneak
Quarterback Holden Moore can have any girl he wants.
Except me: the coach's daughter.

Hail Mary (an Amazon #1 Bestseller!)
Leo F*cking Hernandez.

North Boston University's star running back, notorious bachelor, and number one on my people I would murder if I could get away with it list.

And now?

My new roommate.

The Becker Brothers Series

On the Rocks (book 1)

Neat (book 2)

Manhattan (book 3)

Old Fashioned (book 4)

Four brothers finding love in a small Tennessee town that revolves around a whiskey distillery with a dark past — including the mysterious death of their father.

The Best Kept Secrets Series

(AN AMAZON TOP 10 BESTSELLER)

What He Doesn't Know (book 1)

What He Always Knew (book 2)

What He Never Knew (book 3)

Charlie's marriage is dying. She's perfectly content to go down in the flames, until her first love shows back up and reminds her the other way love can burn.

Close Quarters

A summer yachting the Mediterranean sounded like heaven to Jasmine after finishing her undergrad degree. But her boyfriend's billionaire boss always gets what he wants. And this time, he wants her.

Make Me Hate You

Jasmine has been avoiding her best friend's brother for years, but when they're both in the same house for a wedding, she can't resist him — no matter how she tries.

The Wrong Game

(AN AMAZON TOP 5 BESTSELLER)

Gemma's plan is simple: invite a new guy to each home game using her season tickets for the Chicago Bears. It's the perfect way to avoid getting emotionally attached and also get some action. But after Zach gets his chance to be her practice round, he decides one game just isn't enough. A sexy, fun sports romance.

The Right Player

She's avoiding love at all costs. He wants nothing more than to lock her down. Sexy, hilarious and swoon-worthy, The Right Player is the perfect read for sports romance lovers.

On the Way to You

It was only supposed to be a road trip, but when Cooper discovers the journal of the boy driving the getaway car, everything changes. An emotional, angsty road trip romance.

A Love Letter to Whiskey

(AN AMAZON TOP 10 BESTSELLER)
An angsty, emotional romance between two lovers fighting the curse of bad timing.

Read Love, Whiskey – Jamie's side of the story and an extended epilogue – in the new Fifth Anniversary Edition!

Weightless

Young Natalie finds self-love and romance with her personal trainer, along with a slew of secrets that tie them together in ways she never thought possible.

Revelry

Recently divorced, Wren searches for clarity in a summer cabin outside of Seattle, where she makes an unforgettable connection with the broody, small town recluse next door.

Say Yes

Harley is studying art abroad in Florence, Italy. Trying to break free of her perfectionism, she steps outside one night determined to Say Yes to anything that comes her way. Of course, she didn't expect to run into Liam Benson...

Washed Up

Gregory Weston, the boy I once knew as my son's best friend, now a man I don't know at all. No, not just a man. A doctor. And he wants me...

The Christmas Blanket

Stuck in a cabin with my ex-husband waiting out a blizzard? Not exactly what I had pictured when I planned a surprise visit home for the holidays...

Black Number Four

A college, Greek-life romance of a hot young poker star and the boy sent to take her down.

The Palm South University Series

Rush (book 1)
Anchor (book 2)
Pledge (book 3)
Legacy (book 4)
Ritual (book 5)
Hazed (book 6)
Greek (book 7)

#1 NYT Bestselling Author Rachel Van Dyken says, "If Gossip Girl and Riverdale had a love child, it would be PSU." This angsty college series will be your next guilty addiction.

Tag Chaser

She made a bet that she could stop chasing military men, which seemed easy — until her knight in shining armor and latest client at work showed up in Army ACUs.

Song Chaser

Tanner and Kellee are perfect for each other. They frequent the same bars, love the same music, and have the same desire to rip each other's clothes off. Only problem? Tanner is still in love with his best friend.

about the author

KANDI STEINER is #1 Amazon Bestseller and whiskey connoisseur living in Tampa, FL. Best known for writing "emotional rollercoaster" stories, she loves bringing flawed characters to life and writing about real, raw romance — in all its forms. No two Kandi Steiner books are the same, and if you're a lover of angsty, emotional, and inspirational reads, she's your gal.

An alumna of the University of Central Florida, Kandi graduated with a double major in Creative Writing and Advertising/PR with a minor in Women's Studies. She started writing back in the 4th grade after reading the first Harry Potter installment. In 6th grade, she wrote and edited her own newspaper and distributed to her classmates. Eventually, the principal caught on and the newspaper was quickly halted, though Kandi tried fighting for her "freedom of press."

She took particular interest in writing romance after college, as she has always been a die hard hopeless romantic, and likes to highlight all the challenges of love as well as the triumphs.

When Kandi isn't writing, you can find her reading books of all kinds, planning her next adventure, or pole dancing (yes, you read that right). She enjoys live music, traveling, playing with her fur babies and soaking up the sweetness of life.

CONNECT WITH KANDI:
NEWSLETTER: kandisteiner.com/newsletter
FACEBOOK: facebook.com/kandisteiner
FACEBOOK READER GROUP (Kandiland):
facebook.com/groups/kandilandks
INSTAGRAM: Instagram.com/kandisteiner
TIKTOK: tiktok.com/@authorkandisteiner
TWITTER: twitter.com/kandisteiner
PINTEREST: pinterest.com/authorkandisteiner
WEBSITE: www.kandisteiner.com

Kandi Steiner may be coming to a city near you!
Check out her "events" tab to see all the
signings she's attending in the near future:
www.kandisteiner.com/events

Made in United States
Troutdale, OR
04/28/2024

19509426R00195